About the Author

Deryn Lake joined the popular ranks of historical detective fiction with the highly acclaimed John Rawlings Mysteries, DEATH IN THE DARK WALK, DEATH AT THE BEGGAR'S OPERA, DEATH AT THE DEVIL'S TAVERN, DEATH ON THE ROMNEY MARSH and DEATH IN THE PEERLESS POOL. Deryn Lake is the pseudonym of a well-known historical novelist who lives near Hastings, Sussex.

Death at
Apothecaries' Hall

Deryn Lake

NEW ENGLISH LIBRARY
Hodder & Stoughton

First published in Great Britain in 2000
by Hodder and Stoughton
First published in paperback in 2001
by Hodder and Stoughton
A division of Hodder Headline

A New English Library Paperback

10 9 8 7 6 5 4 3 2 1

British Library Cataloguing in Publication Data

Lake, Deryn
Death at Apothecaries' Hall
1. Rawlings, John (Fictitious character) – Fiction
2. Detective and mystery stories
I. Title
823.9'14 [F]

ISBN 0 340 71861 7

Printed and bound in Great Britain by
Mackays of Chatham PLC, Chatham, Kent

Hodder and Stoughton
A division of Hodder Headline
338 Euston Road
London NW1 3BH

FOR VIRGINIA AND CHARLES PURLE –

Friends for all seasons

ACKNOWLEDGMENTS

I would like to thank, first and foremost, Lt Colonel Richard Stringer, Clerk of the Worshipful Society of Apothecaries, who was kind enough to let me visit Apothecaries' Hall, and who personally showed me round the many beautiful and interesting rooms, telling me a fascinating ghost story into the bargain. Without him it would not have been possible to write this book. Equal thanks go to Professor Denis Baron, who not only told me all about white arsenic but introduced me to Colonel Stringer in the first place. Again, this book would not have been possible without him. Other stalwarts helped too. Carrie Starren, archivist at Kensington Central Library, who led me to the rate books and let me go through them until John Rawlings, with his neighbours Mr Forgus and Mr Horniblow, duly appeared in the year 1760. My research companion on that occasion was Beryl Cross, whose poems continue to delight many readers. As ever, I am in the debt of P.C. Keith Gotch of the Metropolitan Police Thames Division, for his advice on where and when bodies in the river would surface. Thanks, too, to Victor Briggs for photocopying the manuscript when my printer broke down mid book, and to Mark Newington, for his sparkling wit and unswerving friendship, and Dr Nigel de Sousa, who made quite sure I didn't get flu and so could finish this book on time. Last, but very far from least, I would like to thank my editor Philippa Pride, who poured oil on somewhat troubled waters when a harassed author turned to her for help. With a team like this, who could fail?

Chapter One

'It is not,' said John Rawlings, raising his quizzing glass to his eye to inspect the plant lying on the counter before him, 'the finest camomile leaf I have ever seen.'

'I agree,' answered Mr Clarke, the vendor, somewhat tartly, 'but that is because you asked for *dyer's* camomile, Mr Rawlings. Normally, *white* camomile is what is requested.'

'Yes, I am aware of that. However, I am in need of desperate measures to cure a particular patient of mine.'

'But dyer's camomile is not,' persisted Mr Clarke, who ran the shop attached to Apothecaries' Hall and was therefore considered a great expert on all matters relating to herbs, 'generally used for medicinal purposes. Consequently this specimen is all I have in stock.'

'I know the plant's true usage is as a dye, but I have come across an old Assyrian Herbal which recommends it as an external poultice.'

'May I ask for what purpose?'

'For application to the anus when said orifice makes a pustule. Believe me, I have tried everything else.'

Mr Clarke rolled a pair of pale protruberant eyes. 'Dear me! I dread to think what colour the poor patient's fundament will turn if you put this on it.'

John attempted to look serious and wise as befitted his

1

surroundings but ended up grinning. 'He'd best wear yellow breeches for a week or two.'

'If you add iron as a mordant the mixture will become greenish brown,' Mr Clarke informed him, keeping a straight face.

'Merciful heaven,' said John, reaching into his pocket to pay for the purchase. 'I can't bear to think about it.' Then he gave a laugh which echoed down Water Lane and away towards the Thames and in which Mr Clarke, who was far from a bad fellow despite his somewhat prim appearance and manner, cheerfully joined.

This day, John had journeyed to Apothecaries' Hall by water, hiring a wherry which had conveyed him through the freezing river wind as far as Black Friars Stairs. From there he had walked up Water Lane, passing the imposing arched entrance to the courtyard round which the various buildings of the Hall were situated. A few steps further on and John had come to the shop, above the door of which stood the Society of Apothecaries' imposing coat of arms. This displayed Apollo, the God of healing, slaying the dragon of disease, supported by two unicorns – these taken from the arms of James I who had granted the Society its original charter – a miniature horned rhinoceros raised above all.

It was November, 1758, and as cold as Muscovy, but inside the shop all was warm and cosy, and John, in no hurry to face the bitter journey home, lingered to talk while Michael Clarke wrapped up the Apothecary's various purchases.

'So how are things with you, Mr Rawlings?' asked the other man, making a deft parcel.

'Reasonably good. The shop is doing steady trade.'

'And your apprentice?'

'Coming on extremely well.'

'Any marriage plans?'

John smiled a little sadly. 'I have plans, but the lady concerned does not. She is an actress and currently wedded to her art.'

Mr Clarke nodded wisely. 'Keep her on a slack chain, Mr Rawlings. She'll be easier to capture later on.'

'I sincerely hope so.'

'And what of your father, the redoubtable Sir Gabriel?'

The Apothecary's expression changed. 'I am a little concerned for him, to tell the truth. He is slowing down very slightly. By that I mean he only plays cards and attends routs on four nights a week instead of seven.'

Mr Clarke looked amused. 'Dear man. A remarkable figure about town.'

'He is now seventy-four years old.'

'Gracious, you do surprise me. He is always so imposing in his black and white rigs. I would have taken him for ten years younger at least.'

'As do most people. However, I have thought to buy a country residence. Somewhere he may go for a little peace and quiet.'

Michael Clarke appeared dubious. 'Somehow I wouldn't have associated your father with rural life.'

John grinned crookedly. 'I know what you mean. I thought perhaps Kensington where there is a reasonably good social scene centred round the palace.'

'A place like that would indeed be more suitable for a man of Sir Gabriel's temperament.' Mr Clarke handed over the parcel. 'Now, Mr Rawlings, will there be anything else?'

'No, unless you happen to have some herb true-love.'

Mr Clarke looked interested. 'Ah! Treating a person who has been poisoned, are you?'

'No, I wanted the plant for one of its other uses. To aid a patient with his performance in the boudoir.'

'I see. But be careful, Sir. An overdose, which he might feel inclined to take, can produce delirium and convulsions. However, in moderation, the powdered roots consumed in wine are most effective, while the leaves are excellent for dispersing tumours and swellings in the privy parts, to say nothing of healing filthy old sores.'

John inclined his head in a gesture of respect. 'Mr Clarke, a half-hour in your company is an education in itself.'

The other bowed delightedly. 'Most kind of you to say so, my dear Sir. However, today I have had very little chance to air my knowledge. There is a Livery Dinner in the Hall and my customers have been mainly the mighty of the Society. Not those to whom one should express an opinion.'

'I thought there were a great many craft moored at Black Friars Stairs.'

'That is the explanation.'

John glanced at his watch, a gift from his father on his twenty-first birthday. 'Then it won't be long before they come out. I'd best be off before you get a rush of important custom.'

Mr Clarke shook his head. 'There you are mistaken, Sir. Most did their buying on their way in to the Dinner. Now they'll be in a hurry to get home before darkness falls. So stay a moment or two longer. I have some herb true-love in stock.'

He disappeared to the back of the premises, where hung row upon row of different plants, each one with a neat label attached. Alone, John turned to look out into the street through the shop's window, peering towards the left where stood the arched entrance to Apothecaries' Hall. Sure enough, the Dinner was over. Several dignified figures were leaving the building and were heading through the gloomy afternoon in the direction of the river, their way lit by a bevy of linkmen who trotted briskly beside the Liverymen, flaming torches held high. The Apothecary, knowing that one day he would be called to take Livery, watched with a certain feeling of awe as the procession made its way.

'Ah!' exclaimed Michael Clarke from the storeroom, and came back into the shop, the herb John had requested in his hand. 'Will this be enough?'

'I should hope so. My patient only wishes to enhance his performance, not sire every babe in London.'

'Be careful to warn him about the dangers of overdosing.'

'I certainly will. By the way, how is it used to cure poisoning?'

'Well, you know that the seeds and berries combined are compounded to create the aphrodisiac?'

'Yes.'

'If you ignore those and make a tincture from the fresh plant itself, it not only acts as an emetic but eases the inflammation caused by the poison; a double-pronged attack against the presence of toxins.'

'Once again I stand in awe of your knowledge,' said John, reaching into his pocket.

'That will be one shilling, Sir.'

'A bargain. Good day to you, Mr Clarke.'

'I wish you a safe journey, Mr Rawlings.'

These pleasantries exchanged, the two men bowed to one another and John made his way into the dusk-filled confines of Water Lane. Looking at his watch once more, the Apothecary saw that it was a little after four o'clock, and strode out briskly, hoping that he could hire a wherry with no difficulty, having scarcely an hour left before total darkness fell.

It was just as he reached the top of Black Friars Stairs, at the foot of which he had earlier observed so many craft awaiting their owners, that John felt rather than saw a figure leaning against the wooden balustrade which offered passengers their only means of support as they ascended or descended the perilous steps to the water. The Apothecary's hand flew to the pistol he always carried when travelling late and alone, but a faint groan reassured him that this was probably no footpad lurking in the shadows, though he still kept his weapon close.

'Who's there?' John asked in a sibilant whisper.

'Oh, help me,' came the agonised reply. 'I'm sick to my stomach.'

Sure enough, there came the sound of vomiting and an unpleasant plop as the contents of the man's guts landed in the water below. Hoping that there were no boatmen beneath,

John took a step towards the voice, only to draw in his breath in shock as a Liveryman of the Society of Apothecaries put out a feeble hand in his direction.

'My God, Sir,' John exclaimed, 'what has happened?'

The older man shook his head. 'I've been at the Livery Dinner. There must have been . . . bad meat.' His words ended in a gasp and he was violently ill once more.

'If that is the case, you must rest and receive treatment. Shall I escort you back to the Hall?'

'No, young man, no. My barge waits below. I would sooner return home. I can lie down in the cabin.'

'But if you are suffering from food poisoning, Sir, you should not undertake a journey without assistance. How far must you travel?'

'To Chelsea . . .' The older man's voice died away and he was again seized by a painful spasm which caused him to bend double, his thin hands clutching his stomach.

'You are in no fit state to proceed alone,' John said firmly, knowing what he ought to do but thinking of the warm fire in his father's library and wishing he were already sitting beside it.

'My good young person, I will be all right provided I stay quiet. I am an apothecary after all.'

'So am I, Sir. Though only a Yeoman.'

Despite his pain, the Liveryman chuckled. 'We were all only Yeomen once.' He seemed to recover slightly. 'My barge is moored over yonder. Be so good as to call them in, my friend. I doubt my voice would carry at the moment.'

'And what name shall I say, Sir?'

'I am Josiah Alleyn.'

John descended three of the steps and stared out over the river. Beyond the stairs, where a mass of wherries had collected in the hope of gaining custom, several barges bobbed at mooring. Most impressive of all was the Society of Apothecaries' own barge, today being used by the Master. On ceremonial occasions this magnificent craft was decked overall with banners and streamers of crimson and blue silk, and although it bore no extra decorations that evening it was still a wonderful sight. It rode the river tricked out with the Society's great shield, painted and gilded, while the barge's woodwork displayed exuberant moulded foliage, fluted Corinthian pilasters, and carved figures of the four seasons, all of them dwarfed by the depiction of several gods, including Apollo, Hercules and Neptune, cheek by jowl in a chariot drawn by sea lions. A large dolphin was painted on the rudder, providing the finishing touch to this voluptuous decor.

Beyond this floating tribute to the woodcarver's art lay several smaller, more modest vessels. Cupping his hands round his mouth, John called in their general direction, 'Would Master Alleyn's barge come in please,' and was rewarded by the stirring of six pairs of oars rising in the air simultaneously before dipping into the water and rowing towards Black Friars Stairs.

Conscious of the fragility of the older man, John helped Master Alleyn down the wet and slippery surface of the steps.

As they reached the bottom, John said on impulse, 'I would like to go with you, Sir. That is, if you permit.'

The Liveryman was about to answer, presumably in the negative, when he was sick once more, fortunately missing the steps and the wherries immediately beneath. 'I . . . I . . .' he gasped.

John became terribly firm. 'I'm sorry, Master Alleyn, but no protest will sway me. Short of you actually forbidding me to board your vessel, I intend to escort you to your home.'

The old man was beyond arguing. So weak that the Apothecary almost had to carry him, he made no demur as they struggled aboard his barge.

'Your master has been taken ill. Please head for Chelsea as quickly as you can,' John explained to the tillerman as he assisted Master Alleyn into the small cabin.

'Very good, sir.'

And with that, the Apothecary had to be content as the

oarsmen struck out for midriver and began the long haul back to Chelsea.

There was little space in the interior, but John made the best of what there was, lying Master Alleyn down on one of the two bench seats and placing a chamber pot conveniently close to his head. There was little more he could do except dip his handkerchief in the river and put it on the poor fellow's brow. Cursing that he did not have his bag with him, John watched helplessly as Master Alleyn was violently ill once more.

His sense of ineptitude caused the journey to take on a nightmarish quality. John stared moodily out of the window as the barge drew level with the Venetian-style bridge over the River Fleet, then passed the swinging wooden cranes unloading timber and coal, and the warehouses storing beer and dyes and limes. But with the tide in the barge's favour, the commercialism of these ugly wharves was soon replaced by The Temple, where sweeping lawns and legal chambers formed an open quadrangle to the river. This was the furthest point reached by the Great Fire of London, and though many of the lawyers' buildings had been destroyed in the blaze, Middle Temple Hall and the round church of the Knights Templar still stood intact and visible.

A slight gasp from Master Alleyn made the Apothecary swiftly turn to his patient, whom he was reassured to see had fallen into a doze. Wondering how he would ever get home this night, John continued to contemplate the river in the rapidly fading light of a cold November evening.

They were drawing level with The Strand, and his thoughts turned to his mistress, Coralie Clive, who lived in Cecil Street, one of several thoroughfares leading between the main road and the river. She was as beautiful as night with ravishing dark looks and emerald green eyes. She was also passionate and clever, witty and wise. Indeed, Coralie was everything that he had always dreamed a woman should be, for the Apothecary was not an admirer of loveliness alone. If there was a flaw in the diamond, however, it was that Miss Clive, like her sister Kitty before her, was a committed actress with absolutely no desire at this stage of her life to become anyone's wife.

'I love you but don't push me too far,' John muttered beneath his breath as he considered their relationship, and the wretched Liveryman stirred in his sleep at the murmured sound.

The light was fading fast now and the Apothecary could barely glimpse the Water Tower, the most impressive gateway to the river, built to the east of the Duke of York's estates. And it was fully dark by the time the barge drew level with the Duke of Richmond's beautiful riverside home. The Duke, though the Apothecary saw little of him these days, had always been friendly to John, who, for his part, had been ridiculously jealous of the young aristocrat's flirtation with Coralie, a false alarm as things turned out.

Braving the cold, the Apothecary went on deck to wet his handkerchief once more and cleanse the chamber pot, shivering as the chill river wind cut through to his very bone. Hoping that he would be offered a bed in Master Alleyn's household, he spared a thought for all the other Liverymen who had been at the Dinner earlier that day, wondering whether they, too, had been taken as ill as the poor old fellow lying so miserably in the cabin below.

In common with all those who owned houses of substance near the fishermen's village of Chelsea, Master Alleyn had his own private landing stage. And it was with much relief that John finally felt the barge head for the shore, where two servants waited on the lantern-lit jetty, obviously alerted to their employer's arrival by the lights of the homecoming craft.

Leaning over the side he called in an urgent voice, 'Run to the house and have a bed prepared for your master. He has been struck down with food poisoning and needs immediate treatment.' The two stared at him foolishly, clearly unused to emergencies. 'One of you catch the rope, the other go,' he instructed. Finally the younger of the two, a mindless-looking boy of about fifteen, sped off on spindly legs. Returning to the cabin, John, assisted by the chief waterman, who had put his oar to rest now that they were berthed, carried Master Alleyn out of the barge and up the path, which was lit by flares placed at intervals in the ground. Ahead of them lay the house, a generously proportioned place from what John could see in the torchlight, and coming towards them down the track was someone of equally generous proportions. Mrs Alleyn was running to meet them, an expression of fearful anxiety on her face.

'What has happened? What is going on?' She stopped short on seeing John. 'Who are you, pray?'

As best he could with her husband's head and shoulders in his grasp, John bowed. 'An apothecary, Madam. I happened to come across Master Alleyn as he attempted to board his barge. He had already been taken ill. I fear that he may have suffered food poisoning caused by the Livery Dinner.'

'They should be ashamed of themselves,' she answered roundly. 'What are things coming to? That anyone should be poisoned in the Hall, of all places, is utterly ludicrous.'

John assumed his honest citizen face, layering it with a look of immense sympathy. 'A pretty pass indeed, but then I suppose even the Society's Butler is not exempt from buying rotten provisions.'

'She should know better.'

The discussion was becoming pointless and a groan from Master Alleyn gave John the opportunity to change the subject. 'With respect, Madam, I think we should talk of this another time. I believe our main concern must be to get your husband to bed.'

'Of course. Come with me, my sweetheart.'

Robust though Mrs Alleyn was, however, she could not support the dead weight of her husband, who appeared to have lost consciousness and was now pale as death, a sticky sweat about his ghastly features.

If only I had my bag, John thought for the hundredth time, then hit his head with the palm of his hand as he recalled the other use of one of his recent purchases.

The Liveryman's wife looked at him sideways. 'What is it?'

'Madam, this afternoon I bought some herb true-love when I visited the Society's shop. One of its benefits is against poisoning. If you will be so kind as to let me compound in your kitchen, I can extract from the leaves a tincture which should clear the poison from your husband's system.'

A pair of very round blue eyes surveyed him. 'Who did you say you were?'

'John Rawlings, Madam. A Yeoman of the Society. My shop is in Shug Lane near Piccadilly.'

The eyes grew very tight, an extraordinary sight in Mrs Alleyn's somewhat moon-like countenance. It was perfectly obvious that even while she was helping her fainting husband bedwards she was summing up the stranger. Eventually her expression cleared. A decision had been reached and a half smile appeared, displaying a set of gappy teeth.

'I thank you, Sir, for your concern. My husband is usually treated by Master Cruttenden, a fellow Liveryman, but it is somewhat late in the day to send for him, I fear.'

'Further, if he also attended the Dinner, he might well be ill himself,' the Apothecary pointed out.

Mrs Alleyn's chins fell. 'I hadn't thought of that. You'd best compound your tincture, young man.' She paused. 'It couldn't make my husband worse, could it?'

'Temporarily, perhaps, but once it has cleared his system of the toxins it will soothe any inflammation caused.'

'You are very knowledgeable for one so young.'

John bowed and looked duly modest, omitting to say that he had never heard of the remedy until that afternoon.

At last they reached the bedchamber, which, like everything else in the house, was rather fine and large, echoing the status of its owner. Further servants appeared bearing bowls and towels and fresh white linen and, with relief, John handed his patient over.

He turned to his hostess.

'If I might use your kitchen . . .'

She held up her hand. 'Most certainly not. My husband has his own compounding room. Do not you?'

'Only in my shop alas.' John rather wistfully let his imagination dwell momentarily on a home he would own one day, where one of the first priorities would be a good-sized workplace in which he could not only experiment with herbs but continue his researches into water, an element that held an enormous fascination for him.

Now he followed Mrs Alleyn down a corridor and watched as she threw open a door at the end of it. A gasp of spontaneous admiration escaped the Apothecary's lips as he stepped inside the room that lay beyond. Scrubbed tables lined three of the four walls, each laid with pewter pans set over oil lamps, so that herbs might boil and bubble within. The shelves above stood crowded like an Eastern bazaar with retorts and distilling apparatus, alembics, crucibles and long necked matrasses. Jars of both glass and earthenware, filled with coloured liquids, interesting pastes and exotic powders, rubbed shoulders with vials of oleaginous oils. The remaining available space left was filled with leather bound books, which were crammed into every corner and even piled up on the floor.

John sighed. 'Paradise,' he said.

Mrs Alleyn smiled, her expression softening very slightly. 'Well, here is your workroom, Mr Rawlings. Now go to and quickly.' She paused in the doorway, turning back to see John already putting on a long apron. 'Is Josiah's life in danger? Can food poisoning kill a man?'

He looked up, tying the strings behind him, his gaze dark. 'Yes, Ma'am. It can be fatal.'

The round blue eyes suddenly filled with tears and Mrs

Alleyn's dumpling cheeks bunched as she screwed up her face. 'Oh save him, young man, save him.'

'I'll do my very best.'

She rushed at him, pulling him off his feet in a frantic embrace. 'God be with you,' she said, then was gone from the room like an unhappy breeze.

Half an hour later it was done: the tincture, dark green in colour like its mother plant, cooling in a cup into which John had poured a small amount of white wine in order to disguise the bitter taste. Taking a mouthful in order to test its strength, the Apothecary removed his apron and, picking up a candle-tree, made his way down the corridor, his curling hair, from which he had long ago snatched his wig, glowing cinnamon in the light of the flames. Pausing at the door of Josiah's bedchamber, he wondered briefly what sight would greet him. But one glance at the great bed reassured him. Though white as linen and out of the world, the Liveryman still breathed.

Mrs Alleyn looked up frantically. 'Have you done it? Is the tincture made?'

'It is, Madam. Now fetch me a spoon and let me give it to him, drop by drop.'

It was no easy task to administer the antidote to someone as deeply unconscious as Josiah, but with his wife holding his head, a manservant keeping the Liveryman's jaw open, and John patiently placing droplets of fluid into his mouth, the contents of the cup finally vanished.

The Apothecary turned to Mrs Alleyn. 'I think you should leave the room, Madam. Soon he will be violently sick.'

Her round face glared at him angrily. 'I wed Josiah when I was fifteen, Sir. There is nothing about him that I do not know, no experience that I have not shared. I shall stay where I am.'

'Very well. Best order bowls and towels. The poison will quit him by the usual exits,' John answered drily.

It was over by midnight. Weak as a newborn babe, Josiah lay in a clean bed, the vomiting and purging finally at an end. His breathing had become regular and the colour was returning to his cheeks as the soothing effect of the herb began to take hold.

John looked at a weary Mrs Alleyn, who had survived the ordeal like a seasoned soldier. 'You did well, Madam.'

The round face was like a pale pudding as she returned his glance. 'So did you, young man. He's out of danger, isn't he?'

'Yes. Now all he has to do is rest and recover.' The Apothecary stood up. 'I think I can safely leave the room, so would it be too much trouble for your servants to prepare a bath? I feel a little stained.'

Mrs Alleyn rose also. 'There is nothing that I would not do for you after what you have done for us. A bath you shall have and some fresh clothes. What you are wearing must be taken away and destroyed.'

John shuddered delicately, thanking his stars that he had been relatively soberly dressed for his visit to Apothecaries' Hall for, addicted to high fashion as he was, the very thought of good garments being destroyed by flame was one that he did not care to contemplate.

'It's been a difficult night, Ma'am. To have come through with just a ruined suit is a small price to pay.'

For the first time, Josiah's wife smiled properly, her gappy teeth and apple cheeks suddenly youthful looking. 'You shall be rewarded with enough to buy you several suits, my dear. And when Josiah is fully recovered I shall tell him to look out for your progress. You are a coming man, Mr Rawlings. I feel it in my heart.'

Warming to her enormously, the Apothecary raised her hand to his lips. 'You are very kind.'

'Kind, fiddlesticks. It does no harm at all to have friends in high places. Now, to be practical. Shall a bed be prepared for you?'

'I would like that very much.'

'And in the morning you shall travel back in my husband's barge.'

'In that case I shall return to Apothecaries' Hall. I need to replace herb true-love, and, much more than that, I want to find out how many others were afflicted by this mysterious poison.'

'That,' said Mrs Alleyn, nodding wisely, 'would be very interesting to know.'

Chapter Two

The scene was an exact replica of the one that had taken place twenty-four hours earlier. John Rawlings stood in the shop at Apothecaries' Hall, the November day gloomy outside, buying the herb known as true-love. The only differences being that on this occasion he wore different clothes and both he and Michael Clarke were buzzing with intrigue as they discussed the extraordinary outbreak of food poisoning which had stricken the Liverymen who attended the Dinner on the previous day.

'My dear Sir, today has been utter chaos. Nothing but a stream of servants demanding remedies for their masters. Those who are well enough are prescribing for themselves, and those who are not are relying on me.'

John looked pensive. 'I do believe that Liveryman Alleyn might well have died was I not able to make him a tincture from herb true-love. Thank God you told me of the remedy.'

'And that very afternoon at that. It was fate, Sir. Fate. It was obviously not meant that he should go.' Mr Clarke's eyes bulged.

John shivered slightly. 'What do you think could have caused the outbreak?'

'Bad meat or fish, I presume.'

The Apothecary fingered his chin thoughtfully. 'But the kitchens in the Hall are so well run. I find it hard to credit the

Butler would allow anything to be cooked that she had not examined personally first.'

Michael gave a half smile. 'The Butler, Sir, is in an hysteric. She says, most volubly I might add, that this is a slur on her reputation and is threatening all manner of things from resignation to suicide.'

'And the Beadle?'

'Remaining silent as all wise husbands do.'

'Come now.'

'I beg pardon, Sir. I had forgot your intended wife was of a different breed. Anyway, poor Sotherton Backler . . .'

'A name to conjure with.'

'Indeed, Sir, indeed. . . . is not only suffering from his wife's outbursts but is deeply distressed himself at this turn of events.'

'Small wonder. Was everyone present poisoned?'

'As far as I can tell from the reports I have received so far, all those who attended the Dinner were taken ill to varying degrees. Even the Master vomited.'

John shook his head, overawed by the thought that someone as grand and as dignified as William Tyson could do anything so commonplace.

'What did they have to eat, do you know?'

'A winter menu. I believe venison was served as well as various other dishes.'

'Perhaps it had hung too long.'

'I don't suppose we shall ever discover that,' said Michael Clarke.

'No,' John answered, longing to make further enquiries into the mysterious affair but well aware that it was not his province to do so.

'Well, at least you were able to help poor Master Alleyn.'

'Yes, his wife was more than generous to me in payment for my services.'

'Quite rightly so,' replied Mr Clarke, his attention wandering as yet another servant came in with a written request for a cure for food poisoning.

John stepped from the shop into the cold afternoon, a strange feeling about him. He had left Chelsea that morning, transported to Apothecaries' Hall by Master Alleyn's barge, but that had gone long since and now he had to make his own way home. Walking down to Black Friars Stairs, John hailed a wherry to take him over the icy waters to Hungerford Stairs, from whence a brisk walk across The Strand and up St Martins Lane would bring him to Leicester Fields, and finally to Nassau Street, where Sir Gabriel would be waiting to discover with his usual charm and tact, why his adopted son had not returned home on the previous night.

Much as John had expected, the older man was sitting by the fire in his library. His old-fashioned three-storeyed wig, a quirk of Stuart fashion which Sir Gabriel had never abandoned, had been removed and presently rested on a mock head fashioned from wood which resided in his bedroom. In its place, as was John's father's custom, he sported a stiff black taffeta turban adorned with a short but stunning cockade of white feathers. Draped about his long lean frame, for this early evening Sir Gabriel was most definitely *déshabillé*, was a flowing black gown that would not have disgraced the most affluent of Eastern potentates.

'Sir, you look fine,' said John in admiration, from the doorway.

His father turned his elegant head. 'Ah, my dear, there you are at last. I take it your non appearance was in some way connected with the outbreak of food poisoning at Apothecaries' Hall.'

'How did you know about that?'

'It was reported in *The Public Advertiser*.'

'Good gracious, news does spread. I wonder how they got hold of that story.'

'The gentlemen of the press have their methods no doubt.'

'Clearly they do. But yes, in answer to your question, one of the Liverymen was so ill, a Master Alleyn to be precise, that

I accompanied him back to Chelsea, and there, I say without false modesty, I believe I saved his life.'

'How did you do that?'

'Let me sit in comfort and I'll tell you.' John removed his cloak to display a most extraordinary suit of clothes provided by Mrs Alleyn, which, according to her, had once belonged to one of her sons, and which fitted the Apothecary where it touched and no further.

'Good gracious,' said Sir Gabriel mildly.

John winked an eye. 'Mine was ruined.'

His father quivered. 'Say no more of it. My mind races.'

'Then allow it to race on. Let me just tell you that nobody knows quite what happened yesterday. It would seem that the venison, or some other dish, was mouldy and that everyone present was affected, though none, as far as I know, quite so badly as Master Alleyn. Father, I thought at one point that despite all my efforts I was going to lose him.'

'Describe what occurred.'

John did so, sipping the soothing sherry that Sir Gabriel handed him and going over every detail of all that had taken place on the previous afternoon.

'And you say Mrs Alleyn paid you well.'

'She did indeed, Sir. Much put out that my suit was ruined, she gave me more than enough to buy several more.'

'Then it is your duty to your patient to visit him tomorrow.'

John sighed. 'You are quite right, of course. Despite the difficulties of the journey, I shall make it my business to be there in the morning.'

'Then may I make a suggestion?'

'Certainly.'

'That you leave the shop in the capable hands of Nicholas Dawkins for a day or two, and that you and I set forth in the coach to Chelsea, where we rest for a night, and then on to Kensington, to which benighted place, it seems, you have every intention of retiring me.'

Sir Gabriel's tone was playful but John was not amused.

'Father, really! Kensington is a delightful spot. Not only is there the palace, with a lively community gathered round, but also Holland House. To say nothing of the Bishop of Ely's residence.'

'And these delights are supposed to attract me?'

'It is high time,' said the Apothecary firmly, 'that we had a country retreat. Somewhere we can escape to when the pressures of London become too great.'

Sir Gabriel raised a cynical brow, smiling behind his sherry glass. 'My dearest child, I can envisage it now. I am put out to pasture in a rural backwater while you remain here, sporting with your many friends, particularly Miss Clive I imagine.'

For no real reason, except that he was tired from the night before and in no mood for criticism, however jestingly meant, the Apothecary was deeply stung. He rose to his feet.

'How cruel and how unjust of you. I had thought to buy a house out of town for the sake of both your health and mine. I believed that the sweet air would be beneficial after the stinks of London, but I see that my good intentions have been entirely misread. Good evening, Sir Gabriel. I shall go and seek the company of Miss Clive as you suggest.'

And so saying John rose to his feet in an extremely grand gesture and swept from the house, despite the fact that he was still wearing an ill-fitting suit which had once belonged to a man several sizes larger than he was and in which, if truth be told, he looked more than slightly ridiculous.

Coralie Clive, the most beautiful and talented young woman presently gracing the London stage, at least in the opinion of John Rawlings, was currently appearing at Potter's Little Theatre in The Hay Market in Congreve's *Love for Love*. But at this time of day, it being the hour to dine, she would certainly be at home, so still seething from his father's remarks, the Apothecary angrily hailed a sedan chair and directed it to Cecil Street, a thoroughfare running between The Strand and the Thames, where his beloved lived with her sister, the celebrated Kitty.

This night, however, was destined to be fraught with surprises. Alighting from the sedan, John saw to his irritation that a very grand coach was drawn up before the sisters' house and realised that they must be receiving someone of considerable importance. By now in a thoroughly bad mood, the Apothecary rang the doorbell. Thacker, the ex actor turned manservant whose job it was to protect the sisters, answered the door with a cheery smile.

'Ah, Mr Rawlings. How are you, good Sir?'

'I have been better,' John answered dourly. He indicated the coach with a jerk of his head. 'I see that fine company is calling.'

Thacker's face became inscrutable. 'Miss Kitty is entertaining in her private drawing-room. Miss Coralie is out, alas.'

With the feeling that the entire world was plotting against him, John sighed grimly. 'Out, you say? Has she left for the theatre?'

'No, Sir. Miss Coralie has gone to dine with friends.'

Wishing that the entire afternoon had never taken place, the Apothecary resigned himself to his fate and turned to go. But at that moment there came a burst of music played on a harpsichord and Kitty's voice soared out from a first-floor window in a rendering of a Handel aria. In response, a delighted male voice shouted out in German, 'Kitty, my darling, you sing like an angel.' There followed the sound of a smacking kiss, then silence.

John's lively eyebrows hit his hair. ''Zounds!'

Thacker's expressionless face became even more unreadable, if such a thing were possible. 'Shall I give Miss Coralie a message?'

'Tell her I called and that I shall visit her at the theatre on my return from Chelsea, where I am headed to visit a patient.'

'Certainly, Mr Rawlings.'

'Thank you, Thacker. Good night to you.' The Apothecary started towards The Strand, but once again his progress was arrested by a further sound from the first floor. A distinctly audible groan of ecstasy floated downward. Whoever was upstairs with Kitty Clive seemed to be having a very good time. Wishing it were himself and Coralie, John grimly plodded to The Cheshire Cheese, where he filled his stomach with comforting food and bleakly regarded his father's complete lack of understanding.

Despite the lateness of the hour, candles still burned in Sir Gabriel's library when John finally put his key into the lock and let himself in. Still angry, the Apothecary headed for the staircase and his bedroom, too upset even to wish his father goodnight. He was not quite quick enough, however, and the door of the library opened, revealing Sir Gabriel's figure.

'John,' his father said quietly.

The Apothecary approached, suddenly bone weary and not in the mood for further discussion.

'You're pale,' Sir Gabriel continued, his tone very contrite.

'I'm not surprised after my exertions of last night. I battled to save a man and it was a considerable effort.'

'I know. I am proud of you, which makes my ridiculous jest even more unpardonable. I think I might do very well in the country, particularly Kensington, well favoured by the *beau monde* as it is. John, forgive me. There is nothing worse than an old fool, and I behaved very foolishly indeed.'

The Apothecary gave an exhausted smile. 'Father, please don't talk about it further. I truly must get to bed.'

'Then do so. And in the morning we will travel to Chelsea together and call on Master Alleyn.'

John nodded, his earlier feeling of discontent far from abated. 'As you wish. Good night, Sir.'

'Good night, my boy.'

*   *   *

Despite his exhaustion, or perhaps because of it, the Apothecary slept badly, his irritable frame of mind combining with the general sense of disquiet which had come over him in Apothecaries' Hall. Accordingly he was still in a snappish mood when he descended early the next morning to find Nicholas Dawkins, his apprentice, who lived in his Master's house as was the custom, eating breakfast.

The boy, often referred to as the Muscovite because of an exotic ancestry which could be traced back to the court of Tsar Peter the Great, was now twenty-one, having come to his chosen profession late. That he was going to make a brilliant apothecary, John had no doubt. Full of foibles as regards young ladies, particularly Mary Ann Whittingham, niece of the legendary John Fielding and one of the prettiest, wickedest little things in London, nothing could detract from John Rawlings's fondness for the lad. However, this morning he merely grunted a greeting at Nicholas as he sat down opposite him and carved himself a large piece of ham which he wedged between two thick slices of bread.

'You are not in spirits, Sir?' enquired the Muscovite, his russet-brown eyes anxious in his naturally pale face.

'No,' John answered shortly.

'May I enquire why?'

'I have an uneasy feeling about me.'

'Is it anything to do with the food poisoning at Apothecaries' Hall?'

'How very acute of you. Yes.'

And John proceeded to tell his apprentice all about the incident involving Liveryman Alleyn and the wonderful properties of herb true-love.

'But you saved him, Sir,' Nicholas said when his Master had finished. 'Why are you still distressed?'

'I don't know. Perhaps I am over-tried.' John hesitated. It was beyond the code of conduct between a Master and his apprentice to discuss personal matters, and yet Nicholas was only six years younger than he, and they had been through much together. Longing to tell someone about his disagreement with Sir Gabriel, John threw caution to the winds.

'There's something else as well.'

'What is it?'

'I quarrelled with my father last night about the country home I want to buy in Kensington. He more or less accused me of trying to get rid of him – putting him out to pasture were his actual words.'

'He jested no doubt, but perhaps the jest hid a real fear.'

'What do you mean?'

'He has always been such a leader of fashion that I expect he dreads leaving town. But more than that, he will miss you, Master. And me. And Mr Fielding. And all the things that go towards making his old age interesting and exciting.'

John nodded. 'You're probably quite right, yet I have never suggested that he should spend all his time in the country. He can live here during the week, just as I intend to do.'

Nicholas looked wise beyond his years. 'In his heart of hearts I expect Sir Gabriel knows that once he gets away from town he will find it harder and harder to return. Master, he is growing old in body but not in mind. A hard dilemma.'

John leaned across the table and patted his apprentice's head. 'You're a shrewd young fellow, aren't you? I shouldn't have reacted so badly.'

'Exhaustion makes us all behave out of character. And to spend a night with a vomiting, purging patient must have been tiring beyond belief.'

'It nearly killed me, let alone the poor old man. I just hope that I find him much recovered when I call.'

'And when will that be?'

'Later this morning. Sir Gabriel is taking me to Chelsea in the coach, then we are going on to Kensington to look for a house. Which reminds me. Can you take charge of the shop for a couple of days?'

'Certainly. Do you want me to alert Master Gerard?'

Nicholas smiled fondly at the very mention of the ancient apothecary who willingly came out of retirement to help John when the younger man was called away.

'Only if there is an emergency. You are more than capable of compounding for ordinary ailments.'

Nicholas looked duly gratified and rose from the table. 'Then I'll be on my way, Sir. I hope you find a house that Sir Gabriel likes.'

'Is that a hint that he should do the choosing?'

'It is not fitting that you and he should fall out. You have always been so close. Perhaps the best way to heal the breach is for him to decide where you will live. After all, I feel certain that he will be spending more time in Kensington than you.'

John's crooked grin reappeared at last. 'Were you born old and wise, or is it something you learned along the way?'

'Both, Sir,' Nicholas answered seriously, then he bowed and left the room.

They left London by one of John's favourite routes, wending their way south of St James's Park to the somewhat infamous Tothill Fields. From the Middle Ages onwards, the fields had been used for all kinds of nefarious activities, from bull- and bear-baiting, to duelling and dumping rubbish. During the Great Plague of 1665 the dead had been buried there in an enormous pit. Now the entire area had been turned over to good works donated by Christian citizens and looked innocent enough as Sir Gabriel's stunning equipage, jet black and drawn by snow-white horses, edged round the perimeter, passing along the road that led to the Horse Ferry as they did so.

Looking out of the coach's window, John gazed on all the assembled charity. The Reverend Palmer's Almshouses for Six Poor Old Men and Six Poor Old Women sat rather grimly beside the Gray Coat School, complete with the figures of an orphaned boy and girl attached to the frontage. Close by stood Lady Dacre's Almhouses established for the purpose of bringing up children in virtue. But this was not all. Next door to the Green Coat School, yet another haven for orphans, stood Bridewell, like its counterpart near Fleet Street, a house of correction for women who sold their bodies for cash. John musingly thought as they drove past that he was yet to see a house of correction for the men who hired the poor wretched creatures.

But the feature that the Apothecary loved most of all was the one that he could now glimpse out of the window. The imposing Chelsea Water Works was lying directly in front of them. Created earlier in the century, the Works were fed by the Thames and supplied Westminster with water. Magnificent as its reservoir and streams were to look at, however, John was made more than uneasy by the fact that the river was also used as a sewage outlet and no provision at all had been made by the builders for separating the human discharge from the human drinking product. Not a thought he cared to dwell on.

'You're very quiet, my dear,' said Sir Gabriel, who had been a little over-solicitous following their argument.

'I was just thinking about the water we drink.'

'What about it?'

'If only there were a way of bottling a spring, so that at least we could be sure of its purity. The Thames is full of dead dogs and dollops of dung . . .'

'Please!'

'The essence of which we drink regularly.'

'Dear God.'

'It's a fact, Father. There's no escaping it.'

'But wouldn't spring water be a little tame?'

John's uneven smile appeared. 'Obviously, if you compare it with the rich mixture you're imbibing now.'

'Perhaps if it could be made to sparkle it would become more interesting.'

'Now that,' said the Apothecary thoughtfully, 'is a very good idea indeed.'

The carriage turned right, taking them along a tree-lined path which hugged one of the reservoir's many manmade tributaries. This led, in its turn, to Chelsea Bridge which crossed the southern end of the reservoir close to the point where it was fed by the Thames. Looking back, John could see the Neat Houses, quaint dwellings deriving their name from the word neyte, more commonly called eyot or ait, meaning a small river island.

Now came the most delightful part of the drive, down Strumbelo and Jews Row, passing both Ranelagh Gardens, the most fashionable and the most expensive of all London's pleasure gardens, then the famous Chelsea College or Hospital. Built by Charles II to look after retired or wounded members of the royal bodyguard, it had been Christopher Wren who had created The Hospital of Maymed Soldiers, the first residents of which had been admitted in 1689. John stared with delight at its beautiful proportions as the carriage finally turned towards the river and the home of Master Josiah Alleyn.

Approaching the house from the land and in daylight, the Apothecary was once more struck by the spaciousness of the place.

'A goodly dwelling,' commented Sir Gabriel, reading his thoughts.

'I never knew apothecaries could become quite so wealthy.'

'I believe Master Alleyn owns several shops,' answered John's father. 'Perhaps, my dear, you should emulate him and buy another when we get to Kensington.'

'It would stretch my resources to the limit.'

'I was hoping that you would allow me to have a share in the enterprise.'

'But you bought me Shug Lane.'

'That is beside the point. Ours is a family concern.'

'It seems you are resolute,' said John, patting Sir Gabriel's hand.

'Totally. Any further protest would be a waste of valuable breath.'

'I see.'

They were drawing very near the house and it was now apparent that the front had been built to face the extensive grounds belonging to the pleasure gardens, the back to face the river. There was, John could see, gazing down the length of the estate, another barge beside Master Alleyn's riding at the mooring jetty. And it was then that he noticed many of the curtains in the house had been drawn and that a swathe of black material had been hung round the door knocker. 'Stop!' he called to the coachman, sticking his head out of the window. 'Stop here. I must get out.'

Leaving his startled father to supervise the stabling arrangements, the Apothecary sprinted to the front door, his heart pounding. It was opened even before he knocked by a woman servant in a black dress.

'Master Alleyn?' asked John, his voice full of fear.

'The Master is dead, Sir,' she answered, and burst into tears.

Chapter Three

———◦◦◦◦◦———

As John Rawlings entered through the front door, following on the heels of the servant, the unmistakable sounds of a house in mourning rose to meet him. Voices speaking in hushed tones, the ordinary noises of everyday living unnaturally muted, distant sobbing coming from some room at the dwelling's heart.

He turned to the woman who had let him in. 'When did the Master die?'

She looked at him, her pale face damp with tears. 'Early this morning, at first light. He slipped out of life as dawn broke.'

'Christ's wounds!' cursed John bitterly. 'I could have sworn that he was out of danger.'

'Master Cruttenden said he had a relapse.'

'Master Cruttenden?'

'A very old friend of the family. He is an apothecary too.'

'I would like to talk to him,' said John, his voice harsh.

'He's still here, comforting the mistress.'

'I dare not intrude upon her grief. I'd best come back another time. Perhaps if you could tell Master Cruttenden that I called and need to speak to him on a professional level.' So saying, John produced a card from an inside pocket.

'That will not be necessary,' answered a voice behind him, and both the Apothecary and the servant whirled round,

31

startled, to see the tall figure of a man dressed entirely in grey standing almost on top of them, so silently had he approached.

John bowed deeply, his hair almost touching the floor as he did so. 'John Rawlings, Sir, Apothecary of Shug Lane. I accompanied Master Alleyn home from the Livery Dinner at which he was taken ill and treated him with herb true-love. I would have staked my life on the fact that I had saved his.'

The older man looked down the length of his nose. 'Alas, no, Mr Rawlings. Not all the poison was purged. I applied a clyster but, alas, it was too late.'

'May I ask what substance you used?'

'Certainly,' answered Master Cruttenden smoothly. 'It was the distilled water of devil's bit. The most effective treatment I know for cleansing the body inwardly via the colon.' He smiled, though not broadly.

He was like a seal, John thought, long and grey and somehow giving the impression of smoothness. However, all similarity to that particular species ended with his face which was extraordinarily arresting despite the fact that the man must be around fifty years old. A flowing grey wig surrounded a long thin visage, the most dominant feature of which was a piercing pair of eyes, as glittering and as colourless as quartz. The mouth, too, was interesting: there was a suggestive curve to the lips that John felt certain women would find most disconcerting.

Aware that he was being regarded as something of an upstart, and a junior upstart at that, the Apothecary bowed once more, a mark of respect from a Yeoman of the Worshipful Society to a Liveryman.

'Forgive my curiosity, Sir. It is simply that I thought my treatment had worked and clearly it did not.'

'No indeed. Food poisoning can kill, Mr Rawlings. I myself attended the Dinner and was taken quite ill in the night, vomiting and purging for many hours. Fortunately I treated myself and recovered. Therefore I can only presume that my dear friend took more of the tainted substance than I did.'

'Have you any idea what that substance could have been, Sir?'

Master Cruttenden shrugged and as he did so his long apothecary's gown rippled like water.

'Who knows? We had meat, fish, bread, high sauce, fruit. It could have been any number of things.'

John shook his head in bewilderment. 'I feel so guilty.'

The Liveryman gave a worldly smile. 'Pray do not do so, my young friend. We all of us lose patients from time to time. Why, I have attended the funerals of some of my own and though it is a heartbreaking experience I try to console myself with the thought of all those whom I *have* saved.'

The Apothecary sighed. 'You are right, of course. None the less, I find it hard to come to terms with this particular incident.'

Master Cruttenden looked brisk. 'Well, you have little choice, Mr Rawlings. The truth is that Josiah has died and we must all accept the fact.'

A voice spoke from the doorway. 'I shall never do so, never, never. I married him when I was little more than a child. Over the years we grew as one. This is a blow from which I can never recover.'

John turned to see that Mrs Alleyn, her round face crimson with anguish, her eyes streaming, had come to join them. Dreading the blame that he felt sure she would heap on him, John went over to her.

'Madam, what can I say? I did my best, truly I did.'

She fell into his arms like a small round pudding, clutching him to her dumpling breasts.

'I know you did, my dear. I have never seen anyone try so hard. That is what makes it all the more difficult to bear.'

'God have mercy on him,' said John, and felt his own eyes begin to fill with tears.

'Come,' Master Cruttenden put in, his mellifluous voice soothing, 'you must not distress yourself like this.'

'I'll distress myself how I like,' Mrs Alleyn answered from the depths of John's chest.

The Liveryman laid a commanding arm round her shoulders. 'Now, Maud, let me escort you to your room.'

She shook her head forcibly. 'No thank you, Francis. I wish to talk to Mr Rawlings a while.'

'Then I shall go and gather my things together. But when your conversation ends I really must insist that you rest. Mr Rawlings, *adieu*. No doubt we will meet again.'

Still clutching Mrs Alleyn in his arms, John bowed his head. 'Farewell, Master Cruttenden.'

Francis swirled in the doorway. 'No self-recriminations, now. These terrible accidents do happen.'

'I'll try to remember that.'

The Liveryman left the room, his long gown eddying behind him.

'I don't like that man,' whispered Mrs Alleyn in a small, spiteful voice.

'Why?' asked John, mildly astonished.

'My daughter fell in love with him when she was far too young for such follies. It was always my secret belief, though I could never prove it, that he encouraged her to do so.'

'I see.'

Disengaging herself slightly, Maud looked up at him from sore and puffy eyes. 'After that I never took to him, though he still remained a close friend of Josiah's, who believed that I had imagined it all. He was also Josiah's medical adviser, so they were very close.'

John attempted to steer the conversation in another direction. 'Tell me what happened yesterday. After I had gone.'

Mrs Alleyn took a step back, finally letting the Apothecary go. 'Well, in the morning, after you left on the barge, Josiah slept very peacefully for a long time. He woke in the afternoon and declared that he felt very weak. Remembering what you said about food, I gave him a little clear broth, that is all.

34

In the evening Francis called to say that he had been poisoned at the Livery Dinner and to enquire whether Josiah had suffered the same fate.'

'Go on.'

'Josiah was much better by now, though he did complain of some stomach cramps.'

'Which were natural enough after such a severe poisoning.'

'Anyway, during the night, after Francis had gone, he grew much worse again. There was no way I could get a message to you, Mr Rawlings, so I sent a boy on horseback to fetch Master Cruttenden back again. He gave him a clyster to wash the poison out through the bowel but, as you know, it failed.'

'It's a terrible story. I feel as if my professional reputation has been called into question.'

'Not by me, it hasn't. I saw you strive to save him.'

'Perhaps I should have tried a clyster.'

'There seemed little point when he was purging like he was,' Maud answered grimly.

The Apothecary sighed deeply. 'May I see Master Alleyn's body?'

The newly widowed woman hesitated. 'He has not been prepared.'

'That does not matter. I should like to take my leave of him.'

'Then so you shall.'

They went into the bedchamber together, the plump little woman on John's arm, just as if they were going in to dine. Pausing before the door, Mrs Alleyn took a key from her pocket and unlocked it.

'Why did you do that?' John asked.

'Lock it you mean?'

He nodded.

'I don't really know. To keep nosy servants out perhaps.'

Within, the room was dusky, the curtains drawn against

the light, while on the great bed poor Master Alleyn slumbered in the last sleep of all. John drew close. It would not have been seemly to examine the body with the bereaved woman standing so close by, so instead he merely leant over the corpse and scrutinised it intently.

The face was peaceful enough, but one of the hands had drawn the sheet into a tight knot, suggesting Josiah had died in pain. Of the clyster pipe and bowl there was no sign. Francis Cruttenden had obviously cleared up after himself. For what seemed like the hundredth time, John shook his head in bewilderment.

'I thought I'd saved you,' he whispered.

There was a muffled sob from Maud but other than that, total silence. The Apothecary straightened up with sudden determination. 'I am not satisfied with this affair,' he said, turning to her. 'I intend to get to the bottom of the mystery and find out exactly what happened at that Livery Dinner.'

The widow stared at him, round eyed. 'How can you?'

'I don't know yet, but I am going to do my damnedest.'

'Is it worth it? Josiah is dead and nothing can bring him back again.'

John put his hands on her shoulders and she drew close to him, a warm, comfortable motherly figure whom it was impossible not to squeeze, something he now did.

'I know, I know. But it is for myself. For my own satisfaction. For my *amour propre* if you like. I must know what it was that was so virulent it returned to kill Master Alleyn.'

'Then I wish you luck, Mr Rawlings, for you have a good heart, that's for sure.'

There was a gentle knock on the bedroom door. Before Maud had a chance to answer, it opened, revealing Francis Cruttenden in a long grey cloak. He looked more like a creature of the sea than ever as the rippling material whirled about him.

'My dear, I take my leave,' he announced.

Mrs Alleyn made a very small curtsy. 'Thank you for what you did, Francis.'

'It was nothing.' He turned to John, very much the Liveryman addressing a minor Yeoman. 'Good day, young Sir.'

'Good day, Master Cruttenden.' The Apothecary bowed.

The Liveryman swirled from the room leaving John to hug Maud briefly before he, too, took his leave.

'It's a mystery,' said the Apothecary, his feet propped up in front of him, a pipe in one hand, a glass of claret in the other. 'What on earth could it be that kills one man, yet merely makes others ill? An odd form of food poisoning indeed.'

'Quite so,' answered Sir Gabriel, dressed for an evening's relaxation and thoroughly enjoying being away from home in the company of his son.

They were sitting in The Unicorn, a private snug situated in The Dun Cow, a comfortable inn close to Mr Elphinston's Academy, an imposing building with considerable gardens on the outskirts of Kensington, whose founder had not gone unnoticed by Sir Gabriel as a possible neighbour of substance.

John drained his glass and poured himself another. 'I can't let the matter rest you know.'

'I didn't think for one moment that you would.'

'As soon as we return to London I intend to visit Apothecaries' Hall and somehow or other talk my way into seeing the Beadle and the Butler. For certain they will know more than most about what went on that day.'

'Assuredly they will. And now, John, let us consider our country residence. Where do you think we should look?'

'Perhaps Church Lane. It seems reasonably well populated. It is close to the King's kitchen garden, which means there will be activity. Whilst the church itself is always a good centre for meeting others.' Remembering Nicholas Dawkins' words, John paused. 'But I leave the final choice to you, Father.'

Sir Gabriel leant forward in his chair, holding his wineglass up to the fire to study the rich red claret reflected in the flames. 'Do you believe that I am going to retire here?'

'No, Sir, I don't,' the Apothecary answered roundly. 'I believe that you will regard a house in Kensington as I intend to do, a country retreat which will provide a little relaxation away from town.'

His father smiled. 'I may grow to like the place well.'

Very wisely, John answered, 'That, Sir, will be a matter entirely for your own choice.'

'So in the morning I suggest we ride through the entire locality to see which area takes our fancy most, casting an eye on Church Lane as you suggest. Then we can enquire about landlords and leases.'

John nodded, drained his glass, then refilled it. 'I might leave you in charge of negotiations, Father, once we have settled on somewhere.'

'You're longing to return to town, aren't you?'

'As I told you just now, I am most anxious to see the Beadle and the Butler and ask them a few questions.'

Sir Gabriel, too, emptied his glass. 'Will they be of any help, do you think?'

'That depends,' answered the Apothecary thoughtfully, 'on whether they have anything to hide.'

They left The Dun Cow in the most abysmal weather, rain falling out of the sky in sheets. Thoroughly soaked in the short distance between the inn door and the carriage, Sir Gabriel brushed at his cloak with a long pale hand.

'It is said by those who know such things, that conditions like these are ideal ones in which to find a new residence.'

'How do they conclude that?' asked John, wiping the mud from the back of his stockings.

'Very simply. If a house appeals in dismal light, dripping with wet, then it will seem like paradise on a beautiful day.'

'A logical thought indeed.'

The carriage turned westwards out of the inn yard, passing some important looking residences on the left, though nothing so fine as the enormous gardens of Kensington Palace, the chimneys and spires of which could be glimpsed over the fields to the right hand side.

It had been William III of Orange, husband of Queen Mary, who had retreated to rural Kensington. A chronic asthmatic, he had sought to escape the fogs of London and had set up his court there. Thin, weak, solemn and with a constant cough, the Dutchman had started a fashion for the place, which was now *de rigueur*. A street directory purchased by Sir Gabriel indicated that not only did the Bishop of Ely have a residence in the village but also His Grace the Duke of Rutland, together with the Countess of Yarmouth. Then, of course, there was Holland House, in which currently resided the politician Henry Fox and his wife, the former Lady Caroline Lennox, sister of the Duke of Richmond.

The coach turned right off the High Street, proceeding past an imposing church, and went on up Church Lane. Two rows of houses, elegant and no more than twenty years old, faced one another across the cobbled street.

'A little too close for my liking,' commented Sir Gabriel, gazing out of the rain streaked window. 'If I'm going to live out of town then, damme, I want to feel as if I am.'

The lane grew more rural as the King's kitchen gardens appeared on the right, somewhat damp and miserable looking now but obviously bursting with delicious fruit and vegetables during the summer months. Adjacent to the gardens were one or two cottages, clearly belonging to the gardeners. Opposite these was a neat little row of fifteen houses or so, all with gardens behind and around them. At the end of the lane, before it turned left and became the way to the gravel pits, stood a large and imposing parsonage complete with gardens and fields.

'Rural enough?' asked John.

'Perfectly so. Yet in easy access of all the great houses.'

John hid his smile, well aware that his father was already planning what he would wear as he paid his initial visit to the new neighbours, bearing calling cards. Indeed, it would not have surprised him if Sir Gabriel had announced his intention of leaving one at the palace itself.

'What about you, my dear? Do you care for this row?'

'Very much,' said John, who was already casting an eye over all the garden space and starting to plan where he could grow herbs.

'Then let us go in search of whoever owns these houses and talk of rentals and leases. I must say I quite care for the end of terrace, should that prove available.'

Taking the street directory from his father's hand, John glanced at it. 'The parsonage is occupied by the Reverend Waller, I see. And the next three houses to his are occupied by Mrs Trump, William Horniblow and Mr Forgus. There's no indication which, if any, stand empty.'

'Leave this to me,' said Sir Gabriel firmly. 'I am well versed in the way of finding out such things.'

So saying, he called out to the coachman to turn back to the High Street where, or so he claimed, the professional and trades people were bound to be situated.

An hour later it was done. Though not actually empty, the end of terrace house was about to become so. Mrs Trump, the elderly widow who lived there, was considered by her family to be too frail to be left on her own any longer and was due to leave to reside with her daughter. So it was in the pouring rain and full of the old woman's somewhat smelly furniture, John Rawlings first saw what was destined to become a beloved home.

'I shall take it,' Sir Gabriel announced grandly, having finished his tour of inspection and seen beyond the gloom to the house's intrinsic grace.

John looked at him with much affection. 'You are quite sure?'

'Quite, quite, my dear. I plan to divide my time between this place and town. Not as you will, on a regular basis, but in a more leisurely fashion.'

'So will you mind if I return to Nassau Street in the morning?'

'My dear boy, it would be obvious to anyone who claims even a slight acquaintance with your good self that you are straining like a greyhound before a race. Go back and solve the mystery of why Master Alleyn so sadly died.'

'Yes, that,' answered the Apothecary, 'is what I most certainly intend to do.'

Chapter Four

The downpour continued throughout the journey back to the capital, turning the ways into brooks and Tothill Fields a quagmire. Ross, Sir Gabriel's new coachman, clad in oilskins, cursed his luck, and the four beautiful white horses arrived home bedraggled and spattered with mud to their necks. No one was more thankful than John when the poor creatures were finally led round to Dolphin Yard, situated behind Nassau Street, to be stabled and the carriage housed.

'Let them rest for a day before you return for Sir Gabriel,' he instructed the driver.

'Very good, Sir.'

John answered the unasked question with a grin. 'Don't worry, Sir Gabriel will find himself some sort of conveyance in the meantime, you can be sure of that. He simply has to stand there and people run to serve him.'

'I had noticed that, Sir.'

'Then all of you take a good rest. The travelling conditions were appalling.'

'Thank you, Sir. Good afternoon.'

'Good afternoon.' And John went into the house and sat by the library fire until dinner was served. Pictures came into his mind. Pictures of Josiah Alleyn fighting for his life and seeming to win; pictures of Mrs Alleyn and her unstinting devotion; pictures of settling down with Coralie and becoming as united as the old couple had been.

As usual, that particular train of thought came to an abrupt halt. The younger Miss Clive, though perfectly willing to share her bed with him, seemed equally unwilling to share her life. As he sat there, sipping Sir Gabriel's excellent sherry, his adopted son wondered just how much longer he would be prepared to put up with the situation. Last June he had celebrated his twenty-seventh birthday, and though he was still in no desperate hurry to marry, he now cherished hopes that within the next three years that situation might come to pass. However, the beautiful, ambitious Coralie appeared to have no such plans and though he loved her, was totally besotted with her in many ways, he could not see himself allowing this state of affairs to drag on indefinitely. Something of Maud Alleyn's compassionate love for her husband reached out and tugged at John's heart, and suddenly he found himself wishing that his beloved was a very different kind of woman.

Despite all the differing shocks and sadnesses that he had recently experienced, the Apothecary slept well that night and woke at first light, grey and sullen and wintery though it was.

Downstairs, Nicholas Dawkins was chewing his breakfast before setting off to open the shop in Shug Lane. He looked up, surprised, as John came into the room. 'Master, good morning. I hadn't expected you back so soon.'

'There has been a strange twist in events.'

'Master Alleyn?'

John nodded.

'Not dead, surely?'

'I'm afraid so.'

'But how? I thought you said he was out of danger.'

'So I believed.' And the Apothecary related to his apprentice everything that had happened in the last twenty-four hours. 'What puzzles me is the differing symptoms that the

Liverymen suffered. According to Michael Clarke some were mildly ill, others seriously. I suppose everything depended on how much of the rotten food they consumed.'

'Unless of course the dinner itself were tampered with,' said Nicholas slowly.

John stared at him. 'What do you mean?'

'That some foreign agent were introduced and that some Liverymen received a greater amount of it than others.'

'But what substance could do that?'

'You know perfectly well, Master.'

'Are you saying . . .?'

'I'm saying arsenic, Sir. White arsenic. This may sound fanciful, but if someone with a grudge against apothecaries put poison into their food, arsenic would produce symptoms very much like the ones you've just witnessed.'

'But that's impossible.'

'Is it?' said Nicholas, thoughtfully carving a slice of meat. 'Is it really? I think it is a possibility that should be seriously investigated, not denied.'

'But who would do such a thing?'

'Someone with a diseased mind. Someone who believed that an apothecary was responsible for the death of a loved one perhaps. You of all people, Master, should know that there are some very strange individuals roaming the streets.'

John sat silently, his enthusiasm for enormous breakfasts for once at a standstill. 'You know, you may have hit on something,' he said eventually.

'So when you investigate do you intend to proceed cautiously down that path?'

'How did you know I meant to investigate?'

'Because you are yourself, Master,' Nicholas answered, a rogue's smile transforming his pale features.

'As it happens, I plan to return to Apothecaries' Hall this morning.'

'Then bear what I say in mind, Sir. There's something odd about this business. I feel it in my old Russian bones.'

The frisson of fear that occasionally gripped the Apothecary when a situation boded no good, ran down his spine at the very words. 'I wonder if you could be right.'

'If I am, then you will find it out,' Nicholas answered with unnerving confidence.

'How to begin without upsetting a great many important people? That is the difficulty.'

'Oh, you'll charm them, Sir.'

John looked at his apprentice severely. 'The difference between charming ordinary witnesses and charming the Worshipful Society of Apothecaries is a considerable one, young man.'

'I'm sure it is, Master,' Nicholas answered cheerfully, and swallowing down the last bite of his breakfast went whistling off to work.

'I simply can't credit it,' said Michael Clarke, eyes bulging. 'He must have had a total relapse. The entire occurrence beggars belief.'

'As a result, I feel my treatment has been called into question,' John replied gloomily. 'Almost as if the poor man's death is a slur against my professionalism.'

'But your treatment was perfectly correct. Did I not tell you of it that very afternoon?'

Knowing that this was going to be a powerful weapon with which to persuade Mr Clarke to help him, John put on a sad face and sighed deeply. 'Indeed you did, Sir. Indeed you did.'

'Then my judgement must be called into question equally with yours.'

'It is noble of you to say so.'

Michael cleared his throat. 'I feel, in view of all that has happened, we need to know more about this mysterious outbreak. What caused it and how such a terrible thing can be avoided in the future.'

'So do I. If I am to rest easy in my bed I would like to know what substance it was that could not be cured by normal means.'

'There's only one thing for it,' Michael Clarke said with determination.

'And what is that?'

'Jane Backler must come out of her hysteric and tell us exactly what ingredients went into that dinner.'

'Indeed she must,' responded the Apothecary vigorously, and assumed his not to be thwarted expression.

Moving as one in what could only have been an hilarious fashion, John realised, the two men left the shop and marched purposefully under the arched entrance to Apothecaries' Hall, across the courtyard and through a door on the right that led inside the building itself. Immediately facing them was the mighty wooden staircase rebuilt after the Great Fire, ornately carved and rising magnificently to the Hall above. Beyond that, small but functional, lay an area known as the pantry, the province of the Butler herself.

Tapping on the door, Mr Clarke was rewarded by a faint voice calling, 'Come in.' His pale eyes popping with intrigue, the shop manager beckoned John to follow him.

The Butler was seated on a stool before a wooden table which also acted as a desk, listlessly going through a sheaf of bills. She looked up as the two men entered the room and gave a feeble smile, in that her eyes continued to look hunted and haunted though her lips parted to reveal a set of teeth with an intriguing gap between the front top two.

'Yes, Mr Clarke?' she said politely.

'Mrs Backler,' he replied with a faint bow, 'have you heard the grave news?'

The Butler dashed the back of her hand across her eyes. 'About Liveryman Alleyn? Yes, indeed I have. I have not slept since.'

'How did you find out?' John asked, curious.

Jane Backler gave him a penetrating glance. 'I'm afraid I haven't had the honour . . .'

He bowed low. 'Excuse me, Madam. I forgot myself. John Rawlings, Yeoman of the Society. I attended Master Alleyn when he returned from the Dinner. I chanced upon him by Black Friars Stairs and considered him too ill to travel alone.'

She rose and curtsied stiffly, obviously defensive. 'Everyone is blaming me, Sir, for buying rotten foodstuffs, but I swear to you upon my honour that I did not. The only conclusion I can come to is that the flour used in the high sauce was in some way tainted. God be my witness, I have run a clean kitchen since Sotherton was appointed Beadle. I have taken my duties most seriously. I simply cannot understand what has occurred.'

The gap in her teeth made her look curiously child-like and vulnerable, despite the fact that she must be fifty, and it was all John could do to stop himself putting his arms round her and comforting her. Mr Clarke, however, narrowed a protuberant eye.

'Be that as it may, Mrs Backler, *something* went wrong. However hard you tried, everyone at the Livery Dinner suffered from food poisoning. And now with fatal consequences for one of their company.'

Poor Jane's hand flew to her throat and her cheeks flushed. 'I know, I know. But what am I to do? How can I clear my name?'

John spoke quietly. 'Would it be acceptable for me to search in the kitchen? It is just possible that the source of the outbreak might still be there. Then, if it were something over which you had no control, the matter could be resolved satisfactorily.'

She looked at him curiously, her eyes and face still attractive despite her anxiety. 'But what sort of thing could that be?'

The Apothecary looked vague. 'Perhaps some poisonous substance, yew for example, might have hidden itself amongst the vegetables.'

'But the vegetables were thrown out after the dinner, as

48

were the meats, fish and fruits. Normally I make bundles for the poor with what is left over, but as soon as news came to me of the outbreak of illness, I burnt everything.'

John's heart sank. 'What about the flour? The one used for the high sauce? Has that gone too?'

She nodded, a wisp of light brown hair flying out from the sensible cap she wore. 'I destroyed everything, Mr Rawlings. It seemed wiser to do so.'

Barely disguising a groan of annoyance, the Apothecary said, 'None the less, Madam, I would appreciate a look round.'

Mr Clarke became officious. 'I believe we should take this matter very seriously. I agree with Mr Rawlings.'

Jane Backler turned a stricken face on them. 'I *am* taking the matter seriously. If only something *could* be found to disprove my supposed negligence.'

'One never knows,' John answered, without much hope. 'Lead the way, Madam.'

They fell into step behind her as Jane walked from the parlour, through the entrance hall, then opened a door on the left. From there a narrow passageway led to a large kitchen, a fireplace adorned with spits and hanging cooking pots dominating the far wall.

'Were those used to prepare the Livery Dinner?' John asked, pointing.

'Yes, but they've been scrubbed since.'

'Still, may I look?'

'Of course,' the Butler answered, and began taking the pots down, one after another.

'Will you help me inspect them?' the Apothecary asked Mr Clarke, who was growing ever more large-eyed.

'Yes, but what are we meant to be seeking?'

'Traces of food, traces of anything. In fact any residue at all. Scrape it out with your herb knife.'

They set to, holding the pots up to the light, scouring round the surfaces, removing anything they could find and depositing it on a piece of paper that Michael Clarke hurried back to the shop to fetch.

'What are we to do with all this?' he whispered.

'Analyse it.'

'For what?'

John could not resist looking up and winking a very solemn eye. 'Poison.'

Mr Clarke started violently. 'Did you say poi—'

'Shush!' warned the Apothecary, staring round as if he expected interlopers. He raised his voice to normal level. 'Where did you keep the flour, Mrs Backler?'

'In the big pot up on that shelf. It's empty now.'

And it was. Further, unlike the cooking vessels, there was not a trace of residue left in it. Every last grain of flour had been rinsed away. The pot stood devoid of any clues. Disappointed, John handed it back to the Butler and stood thinking for a moment before dropping to his knees and examining the stone flags that made up the floor.

'What are you doing?'

'Looking for any particles that might have fallen. No disrespect to your housekeeping, Madam.'

Jane sniffed a little, but said nothing as John continued his search, joined after a few moments by an ever more astonished Michael Clarke, who had given up asking and now just followed the Apothecary's lead.

Opposite the fireplace, taking up most of the wall space, stood a rather unusual piece of furniture known as a dog kennel dresser, the name deriving from the arched open cupboard beneath. Laden with plates, the dresser's purpose was purely functional, namely aiding service at mealtimes. John sat back on his heels to examine its solid symmetry, thinking that in earlier times such a piece might well have stood in the dining room, bursting with silver to impress the guests. Then he glanced, almost without thinking, at the open cupboard, the so called dog kennel, situated between the two closed ones.

A mouse lay within its dark recess, unmoving and quite dead, a pathetic little figure despite its nuisance value. Taking out his handkerchief, John gently removed the corpse and wrapped it up.

'Well, I can't think where that came from,' said the Butler, sniffing more than ever.

John raised an admonitory hand. 'Madam, please. If this poor creature died because of something it ate from the floor, it might well be the key to the whole wretched affair.' He looked across at Michael. 'Mr Clarke, may we go to your compounding room?'

'Certainly. It will be . . .' Once more he lowered his voice conspiratorially. '. . . private there.'

The Society had its own laboratory, situated beneath the Great Hall and of much the same size, but the shop manager clearly did not want anyone else to know what was afoot at this stage.

The Apothecary turned to the Butler. 'Do you want me to come back to tell you what we find?'

'Please do. But remember that I go off duty and home for the night at six o'clock.'

'Where do you live? Perhaps I could call on you there?'

'In Pater Noster Row, close to St Pauls. Number twenty.'

'I will make a point of seeking you out, though it may not be until tomorrow evening.'

'Good. Then you can also meet my husband, the Beadle.'

'I look forward to it.'

Both men bowed politely, Mrs Backler curtsied, then they parted company, the two apothecaries hurrying back through the gloomy afternoon to the compounding room at the back of the shop. There they laid the mouse on a cloth on the scrubbed wooden table and, taking a sharp knife from a drawer, the shop-keeper made a neat incision, parting the skin to reveal a small, somewhat bloated stomach. This, too, he cut open, delicately removing the contents.

'Flour!' said the Apothecary excitedly. 'The poor little wretch ate some flour.'

'What are you saying exactly?'

John looked up from where he had been crouching over the minute corpse, admiring Mr Clarke's skill with so tiny an autopsy.

'I'm saying that it is my belief we are going to find white arsenic mixed with it.'

The manager's bulging eyes positively ballooned. 'What?'

'There is something a little too glib about this outbreak of poisoning. Something that doesn't quite ring true. I have a premonition.'

'Shall I do the experiment?'

'Yes. It would be an education to watch you.'

Picking up the lumps of flour with tweezers, Michael Clarke placed them in a copper pan which he held above an oil-lamp, breaking them up and slowly drying out the fluids of the mouse's stomach. Then, when all the moisture had gone, he put them onto a sieve and gently shook the lumps till they turned into grains. These he returned to the pan, adding a cup of water before he heated the contents. Vapour began to rise as the water slowly evaporated.

'Wait till it has all gone and then we'll know,' Mr Clarke said solemnly.

Finally it was done. The water had vanished and with it the remnants of the flour. But lying at the bottom of the pan were a couple of tiny white crystals. Sombrely, the Apothecary and the shop manager each took one on a finger and licked it. Then the two men looked at one another.

'Arsenic,' they said in unison.

'So the food for the Livery Dinner was deliberately poisoned?'

'Clearly yes.'

'What shall we do?'

'In view of Master Alleyn's death this is now a case of murder.'

'You are going to inform the constable?'

John shook his head. 'No, I shall take a hackney straight to Bow Street and there acquaint Mr John Fielding with the facts of the case.'

Mr Clarke looked suitably earnest and impressed. 'The Principal Magistrate himself?'

'There is no one else capable of dealing with such a monstrous crime,' John Rawlings answered firmly as he put the grains of arsenic into a vial and made to take his leave.

Chapter Five

The hackney coach which John Rawlings had been lucky enough to hire in Fleet Street drew to a halt. Turning his head to look out of the window, the Apothecary allowed his gaze to wander over the tall thin house outside which it had stopped, remembering the very first time he had seen the place. That had been in 1754, four years earlier, when he had been barely twenty-three and under suspicion of murder. To say that he had been terrified was a laughable understatement, and his first meeting with the great John Fielding, the Blind Beak, had been even more alarming. It was just as if those sightless eyes could see straight through the black bandage which always concealed them and right into the very mind of the person being questioned. That opinion of the Magistrate's unnerving gift had not changed in the intervening years, during which John had come to know the man solely responsible for keeping the peace in the wild streets of London.

'The Public Office, Bow Street. We're here, Sir,' the driver called down.

'Yes, I know. Thank you,' the Apothecary answered, clambering out and feeling in his pocket for the fare.

'Rather you than me, Sir.'

'What do you mean?'

'They say that the Blind Beak can punish hard if he feels so inclined.'

'Fortunately I'm not in line for correction at the moment. This is a social call.'

But was it? Even as he said the words John knew that in fact this was the start of another exhaustive search for a killer. He and John Fielding had worked together to bring a murderer to justice on five different occasions. Now the discovery of arsenic in the kitchens of Apothecaries' Hall was clearly the beginning of a sixth. With a rather solemn tread John climbed the three steps leading up to the open doorway of the Public Office and went inside.

It was a tradition, founded by the first Bow Street magistrate, Sir Thomas de Veil, that the justice and his family live over the court and public rooms, and John Fielding and his household had followed this custom. Above the functional ground floor there were four more storeys, the last being in the roof itself, where two large dormer windows indicated the servants quarters. However, Mr Fielding's favourite receiving area for social visits was on the first floor, a large comfortable salon where, in summer, the windows often stood open to let in the air. But on this gloomy evening a jolly fire threw its glow onto the walls, setting the shadows dancing and enhancing the candlelight.

The Magistrate turned his head as John entered the room, having knocked politely first. Just for a moment there was complete silence, then the Blind Beak said, 'Mr Rawlings?'

Mr Fielding's intuition was uncanny and, as always, the Apothecary felt daunted. 'How did you know?'

'Your tread, Sir, and the odour of you. Not a foul stink, let me hasten to add, but your own highly individual scent. I would know you anywhere, my good friend.'

Again by habit, John bowed. He had always, in common with so very many others, treated the Magistrate as if he were sighted, and now this habit was totally ingrained.

'As ever, Sir, you astound me.'

Mr Fielding rumbled his wonderful mellow laugh. 'I'll get some hot punch sent in. No doubt you'll need warming after the misery of the streets.'

'It is indeed very raw out there.'

The Magistrate rang a little bell which stood on the table beside him and after a moment or two a light step was heard in the corridor outside. This was no servant coming to answer, however: instead, a ravishingly pretty girl entered the room, a girl barely thirteen years old but already one of the beauties of town. A girl so naughty with her flirting that the temptation to box her ears was never very far away. The Apothecary gave her the most severe glance he could manage in spite of her radiant smile.

'Why, Mr Rawlings,' said Mary Ann Whittingham, Mr Fielding's niece, 'how very pleasant to see you again. I was only thinking the other day that I had not set eyes on you since the summer.'

Vividly recalling how he had rescued her from a brothel where poor wretched children were offered to the old and beastly of London, and thinking that the little madam seemed totally unperturbed by the experience, John looked positively ferocious.

She dimpled at him. 'You frown, Sir. Have I done anything to upset you?'

He stuck out his tongue, happily aware that the Magistrate could see none of this. 'Of course not, Miss Whittingham. How could you?'

He crossed his eyes and made a face like a gargoyle.

'Why,' she answered, grinning, 'I do vow and declare that you grow more handsome every time I see you.'

'Enough,' thundered the Magistrate. 'Mary Ann, stop teasing our guest. Ask one of the servants to make a jug of strong punch and bring it to us as soon as it's ready.'

'Yes, Uncle,' she answered demurely, thumbing her nose at the Apothecary, who thumbed his back.

Mr Fielding sighed gustily as the door closed behind her.

'What a creature! After her fright last summer I swear she's bounced back to be cheekier than ever.'

'She's certainly a handful.'

'Of course my wife, having no child of her own, positively dotes on her. That's the root of the trouble.'

'What are you going to do?'

'Marry her off, I suppose, as soon as she's of a reasonable age.'

John's heart sank at the very prospect of trying to keep the little imp under control for another three or four years.

'My apprentice is still in love with her.'

'She'll settle for no young apothecary, my friend.' The Magistrate sighed again. 'No, I detect signs of vanity in her. I believe she'll set her cap at a title.'

'She's very beautiful. She might easily secure one.'

'What a business it is to rear a daughter,' Mr Fielding replied.

For this was how he thought of the child, brought to him at the time of his marriage by Elizabeth, his bride, who, for reasons that were not quite clear, was raising her niece as her own. John felt fairly certain that somewhere in Mary Ann's background was a bastard birth, just as there was in his own.

John had most certainly been born out of wedlock, and had been a starving three-year-old when his adopted father, Sir Gabriel, had taken Phyllida Fleet, John's beautiful mother, forced to beg on the streets of London in order to survive, into his home. Later he had married her and John had been given all the security and background he needed. But he often wondered about his real father, another John Rawlings, son of the powerful Rawlings family of Twickenham, who had gone to find lodgings in London and never returned.

There was a further tap on the door and a servant appeared bearing a tray.

'Set it down on the table beside me, if you please,' the Magistrate said, then, hearing the tray deposited, proceeded to pour out two glasses of punch without assistance.

'And now,' he said, as the man left the room, 'to the reason for your visit, my friend. I have a feeling that this is not merely a social call. Could you have come to see me about the recent strange events at Apothecaries' Hall?'

John stared, astonished. 'I swear to God, Sir, that you read minds.'

Mr Fielding chuckled. 'Not at all. The outbreak of food poisoning was reported in the newspapers, read to me daily by the redoubtable Joe Jago. At least the important matters are – the tittle tattle and gossip I hear from Elizabeth over the breakfast table. Naturally the latest trends in fashion are duly relayed by Mary Ann.'

The Apothecary laughed, then said, 'Have you heard about Josiah Alleyn, one of the Liverymen who attended the dinner?'

The entire atmosphere in the room changed and Mr Fielding raised his head like a dog to a scent. 'Are you telling me that there has been a fatality?'

'I believe,' John replied slowly, 'that there may well have been a murder.'

The Blind Beak nodded calmly and sipped his punch. 'Start at the beginning, Mr Rawlings. It is always the best way.'

John took a deep draught of the hot comforting liquid and launched into his tale, the Magistrate sitting in silence, the black bandage which hid his eyes turned towards the Apothecary, his head utterly motionless.

'You have the arsenic with you, you say?' he asked eventually.

'Yes.'

'Be kind enough to place a crystal on my finger.'

The Apothecary did so and watched as John Fielding cautiously licked it. 'A strange taste. One I have not experienced before.'

'Only safe in very small doses, I fear.'

'And you believe this was deliberately added to the flour?'

'Yes, I do. In sufficient quantities to make all those who attended the dinner violently ill.'

'And kill one of them.'

'Indeed.'

'Um.' Mr Fielding frowned. 'What an extraordinary mind must be behind this. To murder one person is comprehendible, but to attack a whole group is a different matter entirely.'

'Nicholas, who first alerted me to the idea of poison, thought it might be someone with a grudge against apothecaries in general. A person whose spouse or close relative might have died whilst undergoing treatment.'

'That would certainly seem the most probable explanation.'

'But how in heaven's name do we find such a one? Where does the search begin?'

'Whoever this person is, he or she must have access to Apothecaries' Hall and to the kitchen. To mix white arsenic with the flour suggests that they know where the flour jar is kept. A grieving widow, bemoaning the loss of her husband at the hands of a quack, is hardly likely to have that knowledge, now is she?'

'Possibly not, but the Hall is not barred by sentries. Anyone could walk in.'

'None the less,' said John Fielding, refilling their glasses, 'I feel there must be some prior knowledge in this particular case, so I would suggest that you bend the ear of Mr Clarke and also that of Mrs Backler, remembering, of course, that they are not above suspicion themselves.'

'Surely . . .'

The Magistrate raised an admonitory finger. 'Believe me. They have the run of the place. I know they have been helpful to you so far, but that could merely be a cover for something more sinister.'

'Others have the run of the place too, Sir. What about the Master, the Beadle, and all the rest of the dignitaries? I, a humble Yeoman, can hardly start asking them questions, can I?'

'Clearly not.' Mr Fielding shifted in his chair. 'In the case of the Master, I believe it would be fitting if I called upon him personally. He has to be informed of our suspicions of foul play. As to the Beadle, you can quiz him discreetly. After all, Mrs Backler has invited you to their house and you are quite the master of gleaning information under the guise of a social visit.'

'You make me sound very underhand.'

The Magistrate guffawed cheerily. 'We are deceivers all, and in the belief that the ends justify the means I shall drink to that.'

'And so shall I,' answered John, and clinked glasses with his mentor.

He left Bow Street just before dinnertime, not wishing to foist himself on the Fieldings, who warmly pressed him to stay. But John, despite the urgings of his empty stomach, was longing to see Coralie and headed purposefully for The Strand and the house in Cecil Street. This time there was no important coach parked outside, and suddenly excited at the thought of being with her, as he always was, every time anew, the Apothecary rushed up the steps and rang the bell.

'Miss Coralie is at home,' said Thacker, smiling broadly.

'Is she resting before the theatre?'

'She is not going to the theatre, Sir. She has a night off.'

''Zounds!' exclaimed John cheerfully and briefly clutched the actresses' servant in something of an undignified yet heartfelt embrace.

Coralie was standing at the top of the stairs, looking down at him. 'John, it's you,' she called, her voice filled with pleasure.

'May I come up?'

'Of course.'

Throwing his hat and cloak aside, the Apothecary rushed to join her, holding her at arm's length and taking delight in simply gazing into her beautiful face, remembering all the varied times they had spent together.

They had met four years earlier when she had been working for Mr Fielding, acting the part of a murdered woman in a reconstruction of the night of the victim's death. On that occasion she had saved John's life, on another he had saved hers. But they had only become lovers in the summer of this year, despite the strong attraction she had always held for him. Now, though, having been apart for several days, and regardless of the fact that it would soon be time to dine, John and Coralie went into her bedroom and closed the door behind them.

They were both young and in love and in a matter of minutes they had created that rare kind of magic that sometimes can be found between two people, responding to each other as if they should always be together. John, who had slept with several women before Coralie, caught himself wondering if, now that she had become his mistress, he could ever fall in love again. A practical side of his brain told him that he could, but his romantic self vigorously denied that he would ever find such total fusion of feeling with another person. All thoughts were dismissed, however, as they reached the culmination of lovemaking and lay peacefully in the afterglow, starting, once more, to think about food.

Coralie sniffed the air. 'I think we are to have a side of beef.'

John tickled her under the chin, his delphinium-blue eyes serious. 'Will you marry me?'

'One day, I will.'

'When?'

'When I am bored with theatrical life.'

'That day will never come in my opinion. You are as bad as your sister. The pair of you will end your days as spinsters.'

Coralie propped herself up on one elbow, her emerald eyes slanting. 'My dear, there you are completely wrong.

Kitty has been married. It is just that she and her husband prefer to live apart.'

The Apothecary sat bolt upright, utterly shocked. 'I had no idea. How long ago was this?'

'A good twenty years, when she was little more than a girl. She was just starting out in her career and found that the pull of the theatre was stronger than that of being a wife. I have always vowed never to do the same. When I marry I want it to last for ever.' She gave John an unfathomable look.

'But for God's sake, Coralie,' he said, suddenly annoyed, 'how much longer do you expect me to wait?'

'I cannot understand your hurry.'

The Apothecary could feel himself growing exasperated. 'I am not *in* a hurry, yet I have the urge to live with you all the time. To have you in my bed, in a home that belongs to us both. Coralie, be fair. Look at the situation from my point of view.'

Just for a moment her eyes seemed sad and wistful. 'John, I do try, but my sister's experience has left its mark on me. Neither she nor her husband George are truly happy . . .' Thinking about the ecstatic cries coming from the first floor window the other night, John would have argued that Kitty had sounded very happy with her lover, whoever he might be. '. . . and I do not want to repeat her mistakes. Give me another five years and I am sure I will have explored all the major theatrical roles and finally be content.'

'Five years is a long time. I shall be over thirty and you will be staring it in the face. Surely that is leaving things a little late.'

'For what?'

The Apothecary gave an exasperated sigh. 'What do you think? Childbearing of course. You know very well that I want to have children.'

'Do you look upon me merely as a brood mare?'

It was too much. She had gone too far. Turning a furious face in Coralie's direction, John leapt out of bed and began to pull on his breeches. 'This relationship is clearly going no-where. You ask if I see you as a brood mare. How do you regard me, then? As a stallion?' he demanded as he wrestled with his buttons.

His mistress did not answer, looking aloof and remaining in the bed with her back averted.

'Coralie,' said the Apothecary pleadingly, for he loved her and did not want bad feeling between them.

'What?'

'Be reasonable. I care for you deeply. I cannot bear it when we quarrel.'

She turned over, her black hair tumbling over the white-ness of the pillow. In the candlelight he could see that she was smiling. 'I thought I was being reasonable.'

'Well think again, sweetheart. All I want is to marry you while we're still young enough to enjoy it.'

Her smile deepened. 'Very well, I shall compromise. I shall shorten the five years to three.'

John shook his head. 'You're a witch of the wood,' he said, and sighed. Then he kissed her, though deep in his heart he knew that something sensitive and fine had been wounded irrevocably.

He was weak where she was concerned, John knew it. Despite his earlier anger he spent the night in Coralie's bed and was forced to rise into a bleak November dawning in order to visit his shop before setting off for Apothecaries' Hall.

More than slightly annoyed with himself, John entered his premises in Shug Lane at eight in the morning to find that the reliable Nicholas was there before him, his pale face smiling as he whisked off the covers and generally tidied up.

It was reassuring to stand for a moment, gazing round all the wonderful jars and matrasses that were part of his stock in trade. Breathing a sigh of contentment, John looked at his apprentice. 'Any news?'

'A footman came round bearing a letter from the Comtesse de Vignolles. I took the liberty of bringing it with me, not certain of your movements as I was.' Nicholas grinned, perfectly well aware where his Master had spent the night.

The Apothecary made an attempt at looking severe which failed rather dismally. 'Very kind of you I'm sure.'

'Not at all, Master. I always consider your welfare.'

They both burst out laughing, unusually close in age as they were. 'How is the Comtesse, did her servant say?'

'Very well, despite being close to the end of her term. But then the Comtesse would never allow being *enceinte* to bother her, would she Sir?'

'No, wonderful woman that she is.'

Nicholas looked thoughtful. 'Comte Louis is utterly devoted to her.'

'He wasn't always, you know.'

The Muscovite looked genuinely shocked. 'You do surprise me. To me she appears the ideal wife: beautiful, witty, clever, wise.'

'You do not mention being a good housekeeper amongst her attributes.'

'That would be the least of my considerations.'

'My God, times are changing indeed,' said John with feeling.

Opening his beloved friend's letter he felt even more certain that modern manners were hurtling out of control. Despite being only a few weeks away from delivery of her second child, Serafina de Vignolles was giving a supper party for friends to which he was most cordially invited.

'Is it I who am growing staid?' John asked himself in bewilderment.

He spent the next hour compounding various requests for medicines that had been handed into the shop during his absence, taking particular care with a potion of Delphinium Staphisagria or Staves-Acre. A small number of the crushed seeds, but not too many, were effective in the treatment of clap. This particular request had come from a noble house situated not far from Shug Lane, John was somewhat amused to see. It would seem that young Lord Delamere had been sowing his oats just a little too wildly.

The work done, John put on his cloak. 'Nicholas, I'm off to Apothecaries' Hall.'

'So there *was* arsenic in the flour! Why did you not tell me before?'

'It is enough for one of us to be involved in solving murders, let alone two.'

The Muscovite looked hang-dog. 'I suppose you're right.'

'But I promise to keep you abreast of developments and to ask your advice from time to time.'

Nicholas brightened again. 'I shall look forward to that, Master.'

'And now I'm off to seek out Mr Swann in his brand new premises close to St Andrew-by-the-Wardrobe.'

'Do give him my kindest regards, Sir.'

'And from there I'll make my way to the Hall.'

'I wish you good luck, Master.'

'I shall need every bit of it, you can be assured of that,' John answered as he went out of the door.

Chapter Six

As it transpired, John's visit to Samuel Swann, his large and
exuberant friend who considered himself a sharp wit when it
came to helping the Apothecary solve a crime but whose line
in questioning invariably made things worse, was curtailed.
Samuel was out, calling on an important client, so his
apprentice informed the visitor.

'But I am sure the Master would like you to see the new
premises, Sir. Do you have a moment?'

Knowing that if he were to refuse, Samuel's feelings might
be greatly wounded, John agreed, and was indeed impressed
by the scope of the Goldsmith's new workshop and emporium.

The apprentice, a strangely ugly young man with the
beautiful hands of a fine craftsman, beamed expansively as the
Apothecary enthused.

'I shall tell the Master of your comments on his return, Sir.
But I know he will be sorry to have missed you. May I say
when you will be coming back?'

'Later this evening. I might even beg a bed for the night.
You can tell him that there is much to discuss.'

The apprentice's button eyes, dark as chestnuts and quite
out of keeping with his somewhat florid face, gleamed in
anticipation.

'I shall pass your message on, Mr Rawlings.'

'Thank you, Ezekial.'

Ezekial Semple. As if his ungainly appearance weren't enough to contend with the poor youth even had an unfortunate name.

Having left Samuel's shop, which was situated on Puddle Dock Hill, John strode through a maze of alleyways, one very dark and malodorous, and emerged into Water Street where he turned right to go to the Hall. But he had literally taken no more than a dozen steps when a bevy of people coming towards him made him stop in his path and make a bow. Mrs Alleyn, with various assorted young persons, was approaching.

There was one girl and four men, anyone of whom could have been the owner of the ill fitting suit of clothes which Mrs Alleyn had given him on the night of Josiah's illness.

Recognising John, the recently widowed woman, now dressed in dread black from head to toe, as were they all, gave a warm smile and, having dropped a polite curtsey, hugged the Apothecary, there and then and in the public street.

One of the sons reproved, 'Tush, Mother,' but she took no notice and continued her embrace.

Letting go of John at last, Mrs Alleyn turned to her children. 'This is the Mr Rawlings I told you about. The one who fought so gallantly to save your father's life. God bless him but no one could have tried harder. How are you, my dear?'

John thought rapidly. News of the arsenic in the flour obviously had not reached her. Michael Clarke had clearly sealed his lips. He bowed again, knowing he must say nothing until the Master had been informed. 'Busy, Madam, as ever. But what of your good self?'

'The Master sent for us all to come to the Hall. He wished to offer his condolences in person. He has been most kind but, of course, there is nothing anyone can really say or do.' Mrs Alleyn made a hopeless little gesture to which her daughter responded by taking hold of her mother's hand. Then the girl looked up from beneath her sweeping black hat. She was so tremendously beautiful that the Apothecary audibly drew breath, which he hastily disguised as a cough. 'I must thank you, Sir, for all you did, not only for my father but also my mother. I think you must have been a rock of strength to her.'

'Allow me to present my daughter, Emilia,' said Mrs Alleyn, but the Apothecary could hardly hear her. He was drowning in a pair of angel's eyes, submerged and sinking into their mysterious loveliness.

'Rawlings, John Rawlings,' he heard himself mutter in a voice that he could barely recognise as his own.

Emilia curtsied and he bowed yet again, so deep that his hat fell off at her feet. She smiled as only a heavenly creature could and returned it to him. Somebody shuffled his feet on the cobbles and the Apothecary realised that he had completely ignored the four sons and was behaving with extreme lack of courtesy. He straightened up.

'My other children,' said Mrs Alleyn, almost smiling at John's reaction. 'Thomas, my eldest; Richard, my second; Edmund and Ellis, the two youngest.'

They were all four very alike: squarish young men with rather wooden faces which closely resembled carved toys. The two youngest were clearly identical twins, always fascinating to behold, having the same reddish hair and hazel eyes. John wondered how four such very ordinary brothers could have produced a seraphim for a sister.

Thomas spoke up. 'I believe we owe you much in the way of thanks, Sir. I am only sorry that your efforts finally failed.'

Was there, John wondered, a sting in the tail of that remark? Knowing that it wouldn't be long before rumours of deliberate poisoning crept out, he answered, 'The odds were too heavily stacked against me, Sir. I did my best but I don't believe anybody could have saved your father.'

'Not even Master Cruttenden?' said one of the twins, and again it was difficult to know whether the remark was ingenuous or not.

'Not even he,' John answered.

Mrs Alleyn spoke again. 'The funeral is in two days time, Sir. It would please me enormously if you could be there. It will start from the house at three o'clock.'

'I had intended to pay my last respects,' the Apothecary said solemnly. 'Of course I shall be present.'

'Thank you,' said Emilia, and as she turned her head in his direction a glimpse of golden hair, an exquisite colour, showed momentarily beneath her concealing hat.

The four sons bowed, almost in unison, and gruffly muttered their gratitude. Mrs Alleyn planted a swift kiss on John's cheek, while Emilia, head lowered, gave a neat curtsey. Then the entire party continued on down the street towards Black Friars Stairs where their barge was obviously moored.

John stood staring after them, both his heart and eye taking in the fact that Emilia was just as delightful to look upon from the back as she was from the front. He watched until her small shapely frame vanished from view, then stood a second or two more, regaining his equilibrium, before he turned on his heel and continued up the lane towards the shop.

It was empty, though, judging from the noise, Michael Clarke was in his compounding room and working hard. Again, the Apothecary stood silently, remembering Mrs Alleyn's dislike of Francis Cruttenden, brought about by the fact he had encouraged her young daughter to fall in love with him. Was it Emilia, he wondered? Or was there, perhaps, another sibling whom he had not yet met? The thought of that beautiful girl forming a passion for the grey man Cruttenden was so unpleasant that John was relieved when Mr Clarke appeared from the back of the shop to take his mind off the subject.

This morning the shop manager positively buzzed with intrigue. 'Ah, my dear Mr Rawlings. What news, what news? Have you seen Mr Fielding?' he asked excitedly.

'I have indeed, Sir, and he is taking the matter most seriously. He is coming in person to see the Master and inform him of events. Until that time we should remain silent about the poison.'

'Thank God I have kept my own counsel. But, and here's the truth, I had hardly a wink of sleep last night, mulling over in my mind anyone who might wish to harm the apothecaries as a body.'

'And what answers did you come up with?'

'Three names, Sir. Three! One of which will surprise you enormously.'

'May I know who they are?'

'Certainly. Step into the compounding room where we may be more private and I will give you the list.'

They went into the back and stood by the table on which the autopsy on the mouse had been conducted. Very solemnly Mr Clarke handed the Apothecary a piece of paper. He looked at it and read, 'Sotherton Backler, Garnett Smith and Tobias Gill'. John's mobile brows shot to his hairline. 'But Sotherton Backler is the Beadle!'

'I said you would be surprised. But let me explain. Shortly before the Livery Dinner, that very morning indeed, he and the Master had a great argument. So loud was it that I could hear every word standing at the bottom of the stairs.'

'You were listening?'

Mr Clarke's ears brightened a little. 'I was just on my way into the pantry when the commotion broke out. The Master was bellowing like a bull, it was impossible not to overhear.'

'What was it about?'

'It seems that the Beadle has been claiming for money laid out on behalf of the Court of Assistants, together with further monies for extraordinary services rendered for them. The Master shouted that the Beadle was not to trouble the Court with any more bills for arrears of any nature whatsoever. The Beadle answered that such a reply was both unreasonable and unfair. Then he came storming down the stairs with a look like thunder and a goodly line in oaths coming from his mouth. After that he crashed his way into the kitchen. I saw no more of him after that.'

'But surely you are not saying that he would poison everyone as an act of revenge against one man?'

Michael Clarke looked wise. 'Perhaps, in the heat of the moment, the Beadle didn't think like that. Perhaps he simply thought of what pleasure it would give him to make the Master vomit up his guts.'

'But did Mr Backler not attend the Dinner himself?'

'No, though he should have been there in his role as chief ceremonial officer.'

'What excuse did he make?'

'That he felt unwell,' answered Michael Clarke and his bulging eyes gleamed.

The Apothecary stroked his chin, a sign that he was thinking deeply. 'And who are the others on the list? Tell me about them.'

'Garnett Smith is a prosperous merchant with a fine house in Thames Street. He has everything that money can buy, yet a year ago he lost his only son to cancer and blamed the apothecary treating him for the lad's death.'

'What happened?'

'The boy, he was about eighteen at the time, appeared to develop a type of throatal wen. Anyway, his neck swelled up greatly and the apothecary, a Liveryman no less, gave him root of cinquefoil boiled in vinegar, thinking it would ease the knots and kernels in his throat. Alas, he could not know that these walked hand in hand with a cancer and were beyond cure. The father, in a frenzy, took his son to a physician who said he had seen the patient too late. It was all to no avail. The boy died. Thereafter Garnett Smith blamed the apothecary for not diagnosing correctly and in time.'

'And he has borne a grudge against apothecaries ever since?'

'Indeed he has. He wanders into the Hall from time to time, ranting and raving and uttering threats. Last time he had to be forcibly removed. It was all extremely undignified.'

'I see. And what about Tobias Gill?'

'He is a very different case. An apothecary himself with a shop in a somewhat seedy area of the City. He fell out with the Court of Assistants over some imagined grudge, I believe. Anyway, he never took livery and keeps well away from the Hall. However, and this is the interesting part, he has been heard to state publicly that he wishes the entire Society at the bottom of the ocean and would rather be dead than associate with them again.'

'But surely that is just a figure of speech.'

'Probably, but I thought it worth mentioning.'

'Quite rightly so. Nothing should be overlooked in this investigation.'

Mr Clarke sighed. 'When is Mr Fielding coming to the Hall? It will be most difficult to stop rumours flying, in view of the fact that Mrs Backler knew about the mouse.'

'But she didn't know what we found in the poor creature.'

'Did you not call on her last night?'

'No, I was otherwise engaged,' John answered, and had the good grace to colour a little as he remembered the night he had spent with Coralie.

He turned to Michael Clarke, recalling Mr Fielding's order to trust no one and thinking it was time to find out more about the shop manager himself. 'You have tried hard, Sir, and I thank you for it. Perhaps you would care to come and dine with me one day soon.'

'I should enjoy that very much, Mr Rawlings.'

'Where do you live?'

'Across the river in Southwark, in Bandy Leg Walk. It's very quiet but I enjoy that. I am something of a recluse by nature.'

'Is there a Mrs Clarke?' John asked cheerily.

'Yes, but she, too, prefers the simple things of life.'

Thinking it sounded a horribly dull existence, the Apothecary smiled encouragingly.

'We have one child,' Michael continued, his tone changing. 'Alas, poor boy, he has the falling sickness very badly and
it is not safe to leave him on his own. My wife spends most of
her time caring for him.'

'How very sad.'

'I believe it to be a birth defect,' the manager added
quietly, then he cleared his throat and changed the subject. 'So
what next, my friend?'

'I'm off to the kitchen. I want to conduct an experiment to
see if the arsenic could have been added to the flour in full
public gaze.'

'Surely that wouldn't have been possible.'

'It might if it were done by someone whose presence there
was perfectly customary.'

'Do you mean the Butler or one of the kitchen staff?'

'I'm not quite sure who I mean yet,' John answered, and
with that made his farewells, promising to fix a dinner appointment just as soon as Sir Gabriel returned from Kensington.

As luck would have it, John left the shop at the most fortuitous
time. Just as he approached the arched entrance to the
courtyard leading to the Hall a coach drew up outside, and
from it leapt Joe Jago, Mr Fielding's clerk and right-hand man,
holding up his hand to assist the Blind Beak to alight. Seeing
John, Jago called out, 'Mr Rawlings. How are you, Sir?' And
the Apothecary hurried forward to join them.

One of the Magistrate's legs emerged from the carriage
and swung somewhat uncertainly in the air. Jago placed the
foot on the carriage step, then helped the other foot find the
cobbles below. It was clearly a much practised exercise and
one carried through most smoothly.

'Did you say Rawlings?' asked the Beak, gaining his
balance.

'Yes, he's here, Sir.'

'Good morning, gentlemen,' said John, and bowed.

Mr Fielding returned the compliment, the fact that he was pointing in the wrong direction not mattering at all. 'I've come to see the Master. It is imperative that he is now informed of events.'

'Is he forewarned of your visit?'

'I sent a Runner round this morning with a letter. He came back with the reply that I would be welcome to call.'

'Did you say what it was about?'

'No. It was too delicate a matter to put in writing.'

'He's in for an enormous shock.'

'He is indeed.'

They made their way across the courtyard then into the entrance hall, Mr Fielding taking Joe's arm, John following behind. At the bottom of the Great Staircase all three men drew to a halt.

'And where are you going now, Mr Rawlings?' asked Joe, his fiery hair glinting in a sudden ray of winter sunshine, his light blue eyes narrowing as if he were looking out to sea.

'To the kitchen.'

Mr Fielding turned to the Apothecary. 'How are you getting on with your enquiries?' he asked in a quiet voice.

'Very well, Sir. It would seem that three different people might have had a motive for poisoning the flour.'

'Speak to them all, then come and see me if you will.'

'Gladly, Sir.'

The Blind Beak nodded his head, said, 'Well done,' and started to climb the stairs, his clerk beside him.

John, having seen them safely up, turned right and went into the kitchen. Somewhat to his disappointment there was nobody about. Not the ideal conditions at all for practising sleight of hand. However, within a few seconds the door opened and Jane Backler walked in. She stopped on seeing John and stared at him.

'Mr Rawlings, what are you doing here?'

Knowing that the Blind Beak was at this very moment apprising the Master of the true facts about the poisoning,

John decided to tell the truth, only glad that he had not let the monkey out of the sleeve on the previous evening. 'I've come to tell you the results of the autopsy on the mouse.'

'I thought you were calling last night. I waited for you.'

The Apothecary felt himself grow hot but continued regardless. 'The mouse had eaten flour, within which were grains of arsenic. The poisoning at the Livery Dinner was deliberate.'

The Butler slumped into a chair, plunging a suddenly white face into her hands. 'Thank God,' she said. 'Oh, thank God.'

John looked at her curiously. 'You don't seem surprised.'

'I am surprised, astonished even. But much more than that, I am relieved. My good name has been restored to me. You will never know what I have been through since that accursed Dinner. Sly looks, snide remarks, whispering and gossip, but no open accusations, not one. Nobody had the courage to come out and accuse me to my face of buying unfit food.'

She wept at this, very suddenly, her sobs loud and un-controllable. John let her cry for a few moments then went to Jane's side, laying his hand on her shoulder. 'Mrs Backler, enough of your grieving. The worst is behind you. What lies ahead is the monumental task of discovering who put the poison in the flour, because, since the death of Master Alleyn, that person has now become a murderer.'

With the tears still streaming down her face, Jane stood up, making a heroic effort to rally. 'Yes, you're right. How can I help you?'

'I told you a lie about why I came here. The real reason was to discover whether someone could meddle with the flour in front of a kitchen full of people.'

The Butler looked at him shrewdly. 'Don't waste your time, my friend. Nobody could unless, of course, they were a member of my staff.'

'Quite.'

She took in the entire meaning of that short answer and squared her shoulders before she replied. 'Mr Rawlings, present in the kitchen that day were myself and my two daughters, Abigail and Ruth, who come in from time to time to assist at more important occasions. Also here was a French cook who works for me on the same basis. My husband, the Beadle, put his nose round the door from time to time to see how things were getting on.'

She paused and wiped her eyes with a handkerchief, then looked at the Apothecary very straightly. 'I can assure you, Sir, with my hand upon my heart . . .' she laid it there '. . . that I have no reason for poisoning the apothecaries. They pay me an annual salary of six pounds, and Sotherton's status is much enhanced by his position. Even though we still have a shop, it is from the Court of Assistants that most of our benefits flow. You must believe that I would not bite the hand that feeds me.'

Despite Mr Fielding's warning, John felt certain that she was telling the truth. Jane Backler had a blaze of sincerity about her woebegone features.

'As for my daughters,' she continued, 'the little innocents wouldn't harm a fly. Why, they are scarce out of the cradle.'

He looked surprised. 'Yet they work here? How old *are* they?'

'Fourteen and sixteen.'

John burst out laughing. 'Hardly babies.'

The Butler allowed herself a small smile. 'No, I grant I exaggerate, but, believe me, they know very little of the politics of the Society.'

'Are there politics?'

'There are always politics in every group, large or small.'

'How very true. So that leaves the French cook.'

'He was born here but studied with one of the master chefs. His name is Jacques Genet and he works for himself, hiring out his services to any who will employ him.'

'Could he have any motive that you know of for poisoning the flour?'

'Of course not, but I expect you will want to see him none the less. He lives, so I believe, somewhere near Drury Lane. The Beadle will have a record of his address.'

'Then,' said John, coming directly to the point, 'if none of you tampered with the flour, who did? And when was it done?'

A fearful expression crossed Jane's face, the gap in her teeth suddenly making her look like a frightened child. 'Mr Rawlings, can I say something?'

'Yes.'

'This Hall, beautiful as it is in the daylight, is very different at night. Then it is a place full of shadow. I tell you true, I don't like being here on my own after dark.'

'Are you saying something unworldly poisoned the flour?'

'Of course not. What I *am* saying is that I am not alone in my feeling. That people, men included, don't care to remain here for long when nobody else is about.'

'So?'

'So someone who wanted to steal back after nightfall and put poison in a place where it could do most harm would encounter very little to stop him.'

'But surely there's a watchman?'

'An old fellow who dozes half the night. He could easily be avoided.'

'So that is how you think it was done? By a midnight walker?'

Jane shivered. 'Yes, that is what I think.'

'When did you last use the flour?'

'On the previous day. The Master was entertaining guests and a high sauce was made to go with his meat. After that it was not touched until the Livery Dinner.'

John rubbed his chin hard. 'Does that suggest to you that the killer has precise knowledge of this place? Knows that the watchman dozes in the small hours? And knows exactly where the flour is kept?'

'Maybe not the last. But cooking components are stored in pantries. All that he—'

'Or she,' the Apothecary interrupted.

Jane conceded with a nod of her head. '. . . needed to do was locate the kitchen and the rest would be easy.'

The Apothecary nodded slowly, then he took Jane's hand and raised it to his lips, a gesture that clearly pleased her. 'I shall call on you tonight, if I may. I need to talk to your husband.'

She suddenly looked extremely defensive. 'What about?'

'Just about the situation in general,' John answered vaguely, and hoped that with that reply the Butler would be content.

Chapter Seven

—————◦◦◦◦◦————

It would seem that for the time being John had achieved all
that was possible at Apothecaries' Hall. He had been given the
names of three people with grudges, one against the Master
personally, the other two against apothecaries in general. The
Butler had confirmed that only a member of the kitchen staff
could have poisoned the flour during the preparations for the
Livery Dinner. It was also her opinion that the substance was
tampered with on the night before, an opinion with which
John tended to agree.

Finally, innocent though he believed him to be, the
Apothecary had invited Michael Clarke to dine, in order
that he might question him more closely. With these
thoughts and many more tumbling around in his mind, John
left the Hall in order to get a little air and exercise and clear
his head.

It was fast approaching the hour to dine and dusk was just
starting to fall over the river. Not only that. A November fog
was creeping over the water, vaporous and sinister, its white
fingers curling round the boats that lay moored at Black Friars
Stairs.

John stood silently, remembering how Josiah Alleyn had
leaned against this very railing, sick to his stomach. He had
little thought then what a strange trail would open up from
such an unpleasant but seemingly innocuous beginning. But

then nothing was ever quite what it seemed. Did Jane Backler's gap-toothed smile hide a woman ruthlessly protecting her husband? Or was Michael Clarke's bulging-eyed enthusiasm a mask for a disturbed and cruel mind?

John shook himself, thinking that the fog had entered into his brain, then, for no obvious reason, drew back as the sound of footsteps, firm and confident in their tread, approached the place where he stood. Without seeing the Apothecary, Francis Cruttenden strode by and descended the steps, his rippling grey cloak blending so evenly with the mist that he was scarcely visible.

'Barge,' he called, and at the sound of his voice disembodied oars rose upwards in the fog, and a phantom vessel, or so it seemed to John's overactive imagination, began to make its way silently through the vapour.

Though Master Cruttenden had obviously been at the Hall, seeing the Liveryman was still something of a shock and the Apothecary found his thoughts turning to the glorious Emilia Alleyn, wondering again whether Cruttenden had been the focus of her youthful yearnings, or if it had been another sister who had loved him. On a completely crazy impulse John found himself creeping down the stairs from which the Liveryman had just departed and calling to the sole wherryman who had braved the ghastly night and sat in his boat waiting for a fare.

'Boatman.'

'Yes, Scholar?'

'Keep close behind that barge. I've a mind to see where it goes.'

The waterman spat into the river to show his contempt for idiots. 'It'll cost you, Scholar. Double for the fog.'

'Just get on,' answered John and sat down on the plank seat, the dank atmosphere already settling on his cloak.

Master Cruttenden's barge was ahead of them, barely visible through the ever descending mist, pulling across the river towards the south bank. Not quite certain why he was embarking on such folly, John sat in silence, listening to the quiet dipping of the wherryman's oars, feeling as if he were acting out a part in a dream.

The barge vanished from view, the only clue to its whereabouts the sound it made as its oarsmen strove across the tide.

John leant towards the wherryman. 'Have you any idea where they're heading?' he whispered, breath fluting in the vapour.

The fellow shrugged, his face yellow beneath the lantern he carried on a pole. 'Could be anywhere.'

'What stairs are there on the Southwark side?' John persisted.

'Marygold, Bull, Old Barge House. How would I know which one they want?' His face changed and he held up a hand. 'Listen, they're pulling downstream.'

The Apothecary strained his ears but could hear nothing except the distant stirring of water. But his boatman, with a sturdy heave on the right oar, was turning his craft, also to head downstream, and, eventually, towards the open sea.

'Not Paris Garden,' he muttered.

'How do you know?'

'They would have started to pull in by now.'

'Your knowledge is quite amazing.'

'Nay, Scholar, so would yours be if you'd been born in a boat as I were.'

They relapsed into silence, listening for the sound of Francis Cruttenden's barge, now completely lost to view. Finally, the wherryman pointed a gnarled finger at the shore and nodded his head. 'Mason Stairs,' he whispered.

With absolutely no idea how he was going to get back across the river, John paid the man off, gave a generous tip, and set foot on the slippery stone steps. As he did so, he glimpsed the barge, which was being taken off to a boathouse situated, as far as he could tell through the fog, on the river frontage some further yards downstream. Hoping that he would not lose his quarry, the Apothecary set off in pursuit of

Liveryman Cruttenden, his feet overloud on the crunching gravel, or so it seemed in the silence.

At the top of Mason Stairs a walkway ran to both right and left, whilst ahead appeared the shadowy outlines of a timber yard. Beyond that, John could see nothing. He stopped, listening for the sound of movement, and a faint footfall told him that Francis Cruttenden had gone forward. Cautiously, the Apothecary crept on, discovering as he did so that a rough track lay beside the yard, obviously leading to some dwelling place beyond. With extreme care John followed, peering ahead as he did so.

Directly in front of him the hinges of a gate squeaked as it opened and closed. The Apothecary stopped dead, realising that he had caught the Liveryman up and was in danger of coming up so close behind him that Cruttenden might turn and recognise him. He waited several minutes, then cautiously moved on again, finding himself a moment later in front of a tall and ornate iron gateway. Peering through its bars, John could make out a path leading through a formal garden. Beyond that, and scarcely visible in the fog, reared the shape of a large house. Exercising extreme care, the Apothecary eased the gate open a small amount and squeezed his way through without opening it fully. Wondering what possible explanation he could give if he were caught, he proceeded quietly up the path.

The house emerging from the mist was one of extreme magnificence, and John's head tilted back as he took in its grandiose elevation. His mouth fell open in sheer surprise at such splendour. Francis Cruttenden was obviously a man of great means, if this was indeed his home. If not, the Liveryman clearly moved amongst an élite circle of rich friends.

There was the sound of an opening door and John had literally to throw himself behind a bush as a shaft of light coming from the hall illumined the pathway. Through the open doorway he glimpsed a liveried servant, rich carpeting, paintings upon the wall and a glittering candelabra, before the door closed again and he was once more alone in the fog.

Crouching behind the sheltering shrub, John considered his plan. There was no point in proceeding further. Francis Cruttenden had gone indoors, either to his own home or visiting. Further, there was Sotherton Backler to be called upon, then Samuel, hopefully for a night of claret and jolly conversation. The best thing he could do at this moment would be to find someone to row him back to the north bank, and there visit a tavern where he could appease the grumbling of his empty stomach. Without hesitation John turned on his heel and retraced his steps.

Was it luck or just the appalling weather, or perhaps the large tip he had given him, that led the Apothecary to find the same boatman, smoking a pipe and taking his ease at the bottom of Mason Stairs? A weatherbeaten face was raised through the fog. 'Is that you, Scholar?'

'It is.'

'Did you find him?'

'Yes,' said John, settling himself on the damp plank. 'And very surprising it was.'

'How's that?'

The need to discuss overcame the Apothecary's usual discretion. 'Well, the man concerned is only a Liveryman of the Society of Apothecaries. When I say only, don't misunderstand me. They are great men, advanced men, but I would not have thought their position sufficient to enable them to own a mansion of quite such noble stature as the one I saw tonight. That is, if he does own it.'

The wherryman spat into the water. 'Scholar, are you talking about Pye House?'

'I don't know. It's a huge place set back in its own beautiful gardens.'

'Then you are. There's only one great house round these parts.'

'And who owns it?'

'Master Cruttenden. He's the richest man for miles.'

John gaped. 'How did you come by all this knowledge?'

'I told you I was born in a boat, didn't I? I'm river folk, Sir. Have you not come across them before?'

Remembering all that had happened to him in the great Devil's Tavern at Wapping, John nodded his head. 'Oh yes, I most certainly have.'

'Then I'll say no more,' answered the wherryman as they set off through the mist towards Black Friars.

Sotherton Backler's house was rather like its lady, the Apothecary thought, attractive, not new, and somehow understated. It stood amongst its neighbours, its façade plain almost to the point of dullness, yet with an underlying appeal of simple charm that could not be missed. Within, as John was shown into the parlour, the same quality occurred. The decoration was confined to the lightest and most sparely applied plasterwork, yet the fireplace was exquisite. And the Butler, devoid of her plain and practical work clothes and dressed in rustling skirts, was on the point of being a lovely woman.

'Good evening,' said John, and kissed her hand.

Sotherton Backler rose from his place beside the fire and regarded his visitor with all the aloof grandeur of a dignitary of the Worshipful Society. As Beadle he was its chief ceremonial officer and held a position of considerable importance.

'I believe that you are assisting Mr John Fielding with his investigation into the alleged poisoning at Apothecaries' Hall.'

John bowed low, humble as only a Yeoman could be. 'Sir, I wish that I could concur with the word alleged. Unfortunately the poisoning was a fact. A fact that led to a death.' He straightened and looked the Beadle in the eye. 'If only it were not so.'

Sotherton Backler stared at him with a gaze intended to cut the little upstart to size. John assumed his official face, all the while smiling politely and thinking that Mr Fielding had obviously changed his mind: the tactic of gleaning information by means of social chit chat had been replaced by a smack of officialdom. Wondering what his future would be in the Worshipful Society of Apothecaries in view of all this, John continued to smile.

The Beadle glared. 'According to Mr Fielding an unknown hand deliberately poisoned the flour used in the high sauce. Now what possible motive could there be for that? Personally I find it almost impossible to believe.'

John looked contrite. 'It seems, Sir, from what I have learned so far, that certain persons bear a grudge against apothecaries in general, whilst others have a particular dislike of the Master. It is quite conceivable that one of those people added arsenic to the food simply to make everyone ill, perhaps never dreaming that in one case the dose would prove fatal.'

At the back of the room Jane rustled slightly, then said, 'I am thankful, Sotherton, that the arsenic was found. Up till that moment I had been living with the reproach of others. It was one of the worst experiences imaginable.'

The Beadle looked across at her, then pursed his lips, apparently on the point of speaking. John attempted an encouraging expression. Finally, Sotherton Backler cleared his throat. 'No doubt it is common knowledge that the Master and I fell out on the morning of the Livery Dinner.'

Realising how much it must have cost him to make such a statement to a mere Yeoman, John spontaneously shook the Beadle's hand, then bowed. 'I thank you for telling me, Sir.'

'Had you heard the rumour?'

'No,' lied the Apothecary, saving all kinds of trouble.

Sotherton Backler relaxed slightly, his tall, rather full-bellied frame easing its stance. 'It was over a point of internal business. We did not see eye to eye about a certain administrative matter.'

John nodded but remained silent.

'To my shame I must admit that we shouted at one another and I believe that our voices carried.'

'They did,' said Jane succinctly.

'But . . .' stated the Beadle with emphasis, . . . 'I most certainly didn't conceive the idea of making the Master ill or of disrupting the Dinner. Such a spiteful act would be beneath me.' His light blue eyes, dominated by a pair of bushy black and white eyebrows, stared at the Apothecary with an almost pleading expression.

'I trust that my word is good enough, Mr Rawlings.'

'Of course, Sir.'

'He's telling the truth,' said the Butler, flashing one of her gappy smiles. 'Had he come into the kitchen and gone to the flour pot I would have seen him.'

'Where exactly was the pot kept?' John asked. 'You mentioned something about a pantry.'

'No, it wasn't there. It was on the dresser. A big earthenware jar standing on the bottom shelf.'

'That would indicate that whoever did this knew precisely where it was stored.'

'Not necessarily. I did indeed say to you, Mr Rawlings, that a stranger entering the Hall at night could most likely find his way to the kitchen area and from thence to the pantries.'

'Yes.'

'Equally, if they were looking for something to which to add white arsenic, the flour sitting there on the dresser in a storage jar would prove exceptionally handy.'

John stroked his chin. 'Somehow I don't think your theory is right, Mrs Backler. I believe that the person concerned knew exactly where they were going and what they were going to do when they got there.'

She shivered. 'I don't like that thought.'

'It is not a pretty one, but then murder rarely is.'

'But was it murder?' asked the Beadle. 'Or was it simply the wish to wreak havoc?'

'Whatever,' John answered, 'it has become a killing now.'

Sotherton regarded him steadily. 'How, in the name of heaven, are you going to track the guilty party down?'

'By asking questions and observing, that is the only way.' John changed his tone. 'May I just enquire about something else while I'm here?'

'And what is that?'

'Liveryman Francis Cruttenden. Is it true that he is very wealthy?'

The Backlers exchanged a glance, and Jane spoke. 'I believe he inherited a great fortune. He certainly lives in a grand house with many servants.'

John went out on a limb. 'Is he a married man?'

'Why the interest in him?' asked the Beadle.

The Apothecary shrugged. 'Nothing really. I met him when I tended Master Alleyn. Mr Fielding told you of that?' Sotherton nodded. 'I thought him quite an interesting character, clad all in grey and with an air about him smooth as silk.'

Jane burst out laughing. 'What a good description. Personally I can't abide the fellow, but that is between these four walls. However, I believe the ladies adore him, particularly the younger ones.'

'That's idle gossip,' said the Beadle severely.

'Then he has no wife?'

'Not he – he enjoys himself too much to be tied to one woman.'

'What age is he?' asked John curiously.

The Butler answered him. 'He's prematurely grey, of course. Indeed I do believe he had grey hair when he became a Yeoman. I think he is not much over forty.'

'How interesting.'

Yet again, as she had several times that day already, Emilia Alleyn came into the Apothecary's mind. The question was out before he could control it. 'Do you know by any chance how many daughters Master Alleyn had?'

Jane Backler gave him the oddest glance, but answered, 'Only one. Four boys and a girl were his offspring.'

John smiled. 'I thought that might be the case.'

'But what has that to do with his sad demise?'

'Nothing whatsoever,' the Apothecary answered, and wondered why he felt a pang of disappointment that it was Emilia who had been in love with that grey shadow, Master Cruttenden.

"Zounds!' said Samuel. 'This is going to be one of your hardest enigmas to solve, my friend.' He rubbed his hands excitedly. 'What an excellent kettle of fish. A deranged poisoner stalking through Apothecaries' Hall. Couldn't be better.'

John grinned at his old friend's enthusiasm and poured himself a deep glass of wine. 'I don't recall mentioning the words deranged or stalking,' he said from his place at Samuel's table, where the remains of a hefty supper were still laid out.

'But that's what it amounts to, doesn't it? Clearly anyone who goes in for a mass poisoning has to be crazed,' responded the Goldsmith, tipping back his chair and thrusting his legs forward.

'Why?'

'Well, a hatred for an entire group of people is hardly rational, is it?'

'No, that's true enough. And yet . . .'

'What?'

John shook his head, the idea that had just scurried through his mind gone again like a will-o-the-wisp.

Samuel boomed a laugh. 'You looked downright daunted then. I think you're going to need my help.'

The Apothecary winced, remembering all the occasions on which Samuel had made a gaffe with those who needed delicate handling. 'I'll let you know when I do.'

Typically, his loyal friend mistook his meaning. 'Don't worry about keeping me from my business. Ezekial is more than capable of looking after things for a day or two. When can we start?'

As ever, John groaned within but could not bring himself to hurt Samuel's feelings. 'Well, tomorrow I am going in search of Garnett Smith and Tobias Gill, the two who are known to bear a grudge against apothecaries.'

The Goldsmith looked wise. 'And what of the third, Sotherton Backler? Do you believe him to be innocent of trying to poison the Master?'

'As far as I can tell, yes. Anyway, his wife thinks him to be so, and I imagine her to be a very good judge of character.'

'Even about her own husband?'

'It is possible to look at one's spouse without prejudice.'

Samuel's mind made a grasshopper leap of such predict- ability that John almost laughed aloud. 'Changing the subject, how is Coralie these days?' he asked.

'She is well.'

'No nearer entering the married state?'

'I'm afraid not.' A desperate need to confide overcame the Apothecary and he drew his chair closer to Samuel's, pouring another glass of wine for them both. 'I sometimes wonder if she ever will be.'

'What do you mean?'

'I discovered something odd the other night. Apparently Kitty was married very young, just at the beginning of her career. She chose the theatre rather than her husband, and Coralie is terrified of making the same mistake. I believe it has affected her more deeply than she realises. She may go on and on until she feels herself to be ready for marriage, only to find that she has left it all too late.'

An amazing range of expressions flitted over Samuel's face. 'Are you saying, John, that you won't wait for her for ever?'

The Apothecary sighed. 'Yes, I suppose I am.'

'But you've always loved her.'

'I know, I know. And I still do. It's just that . . .' The worst happened, rather as he had feared it would. A picture of Emilia Alleyn, sharp as reality, came into his mind. 'Oh God, Samuel,' John said miserably.

'My dear old chap,' answered the Goldsmith, putting an arm round his shoulders. 'Tell me everything.'

And with a great sense of relief, John did.

When he had finished, Samuel breathed out gustily. 'I had a feeling this might happen one day.'

'That I would tire of the situation, do you mean?'

'That, together with your meeting someone else.'

'But I hardly know Miss Alleyn. We've been introduced, that is all.'

'Your face when you speak of her is enough.'

'But Sam, I really do love Coralie, you know that.'

'Yes, I do. But still I have often wondered if she is the right woman for you.'

'Because of her attitude?'

'Precisely that.'

'I think,' said John very seriously, 'I might drink rather too much wine tonight.'

'If I were you,' Samuel answered equally seriously, 'I think I might too.'

And with that they solemnly toasted one another and the ladies of the town and set about forgetting everything that was troubling them.

It was, inevitably, a very grey dawning. It seemed to John, who had woken himself by snoring, that the fog which had lain heavily over London and its river all the previous day, had now entered his head. He came to consciousness through wads of it, struggling for air, and when he caught sight of himself in the mirror hanging by the bed, he nearly lost it again. To say he looked ghastly was an understatement. His hair, usually a curly, sprightly, springing mop, difficult to control unless kept short, hung limply round his face, which was an unattractive shade of whey. His eyes, frequently a dazzlingly bright blue, had vanished into two slits out of which peered ugly red marbles.

'God!' said John Rawlings, and stuck out his tongue at his image. It was yellow and he hastily put it back again.

Equally loud snoring to his own, could be heard from the bedroom across the landing. Carefully getting out of bed, the Apothecary padded over and looked within. Samuel slumbered hugely, his large frame occupying the entire bed, his arms flung wide.

'Oh dear,' said John, and returned to his room and slept for another hour.

When he woke again it was to hear cheerful noises from below. Peering down the stairwell the Apothecary saw that Ezekiel and Mab, the only servant Samuel could afford at this stage of his career, were chatting together in the passageway outside the kitchen.

'Could you bring me some hot water?' he called down to her. She looked up, round face startled. 'Oh, it's you, Mr Rawlings. I'll fetch it directly, Sir.'

'Thank you. And could I have a cup of tea as well?'

'Certainly, Sir.'

From the kitchen came the pleasant smell of cooking breakfast, always reassuring to John, who considered it the most important meal of the day. As the door opened to allow Mab in, the Apothecary caught a glimpse of Samuel wielding a pan. It was very much an egalitarian household, with the Master and apprentice taking an equal share of duties with the maid, a concept that was a million miles from Sir Gabriel's formal and fashionable approach, but one that John rather liked. Hurrying back to his room he dressed and, as soon as the ewer of hot water arrived, shaved and washed. He eventually went downstairs, feeling considerably restored.

'Recovered?' asked Samuel, serving a large mess of eggs.

'Was I very drunk?'

'You sang a great deal.'

'I apologise.'

'The songs were of an amorous nature.'

'Oh, God save us.'

The Goldsmith added a vast quantity of fried herrings to John's dish. 'You did not seem quite certain of the dedications.'

'Could you explain that?'

'Coralie and Emilia were becoming confused. In the end I think you were singing simultaneously to both.'

The Apothecary rolled a regretful eye. 'Let us be thankful that only you witnessed this.'

Samuel adopted a solemn visage. 'My advice, dear friend, is to be very careful when in the company of either young lady. It would not do at all for you to call her by the wrong name.'

'Hold your peace, rum guts. It's not going to come to that.'

'We shall see,' said Samuel portentously.

Chapter Eight

⸺⸻◆⸻⸺

A large breakfast consumed, somewhat surprisingly in view of his delicate state, John Rawlings left Samuel's house on Puddle Dock Hill and, accompanied by his stalwart friend, went on foot into the City of London. The fog had rolled away in the night and though bitterly cold the day was crisp and clear with a fine wind blowing in off a waterway that only the night before had been wreathed with clammy tendrils of creeping mist.

Looking towards the Thames from the street named after it, one of the longest thoroughfares in London, the Apothecary marvelled at the river's wild reaches, bright blue beneath the sparkling sky, and planned that when he lived in Kensington he would make regular expeditions to Chelsea and there sit by the waterside and stare at nothing and everything as the day and the ships went by.

On the previous evening he had learned from Sotherton Backler that the shop of Tobias Gill, the disgruntled apothecary who no longer wished to associate with the Worshipful Society, was situated in Pudding Lane, that most notorious of alleyways where on the first of September, 1666, the Great Fire of London had broken out. Not considered a good address, with such a stigma attached to it, it seemed that times were hard for Apothecary Gill.

Thankful yet again that Sir Gabriel had bought him

premises in Shug Lane, Piccadilly, John turned to his companion. 'Do you think I should tell him I'm an apothecary or not?'

Samuel jutted his lower lip. 'I'm not sure. He might take against you just for being a Yeoman of the Society. On the other hand it would give you mutual ground for discussion and break any ice there might be.'

'It might be better to wait till I see him and make my decision then.'

'Good plan.'

In the event, all schemes went awry. Walking into the shop, squeezed unattractively between a butcher's and a pieman's, both John and Samuel were amazed to see a comely young woman step forward to serve them.

'Can I help you, gentlemen?' she enquired, lips smiling, eyes observing.

Forced to say something plausible, John struggled for words. 'I had actually hoped to have a word with the Apothecary, discussing the merits of certain herbs and so on.'

A gaze bright as amber beads examined him shrewdly. 'My father is out at the moment, Sir. Are you an apothecary yourself?'

John was cornered. 'Yes,' he said lamely.

Samuel decided to enter the arena. 'Mr Gill is very highly spoken of, of course. That is why we came to see him.'

The brilliant eyes changed direction and the Goldsmith was treated to an appraising look. 'Really? By whom?'

'By everyone,' he answered, then chortled as if he had said something amusing.

The girl flickered a smile. 'How very odd. He is, in fact, not well liked by his fellows.'

Oh God, thought John, searching for a clever reply.

She was blazingly beautiful, with a cloud of red hair, pale skin, and those amazingly arresting topaz eyes. It seemed to be a time, the Apothecary reflected, for meeting lovely females, not the easiest thing for a susceptible creature like himself.

John heard Samuel give a convulsive swallow, indicating that he, too, was far from immune to the charms of the ravishing Miss Gill.

John came to a decision. 'This I know,' he said.

'That my father is not well liked, you mean?'

'Yes. And for that very reason it is imperative I speak to him.'

The acute expression, which had never really left her face, returned fully. 'Why? What has happened?'

'I can save you the trouble of answering that,' said a clipped voice from the doorway, and the two men swung round to see that Apothecary Gill had returned. 'There's been trouble at Apothecaries' Hall of which I am suspected of being the perpetrator,' the newcomer continued, marching into his shop. He went behind the counter, then turned to stare at them. 'That's correct, is it not?'

'I wouldn't put it quite as strongly as that,' John answered levelly. 'The facts are that white arsenic was mixed with the flour kept in the kitchen at the Hall. It seems that this was done the night before a Livery Dinner. As a result all the Liverymen were taken ill, and one of them, Master Josiah Alleyn, subsequently died. Questions have been asked about those with a grudge against apothecaries and it seems that you fell out with the Worshipful Society some years ago. That is as far as the matter goes. You most certainly have not been accused of committing any crime.'

'I should hope not indeed,' said the redhead forcefully. 'My father was treated badly by the Society, but revenge is not in his capability.'

'Clariana, please.'

'I mean it, Papa. They have no right to accuse you.' She glowered at John, reminding him vividly of a molten furnace.

'No one has accused him,' he said patiently. 'It is merely that Mr Fielding, the Principal Magistrate, who is investigating this particular case, insists that all avenues are pursued. Therefore, Mr Gill, as his representative I have to ask you whether you were at Apothecaries' Hall seven nights ago. Or to put it another way, were you on the premises the night before the Livery Dinner?'

It was a downright clumsy approach and the Apothecary knew it, but it seemed there was no other way out. He had been forced to reveal his hand far too soon and now could only make the best of it.

'No, I most certainly was not. I haven't set foot in the wretched place for years.'

'Get out,' hissed Clariana. 'How dare you come here and bully my father? You have no right and no authority. Mr Fielding's representative be damned. You're just a prying busybody sent by the Master most like. Now go before I call the constable.'

Samuel drew himself up to his full height. 'Madam, you are making a grievous mistake, and are also obstructing the natural processes of the law. You leave my friend no option but to report this matter to a higher authority.'

Tobias Gill sighed. 'Clariana, he is right. It is best that this young man and I converse privately. He will soon see that I am innocent of any connection with this extraordinary affair.' The older man raised the hinged flap in the counter and beckoned John through. The Apothecary stood hesitantly, wondering what he should do about Samuel. 'I did not come here alone, Sir.'

'None the less, I wish to speak to you by yourself.'

The Goldsmith bowed to Clariana Gill. 'Would you mind if I remained in the shop?'

A strange look crossed the redhead's face and John felt that she was giving the matter far more consideration than it merited. Finally she said, 'It would not be convenient, Sir. Some customers prefer to ask for their physick in private.'

Samuel stood up. 'It seems that I will be *persona non grata* wherever I am. I shall go for a short walk, John, and will meet you outside in half an hour.'

Thinking that his friend was growing quite dignified with

the passing of the years, the Apothecary followed Tobias Gill into his private quarters.

It was an hour before John emerged into the bright sharp light of midday, noticing that it had grown bitterly cold and wondering how poor Samuel had fared. There had been no sign of the Goldsmith as John had walked back through the emporium, past a cold-faced Clariana who had done no more than shoot a frosty glance in his direction. For no reason, this had annoyed the Apothecary so enormously that he had made much of bowing fulsomely and several times over at that. 'A pleasure, Ma'am, to make your acquaintance. I do hope that we will meet again.'

Clariana's gorgeous amber eyes had given him a contemptuous glance. 'I doubt that we shall.'

The Apothecary had adopted a cunning expression, as if he knew more than he was prepared to divulge. 'Now that I wouldn't be too sure about. There's going to be many a twist before this skein is unravelled. Good day to you.'

He had swept out, jamming his hat hard down upon his head, allowing his eye to roam backwards to give her a final stare. She had been glaring at him so hard that he had been unable to resist winking, slowly and in a lunatic fashion, before be disappeared from her view.

He caught up with Samuel a few moments later, emerging from a coffee house in Little Eastcheap, looking well fed and warm.

'I was worried about you. I thought you might have frozen to death.'

'Not I, dear friend. I hurried in here and ate buns and watched the world go by. I also watched the exterior of Mr Gill's shop.'

'And?'

'And very interesting it proved. You had not been gone ten minutes when the ravishing redhead appeared, dressed for outdoors in a hat and cloak.'

'Did you follow her?'

'As a matter of fact I did. I slipped like a shadow. She did not see me.'

The Apothecary chuckled aloud at the mental picture. 'What happened?'

'She went up Grace Church Street and thence to Cornhill, where she met a man outside the Royal Exchange. I particularly noticed him because he was dressed all in grey.'

John's jocularity vanished on the instant. 'Describe him.'

'He was tall and thin with grey hair. He did not have a wig on, so I noticed it particularly.'

'What was he wearing?'

'A long grey cloak that rippled in the wind. He looked rather like a seal.'

'Francis Cruttenden,' muttered John. 'What the devil was he doing here?'

'Is he the man you followed last evening?'

'Yes, the same.'

'Surely it's too much of a coincidence? It has to be someone else.'

'Yes, you're right. I've got the bastard on the brain. None the less, the description tallies very closely. What happened?'

'They walked along together, talking earnestly, then they kissed and parted company.'

'Kissed, eh? That sounds like the dirty old wretch. He is besotted with younger women.'

'You sound very vehement. Why?'

'Because of Emilia Alleyn.' And John told the Goldsmith what he had heard from the girl's mother.

Samuel nodded wisely. 'No wonder you dislike him. But what about you? Tell me what happened.'

'We went over all the old ground. Apparently he fell out with the Society over money. He was accused of not paying certain dues and resented the fact. It was all water under the bridge a long time ago but he's one of those small, neat, obsessive men who bear grudges. He has very tiny feet, did you notice?'

'No.'

'Well, he has. They are the sort of feet that I associate with pettiness.'

Samuel laughed rumblingly. 'I've never heard that theory before.'

'That's because it is one of my own. Be that as it may, he resents the Society of Apothecaries and everything they stand for. But for all that, he has an account of what he did the night before the Livery Dinner and was in his shop all day when the event actually took place.'

'Do you believe him?'

'I'm not sure. His story relies very heavily on the word of his daughter.'

'Did you question her?'

'No, I didn't. She had such a look about her when I left the shop that I couldn't bring myself to do so. But I shall return and catch her unawares, I assure you.'

'Do you think the man she was with was Cruttenden?'

'I'm going to make it my business to find out, even if I have to follow her one day.'

'So what do we do next?'

'Catch Garnett Smith before he sits down to dine, and ask him a few pertinent questions.'

'He won't tell you anything.'

'I know that,' the Apothecary answered with a sigh, 'but sometimes what they don't say is just as important as what they do.'

Michael Clarke had given John a rough idea of where Garnett Smith's dwelling could be found in Thames Street, but, as luck would have it, it was at the furthest end from the City, close to Samuel's shop, from which point they had originally set out. Huddled into their cloaks to fend off the cold, the two friends fought their way back, walking into the whipping wind, and arrived somewhat rosy cheeked and out of breath.

'Is this it?' asked Samuel, staring at the imposing mansion with its commanding view over the river.

'Yes,' John answered, looking at the piece of paper that Michael Clarke had given him.

'I doubt we'll gain entry here.'

'You may be right at that. Let's withdraw to your place and formulate a plan.'

Glad to get out of the biting wind, the two men turned up Puddle Dock Hill and hastened into the warmth of the Goldsmith's shop. It was three o'clock, an hour before the time to dine, and Samuel set about mulling some wine.

'I think,' said John, having taken a mouthful, 'that the best thing I can do is go back to my shop, collect some physick and pills, and deliver them to Mr Smith's house, then claim, when he denies ordering them, that I must have come to the wrong address.'

'And what do you hope to gain from that?'

'When he realises that I am a much-hated apothecary, I might be able to draw him out.'

'I suppose it could work.'

'Can you think of a better idea?'

'Frankly, no.'

'I dislike using the official line. I rarely get as much information.'

'You're perfectly right. Today was a case in point. By the way, when is Master Alleyn's funeral?'

'Tomorrow at three o'clock at Chelsea.'

'I shall come and observe,' said Samuel portentously. 'You never know what valuable points I might pick up.'

With a grave expression hiding an affectionate smile, John nodded agreement, then stepped out once more into the icy afternoon.

★   ★   ★

The plan worked. After a delay of some ten minutes, during which the Apothecary insisted that he was to hand the medicines to Mr Garnett Smith and no other, he was finally ushered into a small salon where the man himself sat solitary, imbibing fine sherry. He looked up as the stranger came through the door, beetled his brows and said in a gravelly voice, 'What tomfoolery's this?'

John bowed low. 'I have brought your physics, Sir, as ordered by your servant.'

'What servant? Don't you play your knavish tricks with me, Sir. Who the Devil are you?'

John bowed once more. 'John Rawlings, Apothecary of Shug Lane. A footman came in earlier today and told me you were suffering from the quinsy. I duly prescribed and am now making delivery.'

Garnett Smith shot to his feet. 'Out you go, Sir! Out you go! I swore that no apothecary would ever set foot in this house again, and by God I intend to keep that rule, even if it means throwing you out personally.'

John thought fast, but not a single idea came to him. Suddenly, however, fate played into his hands. Garnett, who was quite clearly halfway to being drunk as a lord, swayed then slumped slightly against the side of his chair.

In a split second John was at his side, laying a cool hand upon the other man's brow, whipping his salts from his pocket, gently easing Garnett to sit down. He spoke in a quiet voice. 'We are not all rogues and villains, Sir. I studied long and diligently to become qualified to heal. All I wanted was to ease the suffering of others. It is obvious that at some time an apothecary has played you false, but I beg you not to condemn the entire profession because of it.'

'You're all bastards,' said Garnett and burst into a drunkard's tears.

'Not all of us,' John answered soothingly, and passed a handkerchief imbued with the faint smell of calming herbs.

Garnett applied it to his eyes. 'I lost my son because of one of your kind.'

'Such words cut me to the heart,' answered John, meaning what he said.

'He had a wen in his neck which swelled to the size of a bullfrog's. When I finally took him to a physician, he said that the apothecary had misread the signs, that the boy had a cancer and he could have saved him had my son been taken to him earlier.'

'That simply isn't true.' John kept his voice free of any emotion. 'No one on earth, physician or apothecary, can cure cancer's spread once it has a hold.'

'Are you saying that the doctor misled me?'

'Yes, Sir.'

'And the apothecary?'

'Tell me what he prescribed.'

'Figwort. He said there was no better herb for removing knobs, kernels, bunches or wens upon the body.'

'Nor is there if those growths are caused by anything other than malignancy. But if a foul tumour is at work, then nothing on God's earth will shift it. I fear, Sir, that your son's case was beyond human help and so I should have told you had he been brought to me.'

Garnett Smith looked at the Apothecary with a bleary eye. 'But he wasn't, was he, young man? It was Master Alleyn who killed him, and now, or so I hear, he has paid for that mistake with his life.'

John stared at him in surprise. 'Master Alleyn?'

'The gossip is all over the City. It is said in the coffee houses that someone stole in to Apothecaries' Hall and poisoned the flour, and that everyone at the Livery Dinner was taken ill. But Master Alleyn died of the poison, I'm told, and I rejoice because of it.'

'Is that not rather harsh.'

'My son's death was harsh. And Alleyn caused it.'

'He did not, Sir,' John maintained stoutly. 'Not knowing

what provoked the wen, he acted correctly in treating it with figwort. When the growth did not respond, he probably realised the truth and advised you to attend a physician. Am I not correct?'

Garnett nodded slowly, pouring out two glasses of sherry and motioning John to sit down. 'It's true enough.'

'Then it simply isn't fair to accuse him of negligence.'

The older man downed his drink in one. 'You're probably right. Maybe I've been a bigoted fool.'

'Did you kill Master Alleyn?' John asked in a quiet voice.

Garnett shook his head. 'No, though I've often felt like it.'

'Did you send a hired assassin?'

'Most certainly not.'

The sherry was going down in large measures now, and the Apothecary knew that this was the moment, just before Garnett became incapable, to pose the last few questions.

'Which physician told you he could have saved your son?'

'Dr Betts of Cheapside,' Garnett answered and started to cry again, the long slow sobs of a weeping drunk. 'My sweet son. He was all I had in the world. He was hoping to marry, had even met the girl of his choice. I should be surrounded by grandchildren. I shouldn't be left to eke out my existence in this vast, empty house.'

His self-pity was becoming very slightly nauseating. 'I'm sorry,' was all John could think of to say.

Garnett gulped but made no reply and the Apothecary stood up to go. 'I'll leave you in peace.'

The older man held out a hand. 'Thank you for spending time with me.'

'I hope that I have been of some help.' Rather disturbed by what he had heard, John none the less turned in the doorway.

'May I ask how you knew Master Alleyn, Sir?'

'His daughter was my son's betrothed.'

John felt frozen to the spot. 'Surely you don't mean Emilia, Mr Smith?'

'Yes, Emilia Alleyn. Why, do you know her?'

'We met once,' the Apothecary answered as he hurried from the room.

Chapter Nine

The funeral of Master Josiah Alleyn was bizarre. The fog, blown away by the bracing wind on the previous day, had returned doublefold, reducing visibility to a mere few feet. Standing beside an unobtrusive gravestone where, somewhat to his astonishment, John discovered Joe Jago already *in situ*, sent to observe by Mr Fielding, the Apothecary had the uncanny experience of seeing the arriving mourners loom through the mist, none looking more like phantoms than the Liverymen of the Worshipful Society. They had turned out in force, clad formally in black gowns, their faces sombre, as they packed silently into the churchyard to await the arrival of the body, remembering one of their own who had been unfortunate enough to die from a poison which had affected them all.

It was an unnerving sight, and Samuel Swann, fractionally out of breath as he came into view from the direction of the river, looked suitably uneasy as he went to stand beside the Apothecary. 'Is Master Cruttenden here?' he whispered out of the side of his mouth.

John shook his head, afraid that his voice might carry, while Joe cocked an inquisitive eyebrow.

As if they had conjured him up, the very next figure to appear, descending from a beautifully polished carriage, was the man they spoke of. Today he was a black seal, a vast fur-lined cloak shimmering about him, a dark hat sitting above a fully curled wig.

Samuel shook slightly with excitement as the Liveryman approached through the vapour. 'That's him! That's the one who kissed the redhead. Beastly old lecher!'

Overcoming a violent desire to knock Cruttenden's hat clean off his head, John stood silently, not wanting to draw attention to himself. But Samuel's hissing sibilants had already alerted the newcomer to the fact that a group of people stood amongst the tombstones. His eyes swivelled round and when he saw John, the Liveryman gave a small and somehow sardonic nod of his head.

'Bastard,' said the Apothecary under his breath, and felt better for it.

It was the custom for mourners to wait outside the church to pay the dead man honour as he was carried within, but on this particular day the tradition amounted to an ordeal as the grievers waited in the fog, quiet as the graves that surrounded them, not one of them escaping the chill of the cloying mist which seemed to penetrate even the thickest clothing. It was one of the eeriest scenes John had ever observed, the people dark as rooks, the tombstones like jagged shards of bone, silence coming back at them from the wall of mist, nobody moving. Eventually, though, there came the distant sound of respectfully muffled hooves, signalling that the wait was over and the cortège was approaching the church.

The first to come into view, grotesque because of his size, was the dwarfish figure of the undertaker's mute, a child employed to lead the departed to his final resting place with solemn tread. Shining black horses bearing black plumes upon their heads appeared behind him like creatures from legend, the glass-sided hearse and the pathetic coffin within, quite unreal.

The Apothecary shook himself to restore a sense of normality. Then a glance at Joe Jago reassured him that life was still on an even keel. The fog had brought a sheen of moisture to that craggy individual's wig, and beneath it could be seen the outline of the tight red curls that always fought wildly with any kind of headgear Mr Fielding's clerk adopted.

Sad and solitary, the casket arrived at the church door, then the great black mourning coaches appeared through the mist behind it. The four brothers Alleyn, even more alike in their identical black clothes, stepped forth from the first carriage and shouldered their burden, assisted by two other young males, presumably Josiah's nephews. There was a momentary pause, then the exquisite Emilia alighted from the next coach, solicitously handing out her weeping mother.

To the Apothecary, already on a flight of fantasy, the girl's stark clothing only enhanced her beauty, to the point at which she appeared to him like a dark rose. As if to endorse his thoughts, Samuel, most inappropriately in the circumstances, whistled beneath his breath and said, 'I see what you mean. She's gorgeous.' Overcome, the Apothecary felt his heartbeat quicken. But there was no time for private thoughts, the cortège, led by a vicar chanting in an unworldly voice, was going into the church. Thankful that at long last they were getting out of the damp, the congregation thronged inside behind it.

As ever on these occasions, John turned his mind away from the actual ceremony and instead observed the reactions of those present. Mrs Alleyn was quite out of control, weeping wildly, all attempts to calm her to no avail. But even as Emilia ministered to her mother, she glanced up. As a trapped hare regards its killer, so she looked at Francis Cruttenden. There was no point in further conjecture, John realised: the grey Liveryman still had the power to reduce the girl to shreds of anxiety. Furious at his own impotence to help her, the Apothecary glared at the older man until the girl finally had the strength of character to look away.

The ceremony at an end, the dismal trek to the graveside began. The brothers shouldered the coffin once more, and Mrs Alleyn wept anew. Emilia, tight-lipped with the effort of keeping control, took her mother by the hand only to release it again as the Master, a late arrival whom John had observed slipping quietly into the back of the church, offered the widow his arm. Thus formed, they went outside and vanished into the fog.

John hung back, wondering if there might be something futher to see, and was rewarded by the sight of Francis Cruttenden leaving for the graveside, joining ranks with his fellow Liverymen, his very walk proclaiming to the world that he was a man of substance and station. Remembering Pye House and the wherryman's assurance that Cruttenden owned it, the Apothecary wondered exactly from which resplendent family the man originally came. He turned to Joe Jago.

'Have you ever heard of the Cruttendens? Wealthy people, I believe.'

The rocky face creased into a frown. 'Can't say I have, Mr Rawlings. Why?'

'No reason really. I met one of them, Francis Cruttenden, when I attended Master Alleyn, in fact he is a personal friend of that family. Since then he just seems to keep cropping up. He owns a luxurious house on the south bank. That's all I know about him.'

Samuel, hovering beside them, decided to elaborate. 'Look for the lady, Mr Jago.'

'And what lady might that be, Sir?'

Irritated but not letting it show, John answered, 'Master Cruttenden was involved with Miss Emilia Alleyn, the dead man's daughter.'

Joe nodded. 'Would that be the beauteous young thing tending to her mama just now?'

'It certainly would,' Samuel answered robustly.

The Apothecary decided to cut the whole conversation short. 'Samuel is attempting to tell you that I find Miss Alleyn very charming, and it's true, I do. That is why her relationship with the somewhat elderly Liveryman interests me. However, it begins and ends there, Joe, I assure you.'

The craggy face did not change, although John could have sworn he saw a twinkle gleam momentarily in the clerk's eye. 'Then I shall do my best to find out more about the man, Sir. Now, do you think we should step into the churchyard?' he said.

The actual grave was nowhere to be seen, invisible in the fog. But a melancholy line of people was winding down a nearby path, obviously making its way to throw earth upon the coffin, a miserable tradition which the Apothecary detested. Back up this path, bellowing and sobbing in a pure hysteric, came Mrs Alleyn, the hapless Emilia one step behind. Behind her again, moving swiftly in his eddying black cloak, followed the man of whom they had just been speaking.

'My dear,' Francis was saying in an unctuous voice, 'my dear, let me take care of her.'

'No,' Emilia was answering determinedly, and, 'No, no, no,' Mrs Alleyn protested at the top of her voice.

Francis Cruttenden lengthened his stride and, catching Emilia up, put a hand on her shoulder. 'Now be a good girl,' he said.

She wrenched herself from his grasp. 'Leave us alone, please. Let me look after my mother as I see fit.'

'But, sweetheart . . .'

It was too much for John who stepped forward, blocking their path.

'Oh my dear young man,' sobbed Mrs Alleyn, and flung herself into his arms.

From his authoritative height, Francis Cruttenden looked down his nose. 'Oh. Mr Rawlings, isn't it?'

The Apothecary, his grasp full of Mrs Alleyn, gave a nod of his head that only just met the standards of politeness. 'It is, Sir.'

'It seems we are destined to encounter one another on occasions of great sadness.' His eyes ran over Samuel in a contemplative manner. 'Have we met before, Sir?'

'Indeed not,' the Goldsmith answered heartily, while

John's heart sank at the thought of Samuel's shadowing techniques being on a level with those of his questioning. 'Samuel Swann, Sir,' his friend continued, bowing.

Cruttenden gave a mirthless smile that could have meant anything and allowed his gaze to flicker over Joe Jago. 'And you are . . .?'

Knowing Mr Fielding's clerk as well as he did, John was aware of a slight clenching of Joe's jaw but the bow he gave, though brisk, was polite enough. 'My name is Jago, Sir, and I am here representing Mr Fielding of the Public Office, Bow Street.'

Cruttenden's naturally haughty expression was wiped clean off his face. 'Bow Street? Good gracious, why should they send a delegate?'

'Since the discovery that the flour used at the Livery Dinner had been poisoned, Master Alleyn's death has been treated as a case of murder. And as it is the duty of the Public Office to apprehend criminals, we are in search of the perpetrator.'

'But surely he would not be here?'

'On the contrary,' Joe answered levelly, 'he more than likely is.'

Francis spun round, as if someone wielding a knife might come up the path at any moment. 'What an alarming thought.'

'Surely you're not afraid?' said Emilia, and laughed harshly. Then before he had time to answer, she turned to John. 'Mr Rawlings, if you have the time, would you be kind enough to escort my mother and me home? There will be guests coming back to the house and she needs a few moments alone to recover her composure.'

John released Mrs Alleyn and bowed low. 'I would be delighted, Miss Alleyn.' He turned to Joe and Samuel. 'Will you two be all right to travel back to town together?'

The Goldsmith looked jovial, a sure sign that he was feeling conspiratorial. A fact he endorsed by winking his eye.

If Emilia noticed she gave no sign. Ignoring Francis Cruttenden, whose expression had now become mask-like, she propelled her mother up the path. 'The carriages will be waiting, Mama. I suggest we leave as soon as possible.'

John bowed to the rest of the company. 'Gentlemen, farewell. Sam, Joe, I shall see you again soon. Master Cruttenden, let us hope that the next time we meet no act of foul play has been committed.'

The Liveryman shot him a glance full of daggers, but the Apothecary merely smiled sweetly and went on his way towards the large black coach which had conveyed the principal mourners to the funeral.

Mrs Alleyn's hysteric did not continue long. Having put her to lie down, not the most comfortable of positions on the coach's hard seat, John sent a sniff of salts up her nose fit to lift the poor woman's head off. Seemingly, this did the trick. Coughing and spluttering, she drew a gasping breath and said, 'Oh, dearie me. I think I am a little restored.'

'I'm so glad,' answered Emilia, and kissed her mother on the cheek.

John laid a hand on his patient's forehead. 'You feel cooler, Ma'am. I believe you will be fit to receive your guests.'

Emilia looked up at him and John felt himself drown in her eyes. 'Mr Rawlings, I can never thank you enough,' she said quietly. 'I do believe my mother has a very soft spot for you.'

'As I have for her,' he answered.

'You will stay for the wake, won't you?'

'Do you want me to?'

'Yes.'

'Then I shall,' said John, wishing that Coralie's treatment of him had been kinder and not left him feeling so vulnerable.

The funeral reception was an ordeal, the house packed with dignitaries from the Worshipful Society of Apothecaries.

More than aware of his lowly status, John tried to remain unobtrusively in the background, but this was not easy. Sotherton Backler, for one, engaged him in conversation.

'Well, my young friend, how does it all go? Are you any nearer a solution?'

'No, Sir, I am not. You admit freely that you argued with the Master yet assure me that you did nothing to jeopardise the Dinner. The two men known to hate apothecaries both emphatically deny having anything to do with the poisoning. Therefore I must follow other avenues of enquiry. The investigation has temporarily reached a dead end.'

And yet, thought John, hating having to consider it, but too professional to ignore the fact, there is a loose thread that has not been followed. Garnett Smith's son was betrothed to Emilia Alleyn, of all unlikely things. Could such a situation be mere coincidence? Or was there a sinister web, whose strands he was only just starting to glimpse, to be uncovered here?

Knowing that this was neither the time nor the place to question her about it, John decided on a move that would be to his enormous advantage. Picking his moment, one indeed in which the girl looked decidedly tearful, John approached.

Emilia looked up, blinking her eyes. 'Oh Mr Rawlings, it's you. This is a very sad occasion. You must excuse me.'

He took her hand in genuine solicitude. 'Miss Alleyn, forgive me for intruding on your grief, but there is something I have to explain to you. Yet I truly feel that now is not the right moment. I wonder if some time during the coming week you might allow me to call on you and discuss the matter more fully?'

She smiled unhappily. 'You may call whenever you please, Sir, but I beg you to tell me what is on your mind immediately. I don't think I can cope with worrying about it if you don't.'

'This really isn't an appropriate occasion.'

'None the less, I insist.'

John squeezed the hand that he was continuing to hold.

'You are aware that the flour used in the banquet was poisoned?' She nodded. 'As you heard Mr Fielding's clerk say at the funeral, the Public Office are now treating your father's death as a case of murder because of it.'

Emilia went extremely pale but still said nothing.

'So I feel it only fair to tell you that I am assisting the Principal Magistrate with his investigations.'

She looked frankly astonished. '*You* are? Why? I thought you were an apothecary.'

'I am. It's simply that I know Mr Fielding. Some years ago I found a body in the Vaux Hall Pleasure Gardens and as a result of that discovery was asked to help track down the dead girl's killer. Since then I have assisted the Beak on several occasions. Now I am doing so again.'

Emilia looked enthusiastic. 'But that is good news surely. I would hate to think the villain responsible for my father's death might escape undetected.'

John swallowed hard and finally released her hand. 'What you don't realise is that it will mean asking questions – of you, your mother, of your relatives. The questions may well be about the past, and personal at that. I wouldn't wish, Miss Alleyn, to lose your friendship over this.'

'I wouldn't like that very much either,' she answered and made to move, then turned. 'When do you want to start your enquiries?'

'As soon as possible.'

'Then how about the day after tomorrow?'

'Will you be up to the ordeal by then?'

'I shall make absolutely certain I am,' she answered determinedly, and walked away to join her mother.

It was so pleasant, John thought as he went through the front door of number two, Nassau Street, to feel his father's presence in the house once more. The place, which had been somewhat cold and empty over the last few days, was now full of the smells of good food and wine, and the glow of many candles, in fact all the things that the Apothecary associated with the years of his childhood.

Throwing off his great coat and hat and heading for the library, John delivered his parent a smacking kiss on the cheek. 'Welcome home.'

'My dear, welcome to my London home, you mean. I left our country place this morning, and very grim it looked too.'

'Grim?'

'The respectable widow and her incontinent canine have moved out and a veritable army of workmen are decorating afresh. I have spent a fortune on furnishings, to say nothing of pieces of furniture. La, running two places of abode is not for the faint hearted.'

'You are to stop spending money at once,' John said firmly. 'The rest of the expenses must be my responsibility.'

Sir Gabriel smiled the smile of an indulgent parent. 'We shall see about that.'

'Yes, we shall,' the Apothecary answered, underlining every word.

This said, the two men, as was their custom before going in to dine, settled by the fire with glasses of sherry, an occasion that John always relished.

'So how are the investigations into the strange affair at Apothecaries' Hall?' asked Sir Gabriel. 'I missed hearing about it while I was away.'

'Somewhat at stalemate alas.'

'How so?'

'Because somebody, somewhere, is lying, I imagine.' And John described quite fully everything that had happened and everyone he had met, though only giving the scantiest detail about Miss Emilia Alleyn and uttering not a word about the mysterious and somewhat magical effect she had on him.

Sir Gabriel gazed into the flames and with the extraordinary way he had of appearing to read John's mind, said, 'You seem to have had little time for yourself, my boy.'

'I spent an evening in Samuel's company, which was very amusing, albeit somewhat wine laden.'

'And what of Coralie? Have you seen much of her?'

'Not much.'

'She is busy in the theatre, I take it?'

John flicked a covert glance at his father, but Sir Gabriel's face was quite impassive. 'Yes, very.'

'Ah.'

'Ah, what?'

'Nothing, my son. I merely sighed.'

'I see.' The Apothecary determinedly changed the subject. 'Do you know anything of a family named Cruttenden, Sir? I think they must be wealthy merchants of some kind. Have you ever come across them?'

'Cruttenden.' Sir Gabriel repeated the name several times. 'No, I don't believe I have.'

'It's very odd that. Joe Jago didn't know it either, yet the man lives in a vast mansion on the south bank, across the water from Apothecaries' Hall. He can't have made his money just by being a Liveryman.'

'Perhaps he has a rich wife.'

John shook his head. 'He's not married.'

'A wealthy patron?'

'It's possible, I suppose.'

'You don't like him, do you?' asked Sir Gabriel, darting a quick look at his son's dark face.

'Not in the least. He hangs around younger women like an old vulture. And he's smooth as cream and just as glutinous.'

'How very unpleasant.'

John downed his sherry. 'He's horrid, Sir. Horrid.'

His father laughed. 'Somehow I must attempt to meet this creature. It sounds as if it might be an interesting experience.'

'I don't know how we would contrive it, but I would most certainly like to have your opinion of him.'

'Then I shall think of something.' Sir Gabriel emptied his

glass. 'You haven't forgotten Serafina's soirée tomorrow, have you?'

Somewhat shamefacedly, John nodded. 'I'm afraid I had.'

'It is only to be a small gathering of intimate friends. Her child is due very soon and she can no longer entertain the *beau monde*.'

'I look forward to seeing her.'

'I have heard that Coralie is to be there,' said Sir Gabriel slyly.

The Apothecary did not move a muscle. 'Then I look forward to the occasion all the more.' He rose to his feet. 'Shall we go in to dine?' he said, and stood to one side to let his father leave the room first.

Chapter Ten

The letter came early, delivered by one of the Beak Runners. Opening it while he consumed his breakfast, John read the following:

> My dear Mr Rawlings,
> I write in Haste and send this out with Hope that said Communication will reach you Before you Leave for your Premises in Shug Lane. May I Presume to Ask that you Meet me at the Apothecaries' Hall at Ten O'Clock. The Master has Requested Such and I Wish to Oblige Him, though not at Gross Inconvenience to Your Good Self.
>   Signed, ever your Friend,
>   J. Fielding.

Very slightly put out as he had hoped to spend the morning compounding with Nicholas, John bolted the rest of his food and took a hackney coach to his shop in order at least to see that all was well. There was a goodly crowd within, all apparently buying, and the Apothecary, making his way through to the back of the premises, was gratified to see his apprentice handling the situation with apparent ease. Gradually he noticed that most of the customers were female, aged between fifteen and twenty, and vying with one another for Nicholas's attention.

John stared in surprise, never having thought the Muscovite particularly handsome, then considered a fact about which he was becoming more and more positive: that most people possess a hidden attraction only certain others can see, and it would appear that his apprentice's concealed appeal was apparent to quite a few of the young ladies of the *beau monde*, as well as those of less exalted position. Two or three pampered girls, out shopping with their maidservants, were buying beautifying potions, all the while giggling as Nicholas tried to explain to them the various merits of each one.

'Good morning,' said John cheerfully, and was met with hostile looks from the young females for daring to interrupt their delightful flirtations.

A year previously, Nicholas would have died of embarrassment at this, but these days he was quite a man of the world and merely caught John's eye and grinned over the top of the collection of dainty heads. 'Good morning, Master.'

John reflected on the fact that to his own apprentice he was known as Master, although the actual master of them all was the Master of the Worshipful Society of Apothecaries, that dignified bloodhound of a man, William Tyson. An annual appointment, Tyson had succeeded earlier that year following the death in office of his predecessor, Andrew Lillie. John dreaded the thought that one day Liveryman Francis Cruttenden might take on that most powerful of positions.

Going through to the compounding room, John turned to Nicholas who had hurried in after him. 'I can't stay long. Mr Fielding has requested that I meet him at the Hall.'

'How is the investigation going, Sir?'

'Slowly.'

'I'm sorry to hear it.'

'I shall have to see the three people with a possible motive again, there's no help for it.'

'Probably one of them has not told you all of the truth.'

'Or none of it. Anyway, it's a tedious business because this time they'll be even more hostile, having answered a series of questions once.'

'Perhaps you could disguise your visit as a social call.'

John looked thoughtful. 'You may be right at that. I'll give it some consideration. After all, one is the Beadle and the other owns a shop.'

'And the third?'

'Garnett Smith? A far more difficult proposition. Unless . . .'

'Unless?'

But the Apothecary refused to say more and relapsed into a pensive silence until he called Nicholas to his side to start compounding simples.

In the event, the difficulty of questioning Sotherton Backler further was easily overcome. On arrival at Apothecaries' Hall, to which John, Joe Jago and the Blind Beak travelled together, the Apothecary having gone straight to Bow Street from his shop, the three men parted company. Joe led the Magistrate up the stairs to where the Master waited, and John, instructed to join them after fifteen minutes had elapsed, made his way to the pantry and there found Jane Backler in conference with her husband.

Putting his head round the door, John said, 'Am I disturbing you?'

Jane turned. 'Oh, it's you, Mr Rawlings. No, not at all. Please join us.'

Today there was something strained about the Beadle's face, as if the events of the last few days had finally caught up with and hit him hard. 'Are you all right?' he found himself asking.

Sotherton drew back his lips in a parody of a smile. 'It has all been rather terrible. The death of Josiah, the poisoned flour, the suspicion that I might have had something to do with it.'

It was a golden opportunity and John leapt straight in. 'This argument you had with the Master . . .'

'It concerned monies which I had expended on behalf of the Court of Assistants. It was serious but not serious enough to make me wreak revenge.'

John regarded the Beadle closely. 'Tell me, Sir, do you support your wife's theory that someone came in here after dark and poisoned the flour?'

'Yes, I do.'

'I've asked this before, but I'll ask it again. Would that rule out an outsider?'

The Butler started to answer but her husband raised a hand to silence her. 'I believe it probably would.'

Jane exploded. 'Nonsense. Anyone with a glimmering of knowledge could find their way round. The watchman is always asleep. It would be a simple matter.'

John decided to change the topic. 'Have either of you heard of Garnett Smith? Or Tobias Gill for that matter?'

The Backlers exchanged a glance, then the Beadle spoke. 'Of course. They are well known for their views.'

'I believe that Garnett Smith wanders into Apothecaries' Hall from time to time, and on occasion has had to be forcibly removed.'

Jane answered. 'He does it when he's drunk, poor devil. I pity him. The loss of a child must be more than any parent could possibly endure. It's against the natural order of things. A tragedy that the human soul is not built to withstand.'

'I believe it was Master Alleyn who treated the young man.'

'It certainly was,' Sotherton answered. He was silent for a moment, then said, 'You don't think . . .'

'That he was murdered out of revenge? I must say the thought did cross my mind, although, of course, it isn't possible.'

'Why not?' demanded the Beadle.

'Oh don't be silly,' the Butler answered him. 'How could

the poisoner, attacking everyone as he did, possibly know that it was going to be Josiah who would die? His death was a fluke, an accident almost.'

'Still,' persisted Sotherton doggedly, 'it's damned odd.'

John assumed the most innocent face in his repertoire and turned a wide-eyed look on Jane. 'Was there not some family connection between Smith and Alleyn? Weren't they related in some way?'

She smiled her gap-toothed smile. 'Not related, my dear, but connected most certainly. Andrew Smith, the young man who died, was betrothed to Emilia, Josiah Alleyn's daughter.'

'How strange!' John exclaimed convincingly. 'But surely they must have both been very young.'

'She was seventeen, Andrew two years older. Josiah was called in to treat young Smith because he was a friend of the family.'

'With what bitter results.'

Sotherton interrupted. 'It keeps going round and round in my head that Garnett wanted Josiah dead, and that he has succeeded in that wish.'

'If the poison hadn't been spread so randomly I would agree with you. But as the case stands, Master Alleyn just happened to be unlucky,' John answered.

'Still . . .'

The Apothecary nodded. 'I know. It is a weird coincidence.' He pulled his watch from his pocket. 'I'm sorry, I must leave you now. If anything should occur to you, however insignificant, I would be most obliged if you could communicate with me. You have a note of my address of course.'

'Of course,' said the Beadle, and opened the door to let him out.

As he climbed the great wooden staircase towards the Master's private room, John knew that this would be one of the most difficult moments of his life. For a simple Yeoman of the Society to be thrust beneath the Master's nose as a cohort of the famous John Fielding was bad enough, but for Master Tyson to be asked to co-operate with such an underling was surely going too far. With a gulp of apprehension, John gave the tiniest tap on the door then waited nervously in silence.

'Enter,' said a sonorous voice, and he did so, almost on tiptoe.

The sight that greeted him was so convivial, so very much the opposite of what he had expected, that John almost broke into a smile.

The Master, Mr Fielding and Joe, were all seated in comfortable chairs before an extremely healthy fire, drinking pale sherry out of gleaming crystal glasses. 'My dear William . . .' the Magistrate was saying, and John realised he should have guessed that John Fielding, who knew everyone who was anyone in town, was more than likely to have been acquainted even with the Master of the Worshipful Society.

Master Tyson looked round as the newcomer made an extremely self-effacing entrance. 'Mr Rawlings, isn't it?' he said.

'Yes, Master.'

'I hear that you're a sly dog.'

'I'm sorry, Sir?'

'My old friend Mr Fielding tells me that you have assisted him several times in the past and that he thinks of you very highly. Tell me, are you any connection with Sir Benjamin Rawlings who was Master three years ago?'

'I'm afraid I don't know, Sir.'

'What's that you say?'

'I am adopted, Master. The son of Sir Gabriel Kent. My family name was Rawlings but whether I am kin to Sir Benjamin I honestly can't say.'

'How very interesting,' said William Tyson. 'How fascinating to think that one might have relatives walking the streets of London at this very moment, of whom one might be totally unaware.'

'It used to worry me at first,' John admitted. 'But now I never give it a thought.'

'You interest me,' said the Master. 'Take a seat, young man.'

He *was* like a bloodhound, John thought, particularly around the eyes, with their droopy sad expression and heavy bags beneath. Also his legs and arms were rather short for his body, another canine characteristic. But the Master was as alert as the dog he resembled. In fact it wouldn't have surprised John in the least to see him sniff the air in order to detect trouble.

'Would you like a sherry?' Master Tyson asked.

'Yes please, Sir.'

'Then help yourself, young fellow. And you may refill the other glasses while you are about it.'

John gulped audibly, still not believing that he was standing in the Master's room pouring drinks for the great man and his guests, to say nothing of himself. Mr Fielding, whose hearing was extremely acute, growled a laugh at the sound and the Master visibly preened himself that he was being seen to be generous in his patronage.

The Magistrate spoke. 'We have been discussing the matter in hand, Mr Rawlings and certain conclusions have been reached. Before we go further I wonder if you would report your findings so far.'

'They are precious few, I fear,' John stated nervously. 'Three names were given me as people who might bear a grudge against the Society of Apothecaries. One of them – forgive me, Master – is the Beadle, Sotherton Backler, the other two a Garnett Smith, whose son died after a misdiagnosis by Master Alleyn, and a Tobias Gill, who felt he had been slighted by the Court of Assistants. I have seen all three. Mr Backler I am convinced had nothing to do with the matter. Mr Gill I am not so certain about. The most complex of them, however, is Mr Smith who drinks more than is good for him . . .' John became horribly aware of the sherry glass in his hand . . . 'and who has the strongest motive for killing Master Alleyn. Yet the facts don't add up. White arsenic was put in the flour so that everyone at the Livery Dinner would be taken ill. It is mere chance that the victim died.'

'When and how do you think the poison was mixed with the flour?' the Master asked.

The Apothecary looked over at Joe Jago, who whispered to Mr Fielding. The Magistrate nodded that John should continue.

'According to the Butler, it would have been impossible for anyone to have done so on the day of the Dinner itself. There were several helpers in the kitchen at the time – I have yet to see the chef – and unless one of them were responsible, which seems highly unlikely, the poisoning would have had to be done during the night before. The flour was used on the previous day and was untainted then.'

Whilst talking, John had noticed out of the corner of his eye that the Master had been sitting more and more upright, nose in air, the bloodhound in him never more prominent.

'I was in the Hall on the night before the Dinner. In fact I slept here, it being too late at night to travel home,' he stated with a certain excitement when the Apothecary had finished speaking.

'And did you see or hear anything, Sir?'

Well aware that his audience was hanging on his every word, William Tyson cleared his throat. 'As a matter of fact, I did.'

'Well, I'll be blessed,' exclaimed Joe Jago, never a one to stand on ceremony.

'What was it?' asked the Blind Beak.

'I was woken in the small hours by a distant sound. It appeared to be a crash, as if someone had fallen over something in the darkness.'

'What did you do, Sir?'

'I lit a candletree and went downstairs.'

'And?'

'There was nobody about, not a soul. I called out to the watchman, who stays in a little cubby hole near the courtyard. He called a reply that all was well, so I went back to bed.'

'What time was this?'

'It was just before two, because the clock chimed as I went up the stairs.'

'Did the watchman answer you immediately?' asked John, a faint notion just beginning to creep into his mind.

'Yes. Why?'

'Oh, no reason, Master, though I would very much like to talk to him. Is he here during the daytime at all?'

'No, but he lives near by, in Holland Street to be precise. He has a room in a lodging house there.'

'Then I might call on him.' John thought rapidly. 'Mr Fielding, at what time do you intend to return to Bow Street?'

'In an hour or so. Do you want to travel back with us?'

'If I may. I've just remembered that the cook lives near Drury Lane. I'll get his address from the Beadle, then try a surprise visit. If there's an hour to spare now, I would like to hear what the watchman has to say.'

The Master, who was most definitely playing the part of benevolent leader, allowed a genial smile to light up his drooping eyes. 'What an eager young fellow you are, to be sure. If you treat your business with the same enthusiasm as you do your tasks for Mr Fielding, I believe you will go very far in your profession.'

The Apothecary was frankly delighted, and a grin, curving upwards at one corner of his mouth, simply refused to be repressed. 'Thank you very much, Master.'

'Not at all. Now, the watchman's name is George Griggs and he lives in Holland Street, as I told you. I believe the number is four, but everybody knows him round there. He'll probably be asleep, though.'

Thinking that the wretched man appeared to sleep all night and all day as well, John refilled everyone's glass, arranged to board the Magistrate's coach within the hour, and bowed his way from the room.

★　　★　　★

Holland Street led off Water Street and ran parallel with the river, a mere stone's throw from George Grigg's place of employment. Enquiries at number four confirmed what the Apothecary had already half suspected, however: the man had two jobs, and during daylight hours worked as a labourer in a nearby timber yard. Cursing his lack of time, John cut through some extremely murky alleyways, passing Lime Wharf, Coalmans Alley, Puddle Dock and Dung Wharf, till he came to his destination, Timber Wharf and its adjoining yard. With no space for finesse, the Apothecary stood at the wharf's entrance and bellowed, 'George Griggs' at the top of his voice.

Several heads turned and one asked, ''oo wants 'im?'

'A message from the Master of the Society of Apothecaries,' John answered importantly.

The speaker dropped the planking he was carrying on one shoulder and approached. 'What's up, cove?'

The Apothecary decided on a blunt approach. 'I represent Mr Fielding, the Magistrate from the Public Office, Bow Street, and you know damnably well what's up. Poison was added to the flour at the Livery Dinner, and all those who attended were taken ill. One Liveryman died. You were on duty the night before the Dinner, and that was the occasion when somebody intruded. Do you remember?'

'Don't give it mouth,' George answered through blackened stumps that once were teeth. 'There was no intruder. Never 'as been since I've been akeepin' watch.'

'There was one then. The Master heard him.'

George spat noisily. 'Wot night are we talkin' about?'

'The one before the Livery Dinner.'

''ow would I know when that was? One shift's just like another to me.'

John clicked with impatience. 'It was the night the Master called out to you to see if everything was in order and you shouted back that all was well.'

George shook his head and sucked his stumps. ''e's makin'

it up. The Master never called out to me. 'e must 'ave been dreamin'.'

The Apothecary snatched off his hat and ran his hand through his curls, his wig still in his pocket where he had placed it when he entered the alleyways. 'Are you certain of this?'

A pair of blue eyes flashed in the grime-filled lines of George's face. 'Certain as me cock's in me kicks.'

'How very interesting,' John answered thoughtfully. 'How very interesting indeed.'

Chapter Eleven

———◆◆◆◆———

Just for a moment, after alighting from the hackney coach which had conveyed him from Nassau Street to the graceful building which was number twelve Hanover Square, John Rawlings stood quietly in the street, gazing up at the four storeyed wide-windowed house, at present ablaze with candle-light and alive with the sound of music and voices, and let memory consume him.

Four years had passed since he had first set foot over the threshold, visiting for the very first time that enigmatic creature the Comtesse Serafina de Vignolles. In the time that had elapsed since, his passionate youthful love for her had matured into friendship of a deep and lasting nature, a friendship that John regarded as one of the most important things in his life. As important indeed as his commitment to Coralie, a commitment which, however, had been delivered a grievous blow by her latest rejection of his proposal of marriage.

He and Serafina had weathered some emotional storms together. John with his penchant for falling in love with the wrong women, she with a husband she did not altogether trust. But now the Comtesse and the Apothecary had sailed into calm waters. Comte Louis adored his wife, was com-pletely in her thrall, while she had given him one child, Italia, and was about to produce another; John, on the other hand, was certain that his future must be with the beautiful Coralie Clive. That is he had been certain until recently, when she had wounded him so deeply.

'Damme,' said John, and kicked the cobbles with his fine buckled shoe. Marching up the steps, he rang the front door bell and was admitted by a footman dressed as smartly as any guest.

Handing over his cloak and hat, the Apothecary made his way up the curving staircase to where Serafina and her husband waited, he dark and French and very splendid, she dressed in flowing white, a ship in full sail.

'My darling,' said John, and kissed first her hand and then her cheek.

Louis, who was quite used to this kind of behaviour between them, bowed beautifully. 'My dear friend, how nice to see you again. This is a very small gathering tonight, just a dozen or so. Our last entertainment before the baby is born.'

'Just to be in your house is pleasure enough,' the Apothecary answered fulsomely.

'Your father is here already,' said Serafina. 'He tells me that you have acquired a place in Kensington.'

'A country home,' John answered. 'You will come and visit us there, won't you?'

'As long as I can bring my children to breathe the fresh air, of course.' Serafina narrowed a knowing eye in a half wink, meaning that nothing would keep her away from her old friend's new residence.

'Children are no hindrance to me,' the Apothecary stated pompously.

'Born for fatherhood, eh?' said Louis, and laughed as the next guest was announced from below. 'Miss Coralie Clive.'

John stood where he was, emotions churning, watching one of the most delightful women in London, a woman who was his companion both in bed and out, ascend with elegance the equally elegant staircase. At that moment, staring at her hair, dark as midnight, and her vivid green eyes, shining as she smiled at her host and hostess, he wanted her more than any female alive. Yet, equally, he was tired and hurt by their situation, wishing for more but well aware that she was going to reject him whenever he suggested their relationship should be formalised.

Glancing up, Coralie noticed him. 'John, my dear, how wonderful to see you. I wondered where you have been.'

Beside him, the Apothecary was enormously aware of Serafina listening, knowing how quick she was to pick up undercurrents.

'Coralie,' he said, and taking his mistress's hands in his he contrived to both kiss them and lead her slightly out of earshot. 'I'm so sorry I haven't called on you. Truth to tell, I've been very absorbed with one of Mr Fielding's cases.'

She gave a slightly mocking smile. 'Last time we met, my dear John, you hurled yourself into your kicks and would have left the house had I not persuaded you otherwise. I think perhaps your absence has been deliberate.'

The Apothecary knew to admit the truth would be fatal so he lied manfully. 'I could never deliberately keep away from you. It is merely that fate, together with the Blind Beak, has directed me elsewhere these last few days.'

'Still the strange affair of the poisoning at Apothecaries' Hall?'

'Yes, still.'

'How are you proceeding?'

'The more I learn the less I know.'

Coralie smiled. 'Like life itself.'

'Yes,' said John, a fraction sadly. 'Just like life itself.'

The actress slipped her hand through his arm and together they walked into the first floor drawing-room, where Sir Gabriel, stunning in black satin, a diamond brooch carelessly clasped in his cravat, was chatting with a fascinating redhead of middle years. Samuel, who adored going to any type of social gathering, was laughing heartily at somebody's joke, while Dr

Drake, a fat old favourite of John's, was in earnest conversation with a man that the Apothecary half recognised.

He bowed in the direction of them all, took a glass of champagne from a passing tray, and went to speak to Mr Sparks, a fellow actor of Coralie's and an outrageous queen who had the whole of London at his feet as a result of his high antics.

'Beloved,' said the actor, and kissed Coralie soundly, before kissing John, who smiled as best he could.

'How lovely to see you,' she answered. 'Do you know my friend John Rawlings?'

'The honour's mine, Sir.' Mr Sparks minced a step then gave a bow fit for an Emperor. 'La, but you're a pretty fellow. You must bring him backstage, Coralie, so you must.'

Making a responding bow, John told the truth. 'I hardly know what to answer.'

Mr Sparks, who had obviously been on the champagne for some while, cut a caper. 'I'm sure we could find ways of making you speak.'

'But I might not say the right things,' John countered.

Mr Sparks fluttered his eyelashes. 'Oh, a wit into the bargain. You should join the charmed circle, young person.'

'Leave him alone,' said Coralie. 'He's mine and there's an end to it.'

They all three laughed but, for all that, John was decidedly grateful when someone at his elbow made a bow and said, 'So we meet again, Sir.'

The Apothecary turned and could hardly believe who he saw. Dr Florence Hensey whom he had first encountered in a Flying Coach on the way to Romney Marsh and who had brought him back to consciousness after a crunching blow from the fist of a reprobate called Lucius Delahunty, was standing beside him.

John forgot his good manners and embraced the physician heartily. 'My very dear Sir. What a great pleasure to see you again. And what a surprise.'

'Isn't it indeed. I have recently become acquainted with the Comte de Vignolles and he was good enough to issue me with an invitation for his wife's soirée.'

'Were you aware that I knew them?'

'Yes, your name did come into the conversation when we discussed matters medical.'

'Did you never meet the Comte when we were all down on the Romney Marsh?'

Dr Hensey frowned. 'I didn't realise he was there.'

Fearing that perhaps he had made a *faux pas*, as Louis at that time had been employed by the Secret Office, John covered quickly. 'He came for a short visit only. You probably wouldn't have run into him.'

Serafina came to join them and the conversation changed course. 'I feel enormous,' she said, 'and vowed that I would not see another soul until this little creature had made its entrance into the world. But, truth to tell, I grew so bored and missed everyone, and the thought of another three months without seeing a friendly face was too much to bear.'

'Am I not then friendly?' asked Louis, joining them.

'Too friendly,' Serafina answered, and touched the roundness beneath her loose robe.

Mr Sparks, a little put off by all this natural talk, shrieked an hysterical giggle and the company burst out laughing, at his reaction as well as at the Comtesse's words.

Serafina turned to him. 'I am relying on you for a recitation later, Sir.'

'You shall have one, dear lady. A sonnet, I think. "Shall I compare thee to a summer's day?"'

'You may if you wish,' Serafina answered, and everyone laughed again.

Samuel, hearing the fun, arrived to join the group, but it was already fragmenting, and John took the opportunity to move slightly away, taking the Goldsmith with him.

'There's something odd about this case,' he murmured.

'What's happened now?'

'I saw the French chef this afternoon, as honest a soul as ever did a day's cooking. He is prepared to take an oath that no one went near the flour pot. For sure, the poison was added the night before.'

'Yes, but . . .?'

'The Master, of all people, was sleeping in the Hall. He says that during the night he heard a noise and went down to investigate. There was nobody there but he called out to the watchman, who called back that all was well. However, and here comes the stumbling block, the watchman denies that anyone intruded. Says the Master is making it up.'

'You surely don't believe that?'

'No, I don't. Clearly there are two possible explanations: one is that the watchman was asleep and it was the intruder who called out; the other, that the man was bribed to keep quiet about what he saw.'

Samuel's eyes widened and he rubbed his hands together. 'This is becoming very deep.'

'There's something else too,' John said slowly.

'What?'

'I told you of Garnett Smith who has a hatred for all apothecaries?'

Samuel nodded.

'Well, it seems that his son was betrothed to Emilia Alleyn, and that his specific loathing was for Master Alleyn.'

A series of expressions ranged over Samuel's jolly countenance. 'The beautiful Emilia, eh? She seems to be involved at every level. And it was Master Alleyn who actually died, even though all the others were poisoned as well.'

'Something is eluding me,' said John, shaking his head and frowning. 'There's something I should be realising but can't quite grasp.'

Samuel looked nonplussed. 'Well, I don't know what it is.' He took two glasses of champagne and handed one to John. 'What's next?'

'More visits. To the watchman, to Tobias Gill and also to

Garnett Smith, God help me. And tomorrow evening I am due to question Miss Alleyn about her past.'

'God help you with that too,' said Samuel heavily. He let his eyes roam towards Coralie. 'What are you going to do, my friend?'

'What do you mean?' the Apothecary asked cautiously.

'You're in love with them both, aren't you?'

'Of course I'm not. I hardly know Miss Alleyn.'

' "Whoever loved who loved not at first sight." '

'Stop quoting at me. We've enough of that from Mr Sparks.'

'The queer garter?' said Samuel loudly, and John died the death as the actor looked over and gave a little wave.

'Yes, him. Now will you change the subject please. Here comes Coralie.'

It was true enough, though, John thought as he stood quietly, sipping his drink and watching his mistress chatting animatedly to his best friend. Despite her treatment of him, he loved the actress with all his heart, and yet Miss Alleyn exerted a certain spell that he couldn't deny, nor even wanted to. Truth be told, he felt quite powerless to extricate himself from the situation. So much so that rather than wrestle with the problem and spoil his evening, the Apothecary threw himself into the spirit of the soirée and temporarily put his problems behind him.

After an excellent cold collation, ending with a delicious water ice, Mr Sparks and Coralie gave a short entertainment which provoked much laughter and applause. Then the company went in to play cards. Serafina, who in the early days of her marriage, before she had settled down, had been London's notorious Masked Lady, the most cutthroat gambler of them all, promised not to play deep, much to the disappointment of Sir Gabriel, who was no poor gamester himself. The others, being less accomplished, played moderately, though intently, and it was not until after midnight that the coaches came round to take everyone home.

Dr Hensey bowed low to John. 'My very dear friend, will you call round to see me?'

'Are you still at the same address?'

'Indeed I am.'

'My recollection is that *I* owe *you* dinner, Sir. Would the afternoon after next be convenient? I also intend to invite Mr Clarke, who runs the shop at Apothecaries' Hall. He is most learned and the conversation could well be interesting.'

'It most certainly would. I should be delighted. You live in Nassau Street if memory serves.'

'Yes. At number two.'

'Would four o'clock be convenient?'

'Make it a little sooner and then we can have sherry before we dine.'

'Excellent,' said Dr Hensey, and on that happy note the evening ended.

Despite the rigours of the night before, John rose early, even before his apprentice, and went off to Shug Lane as soon as he had breakfasted. Truth to tell, though he would never have admitted as much to Mr Fielding, he did feel that he was neglecting his business, particularly the compounding of special physicks and pills ordered by his regular customers, a job he would not leave in the hands of Nicholas, however capable he considered the young man to be. This task took a good hour, by which time the Muscovite had arrived for work, dusted throughout, swept the floor, then opened the shop with a cheerful grin. He was just on the point of making his Master tea, something to which John was looking forward before he set off into the cold streets, when the door opened, the bell clanged, and a man came in.

'Is Mr Rawlings in?' John heard him ask, hidden in the compounding room as he was.

'May I ask who wants him, Sir?'

'Apothecary Gill. Tobias Gill.'

Much surprised, John stepped through the opening and made a bow. 'Master Gill. To what do I owe this pleasure?'

'I thought, Sir, to discuss the merits and demerits of various simples, that is if you can spare me the time.'

Even more surprised, John stared at him, but the older man avoided eye contact. He had really come about something else, that much was obvious.

'Certainly, Sir. I am at your disposal. Would you care to step into the compounding room? We can be private there. My apprentice was on the point of making tea.'

Over the top of Gill's head, John winked slowly, indicating to Nicholas that he would like tea then total privacy. The Muscovite nodded briefly and made much of fiddling with the kettle. Five minutes later all was done, and the Apothecary and Tobias Gill sat opposite one another on either side of the compounding table.

'Now,' said John, 'exactly what simples would you like to discuss, Sir?'

Tobias Gill leant forward as if he trusted nothing and no one. 'It's not really about that that I came,' he answered.

'I see.'

'It's actually about my daughter.'

'Your daughter?' John both looked and sounded astonished.

'Clariana. You saw her in the shop. A beautiful girl but a lonely one.'

The Apothecary could hardly believe his ears, wondering what the old man could possibly be on the point of suggesting.

'She lacks the company of people her own age,' Gill continued.

John, fearing the worst, could only answer, 'Oh.'

'So I wondered, Mr Rawlings, if you might come to dine with us. It would do her good to talk to a contemporary.'

'Has she no friends at all?' asked John, vividly recalling Samuel's description of her behaviour with Francis Cruttenden.

Gill pulled a face, obviously hesitating on the brink of saying something. 'Well . . .'

The Apothecary decided to help him. 'Might she be involved with someone unsuitable perhaps?'

The floodgates opened. 'That is just the point, Sir. She is infatuated with a man twice her age and more. She considers herself deep in love with him. As for me, I hate him. He is one of the Liverymen of that accursed Society of Apothecaries with its beastly Court of Assistants.'

'Is that the only reason you think him wrong for her?'

'Of course not. Even I, who dislike their hierarchy right well, would not be quite so narrow. No, Mr Rawlings. I do not trust the fellow. There's something about Master Cruttenden that I find quite sinister. Yes, that is the correct word. Sinister.'

John sat silently, wondering how much he should say, and decided on very little.

'I know him, of course. I must admit that he is not the sort of man of whom I would like to make a close friend.'

Mr Gill positively seethed. 'He is hateful, detestable. I am sure he is making my poor daughter fall in love with him.'

Almost the same words used by Mrs Alleyn, John thought. He smiled sympathetically. 'I will gladly come to dine with you if you think it will do any good, but quite honestly, Mr Gill, I met Clariana in the shop when I came to question you about the murder of Master Alleyn and I received the strong impression that she didn't like me at all.'

'That is because she is being controlled. Her thoughts are no longer her own.'

'Then if I can assist in any way, I will.' John paused, then said, 'Mr Gill, have you told me everything you know about the death of Master Alleyn?'

'Of course I have. I was in my shop all day on the occasion of the Livery Dinner. Indeed I didn't even know about it until you, Sir, drew my attention to the fact. Many people saw me on my premises, I can assure you.'

'I think I mentioned to you that the investigation is also focusing on the night before the Dinner. Did you not say that you were with Clariana all the evening?'

'Yes.'

'But after she retired, surely you could have slipped out for a while?'

'I could have, but I didn't. Please don't annoy me, Sir.'

'I'm sorry. I really don't mean to do so. It is just that it is my duty to pursue every possibility.'

'Why are you interested in that particular night? What is your theory?'

'That someone either crept past or bribed the night-watchman, then stole into the kitchen and poisoned the flour.'

Tobias Gill looked triumphant. 'Then you can rest assured that it wasn't me.'

'Why?'

'I told you that I vowed never to set foot in that damnable place again, and I have stuck to that vow. I would not sully my shoes with their cobblestones.'

It was said with such an air of finality that it left the Apothecary little choice but to accept the statement at face value. Yet how odd that the thread led yet again to Francis Cruttenden and, indirectly, Josiah Alleyn.

John adopted his honest citizen expression. 'When would you like me to dine, Sir?'

'Tomorrow?'

'No, I am entertaining.'

'Then the next day?'

'That would be very convenient. What time shall I call?'

'Four o'clock at Pudding Lane. I shall make sure that Clariana is there.' Tobias Gill bowed. 'Thank you for helping someone you know hardly at all.'

Knowing that the occasion would provide him with a great deal of information, John felt a pang of guilt. 'I look forward to the meeting with a great deal of pleasure.'

Mr Gill turned in the doorway. 'It should have been that wretch Cruttenden who died. Not the other poor fellow.'

This said, he set off down the street at speed, leaving John with the strong impression that Apothecary Gill would be more than capable of murder if the necessity should so arise.

Chapter Twelve

It was busy on Timber Wharf that noon. A large vessel was in, unloading its cargo, and the place was crammed with people, scurrying about in what appeared to be a completely chaotic manner. In fact though, John soon realised, every man knew exactly what he was doing, hauling and swearing and heaving as he loaded timber onto the waiting carts or stored wood in orderly heaps inside the warehouse.

It was difficult in a scene of such intense, sweating, good-natured activity to attract any attention at all, but eventually, after searching the crowd with his eyes, looking for the watchman, John managed to get a word with a burly work-man pausing momentarily for a breath. 'Is George Griggs here today, do you know?'

''e could be, cove. Can't say I've seen 'im though.'

'Is it like him not to turn up?'

'No, 'e's better than most, not getting too drunk of a night because of his other job.'

'Then I'd better try a closer look.'

Attempting to weave his way through the mob proved both difficult and dangerous, however. The workmen stopped for nothing and no one, and after nearly being brained by a piece of passing planking, the Apothecary thought better of it and retired to the sidelines. Another visual search still revealed no sign of the missing Griggs, and, with the first faint whiff of something not quite as it should be, John made his way to the watchman's lodging house.

The handing over of a coin allowed him access to Griggs's room, a smelly, mucky pit if ever he had seen one. But an inspection of the noisesome heap which passed for a bed, difficult though it was to tell from the various grimy indentations which looked as if they had been there for years, proved that it had not been slept in recently.

Slightly alarmed now, John made his way to Apothecaries' Hall and to the pantry of Jane Backler.

He came straight to the point. 'I'm looking for George Griggs, the watchman. Did he report for duty last night?'

'No, he did not. The Master, who was here late again, persuaded a member of the watch to take over. He is threatening Griggs with the sack.'

'That is if he can find him.'

'What's that?'

'Griggs has gone missing,' John answered tersely, the certainty that something was wrong growing with every second.

Jane stared him in the eye. 'Why did you say it like that? Do you think this might have any connection with the poisoning?'

'Yes, I'm afraid I do.'

'But why?'

'I think Griggs saw the poisoner and recognised him.'

'Dear God!' The Butler sat down suddenly.

John thought fast. 'May I borrow pen and paper? I must get word to Mr Fielding but as I have to leave for Chelsea shortly I can't go in person.'

'Of course. Come through to the Beadle's office. It will be more comfortable there.'

Seated behind Sotherton Backler's desk, John hastily wrote a letter to the Blind Beak requesting help in the search for the missing watchman, and despatched it in a hackney coach. This done, he made his way to the shop, where the manager was busy with a customer.

'My dear Mr Clarke,' he said as soon as the other was free. 'I wondered if you might do me the honour of dining with me tomorrow. I have also invited an old friend, Dr Hensey.' John determinedly kept his tone light, feeling it would not be politic to spread word of Griggs's disappearance to anyone further.

The other man's eyes bulged slightly. 'I would be most obliged, Sir. But there is a favour I have to ask you.'

'And what is that?'

'My wife has expressed an earnest desire to meet you. I mentioned that I expected an invitation from you, and she cajoled me into requesting that she might join us. We have a neighbour who cares for our boy, so Harriet can make herself available at any time.'

'It would be my pleasure,' John answered, glad that a female would be present to lighten the all-male company.

Michael Clarke looked overjoyed, endearingly so. 'I know she will be delighted. Harriet does not get out a great deal because of Matthew.'

'Then I must make the occasion special for her.'

'You have a very good heart, Mr Rawlings,' said Michael, his voice quivering a little.

'I'm not so sure about that,' John answered, thinking of the evening that lay ahead of him and wishing that he did not feel quite so wildly excited at the prospect of seeing Emilia Alleyn.

He wanted to reach Chelsea before the light faded, not enjoying the river on a bitter night, when the wind cut through to the bone. Hailing the strongest waterman he could see, burly as an ox and surly with it, John stepped into the boat and urged the man to pull mightily, with the inducement of a large tip. So, with the tide in their favour, the fog gone and John's verbal encouragement, the wherry eased into the Alleyn landing stage at dusk and the Apothecary scrambled ashore, well pleased that it was no later.

The hour to dine had passed but as he approached the house, a certain clatter of dishes told him that the family was still seated at table. Instructing the servant who answered the bell to show him into an ante chamber, John was slightly ruffled when the door to the dining room flew open and Mrs Alleyn herself appeared in the doorway.

'Is that you, Mr Rawlings?'

'It is indeed, Ma'am.'

'Then come and join us, do. We dined late tonight and are still on the meat course. I had prepared an extra place in case you were early.'

Suddenly nervous, his heart lurching, John followed his hostess in and took a seat to her right. Sure enough, a cover had been set there and John sat down in a complete flurry, acutely aware that Emilia Alleyn was seated on the other side of the empty space.

'Good afternoon, Mr Rawlings,' she said, and with his emotions still out of control, John turned to look at her.

He was drowning again, sinking into those heavenly eyes. Just before he disappeared completely, the Apothecary prayed that his feelings were not written over his face for all the world to see.

'. . . at least the fog's gone,' said a man's voice, and John shot to the surface, gasping a little.

It was one of the twins who had spoken, their identical faces turned in his direction.

'Yes,' he said, trying to look intelligent, 'but the wind's very cold.'

It was banal. Here he was, sitting with four bereaved people, with one of whom he was exhibiting all the signs of falling passionately in love, and the only thing any of them could talk about was the weather. With a tremendous effort of will, John got a grip on himself.

'I am sorry to intrude while you are dining, but am most grateful that you included me at your table.'

'My dear friend,' said Mrs Alleyn, 'I feel we owe you a

debt that can never be repaid. You are always welcome in this house.'

Wondering if he would be quite so welcome after he had finished questioning them all, John smiled, deliberately avoiding a glance at Emilia, who was regarding him solemnly with her devilishly lovely angel's eyes.

The meal continued, Edmund and Ellis – which was which? John wondered – making small talk of a trivial kind, Emilia mostly remaining silent, and Mrs Alleyn fussing like the motherly figure that she was. Finally, though, the ladies left the room, but not before Mrs Alleyn had pressed the Apothecary into staying the night, declaring, quite rightly, that it was too cold to contemplate returning.

Left with the twins, John struggled to glean information, but they were either far too stupid or too clever to reveal anything other than that their two elder brothers were married and lived elsewhere, that they were both twenty-three years old, had just completed their apprenticeships as furniture makers, and were looking forward to going out into the world. About the death of their father, they seemed utterly nonplussed.

'I just can't understand why he should have consumed more arsenic than everyone else,' said one of them.

'Nor me,' added the other.

'Nor me,' echoed John.

They stared at him. 'We thought you knew all about it,' they replied in chorus.

He shook his head. 'The only explanation is that the portion of sauce your father consumed was more heavily tainted than anyone else's.'

'But who put the poison in there anyway?'

'If I knew that, I'd know the identity of Master Alleyn's murderer.'

'It must be someone who hates all apothecaries.'

John sighed, rather more noisily than he had intended.

'That is the main line of our investigation. Tell me, does the name Garnett Smith mean anything to you?'

If it were at all possible, the wooden faces became even more set. 'He was a great friend of our family, that is until the death of Andrew. After which Mr Smith fell out with us. That's all we know.'

Were they downright unhelpful or just plain obtuse? John wondered again. Whatever, there seemed little point in questioning them further. He finished his glass of port. The twins simply stared at him and in the end it was left to him, the guest, to say, 'Shall we join the ladies?'

Mrs Alleyn and her daughter had withdrawn to the salon, where a fire of coal and wood not only warmed the cosy room, papered in a distinctive red, but enhanced its welcome. On seeing the new arrivals, the widow sighed a little. 'I suppose the time has come to get down to business and talk of poor Josiah's death. What exactly is it you want to know, Mr Rawlings?'

He answered with a question. 'Miss Alleyn has explained to you that from time to time I work with the Principal Magistrate, Mr Fielding?'

His hostess sighed again. 'Yes. I feel so shocked that the Public Office has been brought into this affair. That Josiah should have been murdered is quite beyond my comprehension.'

Aware that Emilia's eyes were fixed firmly on him, John did his best to remain absolutely calm. 'Yet the fact remains that the flour used at the Livery Dinner was poisoned.'

'But why should Josiah die and not the rest?'

Yes why indeed? thought John. Aloud he said, 'He must have had more of the arsenic than the others.'

Again something nagged at him. Garnett Smith, embittered and full of hatred, blamed Master Alleyn for his son's death, and it was Master Alleyn who had died. It was damned odd, to coin Sotherton Backler's phrase. Yet it had to be a coincidence.

Mrs Alleyn was speaking. 'If I can do anything to help you find the poisoner, I am more than willing.'

'Then allow me to gather a few facts. If I could talk to you two ladies separately I would be most grateful.'

'Why apart?' the widow asked with just a hint of suspicion.

'Speaks for itself,' said one of the twins. 'Emilia's not going to say so much with her mama sitting there listening, now is she?'

'Quite right,' put in the other. 'Come along, Mother. Come along, Ellis.' And he shepherded them out of the room. John's respect for the twins rose in leaps and bounds.

Emilia stood up. 'Where would you like me to sit, Mr Rawlings?'

'In the conversation seat, perhaps. Then we can converse.'

It was a feeble joke and she didn't even smile, but took her place in the elegant chair for two, each seat side by side but facing in a different direction, a curving arm dividing the pair. Despite this barrier, she was unbelievably close to him, and the Apothecary breathed deeply, terribly aware of her heady perfume.

'Where do you want me to begin?'

'At the beginning perhaps. Tell me about your life.'

'What bearing could that possibly have on my father's death?'

The Apothecary's lively brows rose. 'Sometimes events from the past are the key to the present. Mr Fielding taught me that.'

'But my father was killed at random, you said so yourself. How could my past affect a chance poisoning?'

She had hit on the stumbling block that he could never seem to get beyond. John decided to be honest. 'I don't know is the answer to that, but humour me, Miss Alleyn, please. The whole situation puzzles me as much as it does you. Yet something, somewhere, must throw some light on it. Maybe a chance remark of yours could prove to be the key.'

She turned a slightly frozen profile away from him.

'Tell me about your childhood. Were you happy?' John asked almost pleadingly.

'Very. With four older brothers I was extremely spoiled.'

'And what of Andrew Smith? Was he a friend of your brothers?'

She gave him a cold look. 'You know about him?'

'Yes, I do. Now don't get in your high stirrup, Miss Alleyn. His father's name came up as someone who hated apothecaries. It was obvious that it would. This led directly to you, I'm afraid.'

She was silent for a moment, clearly thinking things through. Then said, 'I met Andrew when I was fifteen. He was a friend of the twins, in fact he was at school with them. I became betrothed to him when I was seventeen, he two years older. Six months later he died of a wen in his neck. My father treated him but he could not cure Andrew despite all the care lavished on him. The physician he was taken to declared it was a cancer and it was too late to save him. He accused my father of misdiagnosis. I suppose it was true in a way.'

'An easy mistake for an apothecary to make. I might well have done the same.'

She turned a fraught little face on him. 'But my father was a Liveryman and Andrew his future son-in-law. It was a bitter blow for Papa.'

'Not as bitter a blow as it must have been for you.'

'I thought I would never stop crying, but later I came to realise that what I felt for Andrew had been, after all, nothing but an adolescent attachment.'

John froze with sudden fury. 'Was it Master Cruttenden who told you that?'

Emilia drew in her breath with a hiss, then her hand flew out and struck the Apothecary stingingly on the cheek. 'How dare you ask, you arrogant poppinjay?'

The pain made his head rock back and he caught her wrist between his fingers almost as a reflex action. They were an inch apart, glaring at one another over the dividing arm of the chair. Instinctively pulling her towards him, John Rawlings did what he had wanted to from the moment he had first seen her. His mouth found Emilia's and he just had time to register that instead of fighting and hatred he was greeted with warmth and tenderness, before he and she were lost in the first kiss of love.

How long it lasted he never knew. All he did know was that he had drawn her across that silly divider and onto his lap, where he could hold her close and touch her beautiful breasts. Then the sound of feet on the wooden floor outside had them jumping apart and back into their places. There was a breathless pause before the footsteps passed and John looked at her contritely. 'If you had asked me to stop I would have done.'

'I didn't want you to.'

'Emilia, this is very dangerous.'

'Why? You're not married, are you?'

'No, I'm not,' John answered.

'Then why?'

'Because I am investigating a murder and should be treating you in a professional manner.'

She smiled suddenly and his heart leapt. 'I will tell you all you want to know then you can stop being an investigator and we can be friends instead.' She paused. 'That is what you want, isn't it?'

'By God,' said John Rawlings, 'more than anything else in the world.' And he knew as he said the words that he spoke the greatest truth of his life.

Emilia stood up and returned to his lap, but this time like a child, the passionate sexuality which was so obviously part of her makeup, totally subdued.

'I was still recovering from Andrew's death a year later, when one day I noticed Francis Cruttenden looking at me in a strange light. I'd always known him, of course, ever since I was a child. But this particular day he looked at me as if I were a woman.'

'Filthy old bastard!' John exclaimed furiously.

She laughed, then became serious. 'He seduced me, took me to his bed, taught me the meaning of desire . . .'

'I'll kill him.'

'. . . until I suddenly sickened of him. My parents knew nothing of it.'

John remembered Mrs Alleyn's comments but said nothing.

'He didn't want to let me go, but eventually did so. I have hated him ever since. In my mind he took ruthless advantage of my youth and situation.'

'Has there been anyone else?'

'No, a certain revulsion crept over me every time I thought of him, and I have kept myself to myself as a result.'

'Is that over now?'

'It's over,' said Emilia, and they kissed again.

This time the door did open, and they were hastily drawing apart when Mrs Alleyn came into the room. She stopped in her tracks, staring open mouthed. 'Mr Rawlings, this is not proper,' she said.

'On the contrary, Mama, it is the most proper thing that has ever happened to me,' Emilia replied with spirit. 'Now come and be questioned. It is high time that our guest solved this case and became an apothecary again.' And that said, she curtsied to her mother and left the room.

What is it, John thought, about kissing and cuddling that suddenly makes the whole world seem more cheerful? It was cold as Christmas and he was sitting in a leaking boat, huddled against the wind and inadequately dressed for the occasion, yet he hadn't felt so happy in months. He simply could not get from his mind, nor did he want to, the picture of Emilia's face as she embraced him, the look of total contentment that had covered her features.

'Oh yes,' he said aloud, and the boatman gave him a knowing glance.

'Successful night, friend?'

John felt at one with him, as rough and robust as he was. 'It could have been even better.'

'I see. Well, good luck next time.'

But he'd court her slowly, John thought. The last thing he wanted to do was ruin his chances by rushing events. And then a cold chill, not caused by the elements, swept over him. Between himself and any intended courtship stood the figure of Coralie Clive, the woman who until just now he had wanted more than anyone else in the world.

'What a damnable mess,' the Apothecary said beneath his breath, and suddenly knew that he must see his father, for though Samuel Swann or any other contemporary might be sympathetic and offer solace, none would be as sharp as that wisest of all wise birds, Sir Gabriel Kent.

'Drop me at Hungerford Stairs,' he said to the boatman. 'I think I'll go home before I go to work.' It was still only eight o'clock in the morning and there was time enough. 'Very good, Sir.'

His earlier mood of total happiness was vanishing fast, and now John felt he had just one objective: to talk to Sir Gabriel, even if it took several hours and Nicholas had to cope with the shop. To save time, where normally he would have enjoyed the walk, John hired a hackney coach in The Strand and bowled home at speed.

All was quiet as he went through the front door but investigation of the breakfast room revealed his parent, still *déshabillé*, reading the newspaper and drinking tea.

'Father,' said John, and went to sit down opposite him, removing his hat and cloak as an afterthought.

Sir Gabriel looked up. 'My boy, you appear somewhat rough. Why, I do vow and declare that you have not shaved.' The golden eyes narrowed. 'But there is a definite air about you, what escapades have you been up to?'

'I went to Chelsea last night,' said John, carving a piece of ham that would have daunted an ogre.

'And?'

'And there I questioned the family of the late Master Alleyn.'

'Remind me again who they are.'

'Well, the widow, of course. A kind and comfortable woman who thinks highly of me, at least I believe she does. There are also four sons, two of whom are married and no longer at home, and twin boys, still in residence, together with the daughter, Emilia.'

'Of what age might she be?'

'She is twenty-two, Father.'

'And still unwed?'

'She has had two rather unfortunate love affairs, one of which is connected to the case currently being investigated by Mr Fielding.'

And John spoke at some length about Garnett Smith, about Andrew, about Emilia, and finally about Francis Cruttenden.

Sir Gabriel put down his newspaper. 'You mentioned this man to me before and said we ought to engineer a meeting. I now think this becomes imperative. I don't like the sound of him at all.'

The Apothecary drank two cups of coffee. 'Sir, it is about Emilia that I wish to speak to you.'

His father smiled, a wonderful, worldly smile. 'My son, there is a softening about you this morning. You are alive as I have never seen you before. Is it possible that you have met the right woman at last?'

'But Coralie, Father. I love her. What am I doing? I think perhaps I have lost my senses.'

'Lost and found, John. You have been Coralie's devoted slave for many years. Oh, I know there have been indiscretions along the way but you are young and fit, what man would not make them? But these last few months you have offered her your hand and heart and she has refused them because she has a greater love.'

'The theatre?'

'Just so.'

'But that is the understanding on which our relationship began: that she would come to me when her ambition was finally fulfilled.'

'Alas, time changes everything. No situation, no one of us, is static, even from day to day. An agreement made some while ago must now be measured by today's circumstance. I do believe, my child, that you have outgrown the relationship that Coralie offered you.'

'But I love her,' John repeated. 'I have always loved her.'

'On her terms, not on yours.'

The truth of that hit the Apothecary like a body blow.

'She had her chance with you,' Sir Gabriel continued, 'but she misjudged your patience. She would like your situation to drift on for years, maybe for ever, but you are not done with the world, are questing after whatever is to happen next. You must face her with the facts, my son. And move on.'

The Apothecary wept, over his ham and into his coffee cup. He was a child again, vulnerable and silly and sad.

'She meant so much to me.'

'And maybe always will, but take your happiness while you can, John. If Emilia Alleyn is to be your destiny, then follow your star. If she is not, then at least you have progressed. I believe that your liaison with Coralie was beginning to go down a road to nowhere, except where it suited her.' Sir Gabriel picked up his paper, the conversation at an end.

Getting to his feet, the Apothecary made his way to his bedroom where, somewhat tired after the fitful sleep of the night before, waking every hour, terribly conscious of Emilia slumbering in a room not far away from his, he lay down on the bed and fell deeply unconscious.

He woke an hour later and looked at himself in the mirror.

He was haggard, admittedly, but he radiated something that was difficult to put into words. The Apothecary supposed that he was in love for the first time and that everything in the past had been a snare and a delusion, yet it was hard at that moment to distinguish one from the other. Perhaps he had loved all the girls who had meant something to him, he thought. Perhaps love was like a staircase and with each step one drew nearer and nearer to the ultimate. Perhaps, John Rawlings decided very wisely, love was such a complex emotion that it was impossible to work it out. So determining, John washed, then cleaned his teeth and prepared to face another day.

Chapter Thirteen

————❦————

He spent the morning being brisk about his shop, dealing with customers, including the most petulant and grumpy in town, or so it seemed to John, then rushing out to help a child in the street with a piece of apple caught in its throat. Nicholas came with him and watched with admiration as the Apothecary swung the girl upside down, then hit her on the back hard until the apple dislodged and fell out on the cobbles. The mother, duly grateful, wept copiously, her voice combining with that of her wailing daughter.

'Why are you crying?' asked the Muscovite, astonished. 'Your child is no longer choking. Mr Rawlings saved her.'

'It's the thought of what might have happened,' the woman answered, and pressed a very small coin into John's hand, which he took to maintain her dignity.

As they went back inside, the Apothecary turned to his apprentice. 'She's right you know. I have heard of a child choking to death on a piece of apple. It's not always possible to remove it.'

'You struck her very hard.'

'My Master told me that you cannot be hard enough, the situation is so dangerous.'

'I'll remember that.'

The rest of the hours they spent together were not nearly as dramatic, but for all that very concentrated. Physicks and pills were compounded, and John spent a considerable time with his new machine for making suppositories, an excellent invention, recently arrived from the manufacturer. Finally, and with some regret, the Apothecary handed over his prize acquisition to Nicholas, panting to have a try at rolling and pressing, and set off for Bow Street. The court was still in session, and every seat being taken, John stood at the back and watched justice being administered by the famous Magistrate.

It was partly the fact of John Fielding's blindness that drew the *beau monde* to the court in droves – this, coupled with the widespread belief that the man could recognise over three thousand villains just by hearing them speak. Such legendary behaviour, to say nothing of the Blind Beak's dramatic entrances into and exits from the court-room, a switch twitching before him to guide his path, had led the Principal Magistrate to become one of the main attractions of town. Vowing to get to court early one day in order to obtain a seat, John resigned himself to standing for the rest of the session.

Today the Beak was in a sombre mood, listening carefully and questioning down to the last detail before delivering sentence. The Apothecary wondered whether this had any-thing to do with the fact that Mr Fielding was himself currently being pursued through the courts. Earlier in the year he had committed a young man named William Barnard to prison simply on a verbal charge made by the Duke of Marlborough, namely that Barnard had made a nuisance of himself to the Duke's household. This sentence had so insensed the boy's father that he had laid an information against the Blind Beak for committing his son without due evidence. Judgement in the affair Rex *v.* Fielding was yet to be reached, but all of London society knew about it and was gossiping to its heart's content.

Sad for his friend, John listened to the cases of the day. A group of sky-farmers, some twenty in all, stood squeezed into an overflowing dock, glowering at all the fancy folk sitting agog in the galleries, hanging on every word the Principal Magistrate uttered.

'Sky-farmers,' Mr Fielding was saying, 'execute their schemes in the following manner. One of them dresses himself extremely genteel, and takes upon himself either the character of a private gentleman or reputable tradesman. He is attended by two men in the character of country farmers, with clumsy boots, horseman's coats and so on. The objects pitched upon for imposition are good old, charitable ladies, to whom the trickster tells a dreadful story of losses by fire, inundation, etc., to the utter ruin of these two poor farmers and all their families – their wives are big with child, their children down in the smallpox, or other dire diseases. A book is then produced by the trickster, who undertakes this disagreeable office purely out of good nature, knowing the story to be true. In this book are the names of several of the nobility and gentry set down by himself, who have contributed to this charity; and by setting out with false names, they at length obtain real ones.'

Cries of 'Shame' rang out, particularly from those present entitled to wear a coronet.

'Therefore,' Mr Fielding continued, 'being faced by a whole gang of such villainous fraudsters, apprehended by the diligence and fortitude of the court Runners, I have no option but to pass the severest sentence on them all. One year in Newgate, and the press gang to be waiting at the door on the day of their release.'

'That'll show 'em,' said a high-voiced little fellow, beautifully painted and dressed as any butterfly, fanning himself as sentence was passed.

A scuffle broke out as one of the sky-farmers, furious at his words, broke free from the warders, rather too few in number to be effective, and not only lunged at the butterfly but started to beat him with his fist. There was a scream and women began to climb on chairs as the officials rushed to stop the affray, thus leaving the rest of the gang unattended. At this there was general chaos as the sky-farmers started to charge round the court forming a knot into which Joe Jago, tossing his wig high, plunged head first in the manner of a high diver. John, somewhat reluctantly as he was giving a dinner party that night and had no wish to return home battered, joined in and threw a punch at a sky-farmer.

'Silence! Order!' bawled Mr Fielding, but nobody took any notice.

Dodging a hand big as a ham, the Apothecary managed to weave his way towards the beau who was bleeding from the lip and nose and weeping with the pain of it. His carefully applied macquillage was by now streaked with blood, and he looked at John from eyes around which the kohl had started to run. 'Help!' he called shrilly.

'Here,' the Apothecary replied, and snatching the beau's lace handkerchief applied it to his dripping wounds.

'Blood!' shrieked the little man, glancing down, and passed clean away in the Apothecary's arms.

'Oh, good God,' said John with much feeling.

Over the tumult he could hear Mr Fielding bellowing instructions. 'Runners, take the prisoners below. Clear the court. I'll have you all for contempt.'

But it was Joe Jago, his hair like fire as he swung fists and feet, who finally put a stop to it. Lean he might be, but strong he most certainly was. Picking up three sky-farmers by their collars he practically threw them at the warders, who chose the heaviest of their number to sit down hard on all three. This released the others to go after the rest of the gang who were heading for the doors, hoping to make an escape. Aided by several members of the public who liked any excuse for a good mill, they were all tackled to the floor before this could be achieved. John, meanwhile, wandered round aimlessly, carrying his patient, who lay limply in his arms.

Eventually some sort of calm was restored and Mr Fielding's words rang out. 'Joe, what is happening?'

'The prisoners are retaken, Sir. The public have assisted. Don't think it would be right to charge them with contempt.'

'Indeed not,' said an older female, scrambling down from her chair.

'Silence,' boomed the Beak in her direction, and she subsided, even though wobbling with annoyance.

'Is anyone injured?' Mr Fielding continued.

'Several,' said Joe succinctly.

'Is there a physician in court?'

'I'm here, Sir,' called out John, making his way to the front with considerable difficulty, the swooning young man still in his grasp.

'Ah, Mr Rawlings. In for the sport as usual.'

'Yes, Sir,' John answered drily.

'Patch 'em up if you will, there's a good fellow. You can use the Public Office as a surgery. There's water near by and someone will find you bandages.'

'I'll do my best to help, Sir, although I actually came for a word with you.'

'Can that wait?'

'Not really. I have guests for dinner tonight, so am somewhat pressed for time.'

'Um. I shall remain in court till you are done, then we shall converse briefly. To make amends I shall send you home with the two Brave Fellows, that will save a half hour.'

During the last part of this conversation the beau had been making mewing noises and now opened his dark-ringed and very messy eyes, a look of amazement in their depths. 'Who are you?'

'An apothecary,' answered John, setting him on his feet.

'Don't put me down, I'm poorly.'

'You're perfectly all right. Let me have a quick look at your nose and mouth.'

The beau, giving a simply fearful grimace, presented them for inspection then parted his carmined lips in a winsome smile. 'What is your name?'

'John Rawlings.'

'Nice.'

'Just keep still.'

'You're very masterful.'

John groaned aloud. 'The last thing I need is you trying to flirt with me. Just hold your tongue.'

'Why don't you?'

'What?'

'Hold it for me.'

'Oh go away,' said the Apothecary, much aggrieved.

The rest of the patients were far more straightforward; bruises, cuts and one badly damaged nose which John sent straight round to the physician who dwelt near by. Then it was finished, though he glimpsed the beau, hat pulled well down over a rapidly bruising eye, loitering in the doorway. With firm tread, John headed back into the courtroom and closed the door behind him.

Mr Fielding still sat in his high chair, his eyes, as ever concealed by a black bandage, turned towards the sound of the Apothecary coming in. Beside him, Joe Jago said, 'Mr Rawlings is here.'

'My very dear friend, how can I ever thank you enough? What a fracas. Alas, as ever we are underfunded. I need more trained men about me.'

The Apothecary nodded. 'Indeed, Sir, indeed.'

'Now what is it you wanted to talk to me about?'

'You received my letter? The one in which I reported that the watchman had gone missing.'

'Yes. I sent a Runner straight away to make enquiries both at the lodging house and at Timber Wharf. There's no sign of him.'

'I fear that he has been disposed of,' John stated grimly.

'What do you mean?'

'It's my contention, Sir, that whoever poisoned the flour either bribed the man to keep silent or stole into Apothecaries' Hall then realised that Griggs had awoken and was observing him.'

'Are you saying that he has been murdered?'

'Yes, I believe I am. I think he knew the identity of the poisoner and, with the chase beginning to warm up, was proving dangerous and had to go.'

The Blind Beak leant forward, his bandaged eyes only an inch away from John's own. 'Have you any idea who perpetrated this crime?

The Apothecary sighed. 'No, Sir. There were three obvious suspects which I have now whittled down to two. Yet Tobias Gill does not quite fit the bill. As for Garnett Smith, I really don't know. He has family connections with Master Alleyn which do indeed make him highly questionable.'

'What are these connections?'

'Garnett's son Andrew was betrothed to Alleyn's daughter, Emilia. Because of this, it was Master Alleyn who treated the boy before he died. I believe that Smith still blames him for his son's death.' John paused, then said, 'It is very odd that it should have been Master Alleyn who consumed a fatal dose, when he is the object of so much hatred.'

There was a long silence, during which the Magistrate sat so still he appeared to be frozen. Neither John nor Joe spoke, knowing that the Blind Beak was actually deep in thought. Finally he said, 'Is it possible that Master Alleyn was the intended victim all along?'

'But how could that be?'

'Perhaps the Liveryman sitting beside him slipped additional arsenic into his food.'

'But everybody was taken ill.'

'Indeed they were, although that could have been a deliberate ploy. Were we meant to think that a maniac with a grudge tried to poison all the apothecaries, when really the fatal dose was just meant for one?'

'Then how was it done?'

'The poisoner crept into Apothecaries' Hall the night before the dinner. I think you have established that beyond doubt, Mr Rawlings. Then, the next day, at the Dinner itself, he contrives to put extra poison into Master Alleyn's portion.'

'Um. I'm not happy about that. Supposing he were caught in the act?'

Mr Fielding nodded solemnly. 'I agree with you, my friend. The argument is flawed, but for all that, I think we should now begin to look at this case from a different viewpoint.'

'But it would mean questioning absolutely everyone present at the Dinner,' John said unhappily.

'I would not expect you to take on such a thing. You would never get any work done at all. I shall put the Runners on to it, three of them, I think. Meanwhile, Mr Rawlings, I would like you to concentrate on the others – Mr Clarke and Apothecary Gill, imagining for the sake of argument that the mass poisoning was a bluff, that Master Alleyn was the one chosen to die.'

'What about Garnett Smith?'

'You must visit him again with the same premise.'

'But if the murder was committed at the Dinner that would automatically rule him out.'

'Not if he were acting in league with someone.'

John struck his forehead with his hand. 'This is becoming truly complex. Are you suggesting a hired assassin?'

'Anything is possible.'

'I am daunted by the whole prospect.'

'Don't be. You are already starting to peel away the layers.'

'Do you think so?'

'Look at the information you have gathered so far.'

Joe spoke up. 'We are further down the road, Mr Rawlings, even if you can't see it.'

John got to his feet, ready to take his leave. 'Well, I'll continue to do my best. You can be sure of that. Now, what action do you want me to take about the missing watchman?'

'Keep your ears open, that's all. Meanwhile, we'll stay in touch with the morgue keepers in case he's brought in.'

'Whoever this killer is,' John said sombrely, 'he's a ruthless bastard. I fear for anyone who stands in his way.'

'Then have a care for yourself, my young friend. He may already be aware that you are on his trail.'

Thinking of Master Alleyn's cruel death and the swiftness with which George Griggs had vanished, the Apothecary shivered slightly as he left the comforting confines of the courtroom and stepped into the carriage which was waiting to take him home.

Harriet Clarke was not at all what John had expected. Possibly because she had an invalid son, he had formed a mental picture of rather a drab little lady, weighed down by the cares of the world. Instead, a very striking woman was shown into the small salon where John was receiving his guests. A bony but arresting face, dominated by a pair of grey eyes, bright as jewels, immediately caught his attention. Thick hair, dark as a gypsy's, was gloriously abundant beneath her headdress.

'Mr Rawlings,' Harriet said, as she made a formal curtsey, 'I have been so looking forward to this moment.' And she extended a hand with long firm fingers which the Apothecary kissed with enthusiasm.

Away from the shop and dressed for the evening, Michael Clarke presented a better image than that of his work-a-day self, while Dr Hensey, as ever neat and dapper, had put on a canary silk waistcoat embroidered with red and pink roses. In short, though the company was small it was elegant. The only thing missing, in John's view, was a hostess, and his thoughts immediately went to Emilia, and his heart ached as he wondered what she was doing.

Earlier that evening, before the guests had arrived, a letter had been delivered to the door from Coralie Clive. Had its tone been very slightly curt? John had wondered. Commenting on the fact that she hadn't seen him since Serafina's soirée, the actress had said that she would ignore this and went on to invite John to escort her to an Assembly on the following Saturday. Knowing that it would be wrong of him to refuse, the Apothecary had hastily penned a letter of acceptance and returned it with the messenger. And now here he was, standing amongst his dinner guests and thinking of Emilia just as if the last four years, during which he had wooed and finally won Coralie, had never taken place at all. Considering himself a regular wretch, John turned his attention to the alluring Harriet, who smiled enigmatically and took his arm as they went through the open doors in the archway which separated the salon from the dining room.

Sir Gabriel Kent, ever considerate, had accepted an invitation to whist, so that his son might act the role of host without competition. So it was that the Apothecary sat at the head of the table with Harriet Clarke on his right, Dr Hensey to his left, and Michael Clarke opposite.

Murder not being the ideal topic for dinner party talk, the conversation ranged over a variety of subjects including John's adventures at Bow Street earlier that day.

'It's so easy, is it not,' said Michael Clarke, 'to forget about the war, that is unless one has one's nose permanently affixed to a newspaper. It needs something like Mr Fielding's warning that the press gang will be waiting at the prison doors to remind us that it is still on.'

'Of course, it was very much uppermost in our thoughts when I first met Mr Rawlings, nearly two years ago now,' Dr Hensey answered. 'Fate took us to Romney Marsh where it was all talk of spies and such like.'

'Not just talk either,' said John. 'One of them, French as they come, though you would never have believed it to meet him, delivered me a crack on the jaw fair set to put me out for a week. If it hadn't been for Dr Hensey here, I believe I might only just now be regaining consciousness.'

'So you are a physician?' asked Harriet, leaning in the doctor's direction.

'I am, Madam.'

'What do you know about the falling sickness? My poor boy is badly afflicted and there's not one apothecary worth the name – and there's not many of those, I fear . . .'

John thought this quite the most extraordinary remark.

'. . . who can do a thing about it.'

Dr Hensey sipped his wine. 'Strange to tell, the falling sickness is a speciality of mine. I studied in Paris under an eminent man, Professeur Henri Collard, and he had definite theories about it.'

'Which were?'

'The use of certain physicks, combined in most specific quantities, can control it for the rest of the patient's life.'

One of Harriet's strong white hands flew to her throat. 'Do you mean this?'

'I most certainly do, Madam, and it would be my pleasure and privilege to visit your boy if that is what you would like.'

'I *would* like it, I would like it very much indeed.' She turned to her husband. 'Michael, what do you think?'

'Anything that might help our son would be gratefully appreciated.'

'In that case I shall make it my first duty as soon as I have attended my other patients.'

He continued to talk to Michael, who listened avidly, and unable to help himself, John drew Harriet's attention.

'I hate to pry, Madam, but what did you mean by your disparaging comment about apothecaries?'

She smiled a slow and cynical smile. 'My experience of them has not been too good over the years.'

'But you're married to one.'

'Well?'

John was nonplussed, not knowing at all how to answer.

Obviously sensing his confusion, Harriet patted his hand over the dinner table. 'My dear Mr Rawlings . . .'

'Please call me John.'

'John, then. There is no need to look quite so put out. An apothecary tended me when I was pregnant and suffered greatly from sickness. He prescribed such terrible things, terrible things . . .' She paused for a moment and looked positively ill. '. . . that I have never been certain from that day to this whether they had anything to do with my son being born the way he is. That's all. I have nothing against you or my husband. Now, can we talk of other things?'

While she had been speaking Harriet's face had undergone a series of changes, a dark, almost vicious look gradually being replaced by the kind of expression demanded by social nicety. Convinced that there was an underlying message to what she was saying, John felt powerless to question her further. He changed the subject.

'Do you enjoy living on the south bank?'

'It's very quiet but I quite like that. Although I was born in Spitalfields, my parents moved across the river when I was small, so one could say that I am used to it.'

'You must know Francis Cruttenden, a Liveryman of the Society. He lives in Pye House, quite close to you.'

Harriet's sculpted features turned into those of a cat. 'Yes, I know him,' she said.

And dislike him, John thought. He put on his ingenuous face. 'He must be tremendously rich to live in a place of such splendour.'

'I would call it tasteless grandeur.'

'You've been inside, then?'

'Several times, both before Cruttenden bought it and after. The house used to belong to old Mr Harman who made a fortune from importing rare goods. When he died his children sold it on and the Liveryman bought it.'

'How long ago was this?'

'Twelve years or so.' Harriet paused and drank from her wineglass. 'As I told you, I was brought up on the south bank. My father was a furniture maker, quite a successful one, but before he became established, my mother, in order to help out, worked as a servant for Mr Harman. I had the run of Pye

House when I was a child. In fact his children and I were playmates.'

'And after he died?'

'Both Mother and I continued to work as servants there. That was until I married.'

'So Master Cruttenden was your employer?'

Harriet nodded. 'He was indeed.'

It was on the tip of the Apothecary's tongue to ask her opinion of the man, but he held back, aware that he already had the answer. Her earlier change of expression had told him everything he wanted to know. Harriet Clarke disliked the Liveryman intensely. He changed the subject again.

'How old is your son?'

'Matthew? He's eleven. Poor little soul, he cannot lead a normal life, because people hate and revile those who fall and have fits.'

'They do indeed,' said Dr Hensey joining in their conversation. 'That is why my old tutor did all the research he could, to try and redress the balance.'

Harriet turned on him, her face suddenly radiant. 'When can you come to see him?'

'The day after tomorrow. Now tell me where you live exactly.' He started to make notes in a pocket book and Michael Clarke took this opportunity to talk to John.

'Have you heard that Griggs has gone missing?'

The Apothecary nodded. 'I fear the worst.'

'Surely you don't think . . .'

'I believe he saw something on the night the flour was poisoned.'

'And was done away with as a result? Oh, my God, I pray it isn't so.'

'So do I,' answered John, but even as he spoke an inner conviction was growing that anyone connected with the poisoning at Apothecaries' Hall stood in ever-increasing danger from a killer who regarded human life as little more than an expendable commodity.

Chapter Fourteen

———◆◇◆◇◆———

The energy of Sir Gabriel Kent never ceased to surprise his son, who felt fractionally tired after entertaining company for the entire evening. His father, on the other hand, presumably boosted by the fact that he had won handsomely at whist, was sky-blue bright and ate rather more than his usual sparing breakfast.

'My child, I am going to Kensington for a few days,' he announced as he peeled some fruit.

'Today?'

'Yes, as soon as I have made a toilette. I want to see how the labourers are progressing in our new residence.'

'Woe betide them if they have been slacking.'

'I am quite certain that they are working with a will,' Sir Gabriel replied urbanely.

'Unfortunately,' said John, attacking a slice of beef, 'I shan't be able to join you. Tonight I have to dine with Mr Gill and his obnoxious daughter – all in the line of duty, you understand – and tomorrow I am going to an Assembly with Coralie. The day after that, being a Sunday, I thought of going to call on the Alleyns.'

'And Miss Emilia in particular?'

'Yes,' John replied, 'a hundred times yes.'

'Is it wise,' said Sir Gabriel, drinking from a bone china cup, 'to continue to see both young ladies simultaneously?'

'It is very unwise and soon I am going to have to do something about it.'

'Yes, you are, my dear.' Sir Gabriel picked up his newspaper. 'Um, how odd.'

'What's that?'

'There's a report here that spying continues unabated in London. That despite the efforts of the Secret Office to smoke them from their dens, the French are still obtaining undercover information with apparent ease. Damme, but these people have their nerve.'

'One can't help but admire their daring.'

'True enough, but it is hardly aiding our effort in the war.'

'I'm prejudiced,' said John. 'The only French spy I ever met was such a lovable rogue that I can't find it in me to dislike the breed.'

'You'd change your tune if you were staring down a gun barrel.'

'Yes, I probably would.'

'Anyway, to other things. How does the Apothecaries' Hall affair progress?'

'An interesting twist,' said John, and told his father of the Blind Beak's theory.

'It makes perfect sense to me. A mass poisoning always seemed a far-fetched idea. I'm sure Mr Fielding is right. Liveryman Alleyn was the intended victim all the way along.'

'But there's a stumbling block to that, and one that I personally have difficulty in getting past.'

'Namely?'

'How was the fatal dose administered? The amount of arsenic put in the flour was clearly only enough to produce sickness. How was it contrived to give Master Alleyn more?'

Sir Gabriel smiled. 'That, my child, is where your powers of deduction come into play.' And he returned to his newspaper.

Rolling his eyes to heaven, John smiled wryly, finished his breakfast, kissed his father on the cheek, and set off for his shop.

'Visitor,' said Nicholas, meeting him as John put his foot over the threshold.

'Who?'

'A young lady. Wouldn't give her name. Said she wanted to surprise you. I showed her into the back.'

At the very thought that it could possibly be Emilia, John's breathing quickened its pace, and it was with bright eyes and a heart full of expectation that he made his way into the compounding room. And there she sat, lovely eyes turned towards him, her mouth already curving into a smile.

John didn't say a word but simply raised her from her seat and took her in his arms. 'I missed you.'

'And I missed you,' she answered.

'Was your mother very angry with us?'

'No, she thinks the world of you. It's just that she was brought up in the old school. She believes that a young woman, particularly her only daughter, should never, ever be left alone with a young man.'

'That could prove a bit awkward.'

'Are you being rude?'

'Very,' said John, and indulged in a long and hot-blooded kiss which could have left Emilia Alleyn in no doubt about his feelings towards her.

'So how did you escape today?' he said eventually.

'My mother is in town visiting her sister. I pleaded the need for a little air and set off for Shug Lane.'

'What shameless behaviour.'

'Yes. I hope you're not shocked by my lack of decorum.'

'I am so shocked that I am thinking of taking an hour off and walking with you to act as your chaperone.'

'Take me to the park,' said Emilia, 'I would like that.'

'At once,' John answered, and bowed. 'Nicholas,' he called.

His apprentice appeared, attempting to look nonchalant and failing because of his broad grin. 'Yes, Master?'

'I am going for a stroll with Miss Alleyn. Look after the shop for me.'

'Gladly, Sir.' He bowed to Emilia. 'It's a great pleasure to meet you, Ma'am.'

'I return the compliment.'

Nicholas was visibly seen to melt at one glance from her angel's eyes.

'It will be cold in the park,' John said, feeling enormously protective, an emotion he did not often experience with Coralie, who was so very capable of taking care of herself.

'My cloak is quite thick.'

'And I'll stay close to you.'

There was a muffled sound from Nicholas which could have been a cough but might just as easily have been a guffaw suppressed.

The Apothecary stared at his apprentice severely. 'I shall be about an hour or so.'

'Very good, Master. What shall I say if anyone calls for you?'

'That I have gone to see a patient,' John answered, and beetled his mobile brows at the Muscovite, who seemed to be having some difficulty in wiping the grin from his face.

'Goodbye,' said Miss Alleyn, inclining her head politely.

'I sincerely hope we meet again,' replied Nicholas, bowing himself almost in half.

'Have a care,' put in John enigmatically, and left the shop with all the dignity he could muster.

'Was that young limb laughing at us?' asked Emilia, blue eyes bright.

'If we were to go back now we would find him convulsed.'

'Why?'

'It's the thought of me courting a young lady that he finds so amusing.'

'But surely he must have seen that before. After all, he has been with you some years, hasn't he?'

'Several, and yes he has.'

Emilia stared into the middle distance. 'Is there a woman in your life at present, John?'

Dear God, had he ever felt so wretched? 'Yes, Emilia, there is.'

'Tell me of her.'

'I have known her for four years. She is an actress, Coralie Clive. She lives with her sister, the famous Kitty. The relationship is going nowhere.'

'And that is all?'

'Yes, more or less.'

'I presume you are lovers?'

'I became her lover before I met you,' John answered truthfully.

He had said the correct thing. Emilia stopped walking and turned to look at him. 'I really have no right to ask you these questions.'

'What passed between us the other evening gives you every right.'

'So what will you do, John?'

'I will speak to her, of course.'

'And say what?'

'At this moment I really don't know,' the Apothecary answered, and the misery he was feeling must have sounded so clearly in his voice that Emilia said no more, simply taking his arm and walking in silence as they made their way to St James's Park.

He spent the rest of that day in a strange mood, half elated through having been in the company of Miss Alleyn, half weighed down with worry over how he was to conduct himself with Coralie. For truth to tell, his feelings for that young woman were very far from dead. He had walked too long and too close a road with her for all emotion to vanish overnight. As if sensing his Master's pre-occupied state, Nicholas ceased to grin and guffaw, and worked soberly and silently for the rest of the time they spent together.

Then at three o'clock John put on his hat and cloak. 'I have to dine with Mr Gill and his daughter, so I thought I would combine the visit with a call on Mr Clarke. There is something I really must ask him.'

Nicholas said nothing but clearly longed to know what it was.

John put him out of his misery. 'His wife was treated for sickness when she was pregnant and half believes that the apothecary concerned might have contributed to her son having the falling sickness.'

'Was it Master Alleyn?'

'That's what I need to find out.'

'The poor man certainly had his enemies it seems.'

'But how did they get to him? That's what I want to know.'

'When you discover that you'll have the answer to the whole problem,' Nicholas answered cheerfully, a remark which did nothing to boost John's confidence whatsoever.

Just for once Michael Clarke was not in his shop, which was closed and bore a sign saying, 'Back Shortly'. As there was no indication as to what time this had been posted, the Apothecary thought it futile and went marching off into Apothecaries' Hall to see if he could track his quarry down. Sure enough he found him taking tea with Jane Backler in the Butler's pantry. They both looked up as John came into the room, rather guiltily he thought, which made him wonder if they indulged in an occasional flirtation.

Michael got to his feet. 'My dear John, may I say what a very pleasant evening Harriet and I had yesterday. We are most anxious to return the compliment.'

'I should be delighted.' The Apothecary bowed.

Jane Backler, obviously feeling a great deal better than of late, said, 'Sotherton and I would enjoy it very much if you all came to dine with us.'

Polite noises were made, though no actual date was fixed.

'Now, is there anything I can do for you in the shop?' Michael asked. 'I was taking a short break but am due to go back at any moment.'

'Yes, there are one or two herbs I require.'

'Excellent, let us walk together.'

They crossed the courtyard, went out into the street, then in through the shop's door, Michael removing the notice as he did so. He turned to John. 'What can I get you, my friend?'

The Apothecary thought quickly. 'I have a patient who is suffering greatly with morning sickness. I am considering recommending a caudle of balm, made with eggs, sugar, rosewater and juice. What's your view?'

Mr Clarke pulled a face. 'I think you might be better just to give a syrup made with the juice and sugar. The tansy you are thinking of might possibly procure an abortion.'

'Oh, surely not. I give a decoction of the root of butcher's broom to desperate young women. If that doesn't work, a decoction of the tops of centaury, together with the leaves and flowers, never fails.'

Michael looked glum. 'Harriet nearly lost our child through taking such a caudle of balm. If I hadn't intervened, I do believe Matthew would have been voided.'

John contrived to look amazed. 'Then I apologise for my ignorance. But obviously I am not the only one innocent of this. Whoever prescribed such a treatment for your wife must also have been unaware of the dangers.'

'Yes,' said Mr Clarke expressionlessly.

The Apothecary cursed silently. He was being forced to show his hand. 'Might I ask who it was?'

'Her employer at the time,' Michael answered, his tone abrupt.

'Do you mean Francis Cruttenden?' John said, a very strange notion just beginning to dawn on him.

'Yes, him,' the shop manager replied, and refused to be drawn any further.

Pudding Lane by night was even worse than Pudding Lane by day. Wading through sodden mounds of rubbish, avoiding the dark shadows, both animal and human, that slunk in the blackest corners, and elbowing one hopeful cutpurse so hard in the privy parts that he left the man wheezing, John finally came to his destination. With plummeting heart, having no real wish to see either Mr Gill or the truculent Clariana again had he the choice, he rang the bell.

In common with many shopkeepers, Tobias lived above his premises, and while John stood on the step, hoping that no one else would approach him, the sound of descending footsteps, followed by the drawing back of bolts and the turning of locks, was distinctly audible. Eventually the door to the shop opened, and Tobias, complete with candletree, ushered him within.

'My dear young man, how kind of you to come. I had half thought that you might not appear.'

'I've been looking forward to it,' lied John stoically.

'Clariana has too,' Mr Gill answered with a hint of waggishness in his voice.

Thinking that he would believe that when he saw it, the Apothecary plodded up a spindly staircase in Tobias's wake and entered the apartment above.

Considering the terrible area they were situated in, the rooms were very spacious and pleasant. Rebuilt after the Great Fire, Mr Gill's home was large and gracious, with delightful windows, presently covered by curtains. Decorated in tasteful colours and lit by many candles, the apartment proved an excellent background for Clariana, who was dressed in sea green, a colour that greatly enhanced her flaming hair. Her face, however, was pinched and angry. If she was pleased to see the Apothecary, Tobias's daughter was concealing it very cleverly.

Longing to wipe the supercilious expression off her smug face, John made a florid bow, glad that beneath his sensible cloak he was dressed to kill.

'Miss Gill.'

'Mr Rawlings.'

'How kind of you to invite me to dine.'

'The invitation was extended by my father, not by myself.'

'How gracious of him.' He lowered his voice to a whisper. 'A pity that the same courtly behaviour does not extend to you.'

Clariana glowered. 'I will not be insulted in my own home,' she hissed.

'Then step into the street and I'll do it there.'

'You insolent pup.'

'Steady, girl. You'll ruin your looks with all this ill temper.'

She made an involuntary move, as if she were going to strike him. Smiling pleasantly, the Apothecary caught her wrist and raised her hand to his lips.

'Charming,' he said loudly.

Mr Gill, who had been busying himself at a tray of drinks and had therefore missed the whispered exchange, handed round glasses of sherry. 'So pleased you two young people are getting on,' he commented genially.

'Miss Clariana is difficult to resist,' John answered.

She narrowed her eyes but said nothing, smiling through gritted teeth. Sighing resignedly, the Apothecary decided that at least the evening was not going to be boring.

An hour later he was beginning to revise his opinion. Clariana, seething with sulks, had obviously decided on a policy of silence and merely chomped at her food, fixing her eyes firmly on her plate. Mr Gill, clearly uncomfortable at this but unable to do much about it without causing an unwelcome scene, manfully tried to fill the gaps with small talk. It was an excrutiating situation, and John cast about in his mind as to the best way of dealing with it. Finally he decided on shock tactics. Giving Tobias an encouraging smile, in an attempt to reassure the older man, he turned to Clariana.

'I believe you are a great friend of Francis Cruttenden,' he said.

Her gaze shot up and she eyed John ferociously. 'Who told you that?'

'No one,' he answered pleasantly. 'I just happened to observe you with him in the street the other day.'

'How do you know him?'

'You forget that I am an apothecary and he is a Liveryman of the Worshipful Society. I do have a particular interest in him, however. I am friendly with the Alleyn family, the head of which was so recently and so brutally poisoned, and Master Cruttenden is also a friend of theirs. That is why I noticed him.'

Tobias Gill gave John a look of eternal gratitude for not telling the truth, a look which Clariana fortunately did not notice. However, her red hair was not for nothing.

'My father does not care for me to see Master Cruttenden,' she stated boldly.

'Clariana! This is hardly the place . . . ' Tobias remonstrated, but she ignored him, fixing John with a glare and speaking directly to him.

'He believes that Francis is too old to court me, but I don't think age matters when one is in love, do you Mr Rawlings?'

'That depends,' he answered carefully. 'If there is too large a gap it can lead to heartache in the future.' John laughed heartily. 'But I don't suppose Master Cruttenden would agree with me on that score.'

'Why do you say that?'

'Because he clearly has a preference for the younger lady. I believe he was involved with Miss Emilia Alleyn for a while.'

Clariana became molten. 'Mr Rawlings, you are a busy-body and a gossip. I think you have come here to make trouble.'

The Apothecary shook his head. 'No, Miss Gill, not so. You must look to yourself and question. If your trust of Liveryman Cruttenden is so unsure that the very mention of his past rouses you to anger, then your relationship must be built on sand.'

She shot to her feet. 'I will not sit here and listen to another word of this.'

'Go, then,' shouted her father, suddenly and surprisingly losing his temper. 'Go to your room. But know this, Clariana. You have insulted a guest and shown yourself in an appalling light. Any hopes you might have cherished of marrying that evil genius Cruttenden have been finally dashed by your behaviour tonight. By God, even if I have to send you to your uncle in the country to get you away from him, I will not hesitate to do so.'

His daughter flounced from the table, weeping copiously.

Ashen faced, Tobias turned to John. 'My dear young friend, I do apologise. I swear she has only been like this since she fell into Cruttenden's clutches. Underneath all, she really has a very sweet nature – or did have once.'

'It is certainly a terrible situation,' the Apothecary answered with feeling. 'What are you going to do?'

'I shall forbid her to see him, and if that fails I will make good my threat. To the country she goes.'

'Have you thought of talking to Cruttenden?'

Tobias Gill fumed. 'Talk to that jackanapes? Why, he's everything I detest. A vile seducer of innocent young females, and a Liveryman into the bargain. No, Sir. I don't intend to waste my valuable breath on him.'

'Then I wish you luck, Sir, for it's my view he's as slippery a fish as ever flipped out of the ocean, and not the easiest being to get the better of.'

'He won't thwart me,' said Mr Gill determinedly.

'I sincerely hope not,' John answered, and wondered whether Tobias's sudden show of temper had ever been focused on Josiah Alleyn, and if so, with what dire consequences.

Chapter Fifteen

———◦◦◦◦◦———

If John had taken pains with his appearance on the previous evening, tonight he spared himself nothing. Well aware that the Assembly to which Coralie had invited him was being given by the Duchess of Northumberland, a great theatregoer and an admirer of the work of both the sisters Clive, the Apothecary dressed luxuriously. A suit only worn once and fastidiously cleaned after that wearing, was fetched from his clothes press. With much care John, who spent every available guinea he had on high fashion, his greatest weakness, put on a pair of silver breeches decorated with purple flowers and slipped an exactly matching waistcoat over his fine cambric shirt. The throat he had dressed open, as was the fashion, but there was an abundance of fine lace filling the gap, as good taste demanded. Having checked that there were no wrinkles in his white silk stockings, John put on a pair of purple Meroquin shoes adorned with sparkling buckles, and completed the stunning ensemble with its finest item, a white and silver velvet coat. Wrapping himself in a fur-lined cloak and putting on a hat adorned with silver lace, scolloped stiffly, the Apothecary was finally ready to leave the house.

Sir Gabriel having taken the équipage to Kensington, John had sent a servant to fetch a hackney coach to the door. Directing the driver to Coralie's home in Cecil Street, he leant back against the slightly worn interior, confident about how he looked but nervous as a cat about the evening that lay ahead of him.

It would not be fair, he had decided, to tell his mistress about Emilia until the Assembly was at an end. Knowing that Coralie would invite him back to spend the night with her, he thought that that might be the moment, when they were alone and quiet. Then he could go home and leave her in peace, realising that their long association was finally at an end.

But was it? John tortured himself by asking. Could he ever really escape Coralie's profound hold on him? Did he really want to? Racked with cruel and painful indecision, John climbed the steps leading to Coralie's front door and rang the bell.

Almost as if she knew she was under threat, tonight the actress's beauty shimmered, her dark looks enhanced by her ice blue and violet ensemble, colours that brought out the very best in her.

'You look lovely,' John said admiringly.

'So do you. You'll even outshine the Prince of Wales.'

'Is he going?'

'He and the cream of high society. The *beau monde* is turning out in force.'

'Are you sure that I am a suitable escort? Just a humble apothecary?'

'Don't be servile, it does not become you.'

'I'm sorry. But I'm partly serious. Couldn't you have found a more illustrious companion to be seen with?'

'It's you I wanted to accompany me,' Coralie answered. And though John was gratified, his soul sank at the thought of hurting her.

Even though it was deepest November, the Duchess had ordered lights to be hung in the gardens of Northumberland House. A diamond necklace of lamps edged the lawns, swinging from one tree to the next, a most attractive sight to gaze upon through those windows before which rich and opulent curtains had not yet been drawn. Not to be outdone, the house was full of flowers and candlelight, with musicians dispersed throughout the various rooms, somehow contriving to play in harmony rather than discord. Liberal amounts of champagne were being served by white-wigged footmen, and even though the night was young there already came the sounds of laughter and high-pitched voices chattering animatedly.

'Miss Coralie Clive and Mr John Rawlings,' called the major-domo, and there was a smattering of applause and delighted cries from the theatregoers present. Inclining her head graciously, Coralie joined her admirers.

This had been happening more and more of late, a sure sign that the actress was at last achieving the kind of recognition she so hungrily sought. And John, hovering in the background, was pleased for her that her ambitions were being fulfilled but sorry that Coralie was letting the rest of life pass her by.

'Are you Miss Clive's husband?' asked an elderly lady, cupping her ear for the reply.

'No, Madam, just her friend.'

'That's as well, then, for I don't believe these great actresses should be married to anything other than their art.'

It was like a conspiracy, John thought, and fell to studying the pictures on the walls, leaving Coralie to greet her devotees, who buzzed around her like a swarm of bees circling the fabled honey pot. Being slightly removed from her also gave him a chance to look round, a pastime he had always enjoyed.

The place was populated by either members of the aristocracy, the very rich, or the famous. In short, all those who glittered in society. Of the professions and other more ordinary folk there were few representatives. There was consequently a certain decadence in the atmosphere, an effete exhaustion, a kind of hothouse lassitude. Everyone seemed to know everyone else, and the feeling of incestuous gaiety was almost tangible. Wishing that Coralie would free herself of her entourage, John walked towards the musicians who at least were working for their living this night. And then he froze where he stood as the voice of the major-domo rang out.

'Miss Clariana Gill and Mr Francis Cruttenden.'

The Apothecary wheeled round, never more astonished in his life. That Cruttenden was wealthy was beyond dispute, but that he mingled at this level of society was frankly astounding. Liveryman of the Worshipful Society or no, John would never have expected to find him in these distinguished halls.

Cruttenden was dressed in his usual grey, his coat of silk lined with pink, a stunning combination. Beneath it his grey satin waistcoat was embroidered with gold, a theme echoed by his superbly cut breeches, which ended at the knee in fine grey silk stockings. Pink shoes studded with gleaming diamond buckles completed the highly fashionable rig. And Clariana had not been outclassed, for she dripped jewels from hair, neck and fingers, obviously the gifts of her adoring lover. Studying the pair through critical eyes, John reckoned that at least thirty years must separate the couple.

Clearly at ease, Cruttenden stood a moment or two, surveying the company through his quizzing glass. Then his gaze fell on John and after shooting him a contemptuous glance, the Liveryman looked away, although not before whispering in Clariana's ear. Now it was her turn to glare daggers, and the Apothecary distinctly saw her mouth the word, 'Upstart.'

'Who are you staring at?' Coralie had come to join him and was standing at his side.

'Francis Cruttenden.'

'Who?'

'Did I not tell you of him? He's one of the people involved in the mysterious affair at Apothecaries' Hall.'

Coralie gave a small sad smile. 'John, the last time I saw you was at Serafina's party. You have hardly discussed this case with me at all.'

Suddenly guilty, the Apothecary began to make excuses. 'Sweetheart, I really have been very busy—'

She stopped him in mid flow. 'Don't bother to say it, I know you have. Anyway, if this man is one of the suspects, I can tell you now I don't like the look of him at all. He's a lecherous grey lizard. Observe the way he's looking at me through that glass of his. And who's the poor benighted redhead with him? I don't envy her her future.'

'Actually, he's not a suspect, that is, no more than anyone else. Truth to tell, Coralie, we haven't really got any suspects. The obvious ones, with the exception perhaps of Garnett Smith, seem accounted for in one way or another.'

'Do you mean you're no further forward?'

'There's been a mysterious disappearance, if you can call that progress.'

Coralie looked intrigued. 'Who has gone?'

'The nightwatchman at Apothecaries' Hall. I believe that he saw too much.'

'What a tangled web.'

'Isn't it? But let's move on. There is much I would tell you about Cruttenden and his lady love, with whom I had an astonishing argument last night.'

It was just like old times, Coralie's hand on his arm as they progressed through the various rooms, greeting people who knew and admired the actress, even occasionally meeting those who had been treated by John and remembered him. During their perambulations, while they were not talking to others, the Apothecary gave her as much detail as he could about the poisoning, about the Blind Beak's theory that Alleyn had always been the intended victim, about Tobias Gill, Garnett Smith, Harriet and Michael Clarke, and finally about Clariana and her passionate affair with her elderly lover.

'How will you solve it all?' she asked finally, giving him that gypsy-eyed look that he had always adored.

John shook his head. 'I have no idea.'

'Perhaps—'

But her words were interrupted by a call to supper. Feeling quite hungry, Coralie and John made their way through to the rooms set aside for the cold collation and fell to eating with enthusiasm.

Dancing had begun in the ballroom, and as the meal ended so the floor began to fill up. Benches set around the room exhibited rows of ladies in great distress for partners, for many of the gentlemen had retired to the rooms prepared for dice and cards. Fops, fools and gamesters led the way, and John was interested to see that mingling in their wake, generally made up of rakehell aristocrats and younger sons, was none other than Francis Cruttenden. Surprise was heaping on surprise, he thought.

Sets were being formed for the dancing, most of the young gentlemen wanting to be in Coralie's, John noticed, though the caller insisted that ladies from the benches were chosen to partner them. Eventually, there being such an unwieldly number of dancers, the musicians launched into 'The Dumps', a longways set for an odd number of couples. Although mightily popular, this particular dance relied on good timing and there was a great deal of champagne-induced giggling as several couples got out of sequence. Sensing the mood of the company, the caller chose vigorous and jolly capers, and John and Coralie whirled through 'Cold and Raw', 'Green Stockings', 'Half Hannikin' and 'Joans Plackett', ending up with 'Maid in the Moon'. By this time they had expended enough energy and made their way, somewhat hot and short of breath, to the refreshment room for some water ices.

Coralie turned to the Apothecary. 'It's Sunday tomorrow. Can we spend the day together?'

He couldn't meet her gaze. 'No, I'm afraid I have to go to Chelsea to continue my investigations.'

Even though he was not looking directly at her, John was aware of a green glint in the actress's eyes. 'I see.'

He was unable to say, 'See what?' as he normally would have done, riven with guilt as he felt.

'But you are coming back for the night?'

'I'll come for a while.'

She took his face between her hands, forcing him to look at her. 'John, what's wrong?'

He started to protest, was even about to lie, when he was saved by the sound of running feet in the corridor outside the supper room.

A head appeared in the doorway. 'Is there a physician present? There's been an accident outside.'

'I'm an apothecary,' answered John.

'Then come quick. There's a man down and bleeding.'

John was acutely aware of Coralie hastening behind him in her high heels and felt, even in these extraordinary circumstances, a pang of regret that their great love affair appeared to have run its course.

'Where is he?' he asked, as they sprinted outside.

'In the road, Sir.'

'What happened exactly?'

'He was one of the departing guests, just waiting for his coach to come round. All of a sudden, a brute steps out of the shadows and sets about him with a cudgel. I reckon he would have killed him if me and some of the other servants hadn't gone running.'

'Good God! What happened then?'

'The villain took off pretty sharpish.'

'Where did he go? Did you see?'

The footman shook his head. 'Not really, Sir.'

'What's that supposed to mean?' Some instinct, even running full pelt as he was, prompted John to draw a coin from an inside pocket and press it into the fellow's hand.

The footman looked at the guinea and drew breath. 'That's just the funny part, Sir. He stepped into a carriage with a coat of arms on the door.'

Frankly astonished, John could ask no further questions. They had arrived in the street where a small huddle of people stood, gathered round something lying on the cobbles.

'Stand aside,' called the footman importantly. 'Here's the man of medicine.'

John was just about to kneel down beside the victim when he suddenly remembered that he was wearing his very best coat. Carefully removing it, together with his waistcoat, and handing them to the footman, he sent up a silent prayer that his silver breeches would stand the strain, then knelt and turned the victim over.

Francis Cruttenden's face, eyes closed, blood pouring from his head, a wig dyed crimson hanging over one ear, lay a few inches away from his.

The Apothecary heard Coralie's voice. 'What can I do to help?'

'Find the redhead. She may have run away in a panic and be in danger herself.'

The silly high heels skimmed off over the cobbles and, pushing the crowd of onlookers back, John was left alone with his patient. An extremely gentle examination of Cruttenden's skull covered the Apothecary's hands in blood but also revealed that there was no fracture. However, the bleeding from the deep wounds was profuse.

John called over his shoulder, 'Get me some bandages quickly. Rags will do as long as they're clean.'

Someone scurried away into the house, and as a stopgap John, thinking to himself that he wouldn't have minded this sacrifice for a friend but for someone he positively disliked it was too much to ask, tore a sleeve out of his beautiful shirt, ripped it into shreds, then bound the Liveryman's head as tightly as he could. Cruttenden groaned and his eyelids flickered.

A handful of bandages appeared, together with a bowl of warm water and a washing cloth, something John hadn't asked for but was extremely glad to see. Cleansing the wounds as best he could, wishing he had some green balsam made from adder's tongue to rub into them, the Apothecary did as good a job as he was able on the wounded man's head.

The Liveryman moved slightly, calling out at the pain, and finally opened his eyes, staring directly at John. 'What are you doing here? What has happened?'

John did not mean to be crisp – had he not learned long ago that recovering patients sometimes act most untypically? – yet there was something about the way Francis Cruttenden spoke that irritated the Apothecary beyond measure, particularly as he had ruined his best shirt for him.

'You were attacked, Sir, by some brute loitering in the shadows. I can only presume that he meant to rob you. As to why I was called to attend you, it seems that I was the only medical man on the premises other than yourself.'

'Did I not see Dr Ridgeway in the gaming room?'

'If you did, then he is still there.'

The Liveryman grunted, attempted to sit upright, then felt the pain in his head and remained very still, his face suddenly ashen. 'What are the extent of my injuries?'

'Your head is badly gashed in several places but there is no apparent fracture. However, I think it might be as well if you consulted your physician tomorrow. Until then, can you stand or do you need to be carried into your coach?'

'I can manage,' the Liveryman answered. But he couldn't. He was all splayed legs and sliding feet. Taller and heavier than John, he nearly sent the Apothecary flying as he tried to stand up.

'Is Master Cruttenden's carriage here?' John asked a gawping hostler.

'Yes, Sir.'

'Then help me get him into it.'

Many hands turned to at this request, some even taking quite a delight in heaving the snarling Liveryman into his conveyance.

'Wait,' said Coralie, panting into view. 'I have the redhead near by. She has screamed herself into a pure hysteric and Dr Ridgeway has been called from dice to control her. He is well pleased at that, I can assure you.'

'What a night,' said John, his naked arm, devoid of shirt sleeve, suddenly feeling the cold. 'I think I'll go within to have a brandy.'

'I'll come with you,' said Coralie.

They strode in side by side, disregarding the astonished looks at the sight they presented, undressed, bloodstained and, in Coralie's case, somewhat the worse for having run up the street in unsuitable shoes.

'My dears,' said the Duchess of Northumberland, hurrying over to them. 'I hear that you are the heroes of the hour. Apparently some cutpurse attacked one of my guests and you saved his life. Mr Rawlings, how can I ever thank you enough?'

'By handing me a large glassful,' he answered, giving her a smile which, as always, managed to curve up at one side.

The Duchess actually fluttered her lashes. 'But of course. Come and sit down, my dear Sir. Tell me about your shop.'

'I think he's a little short of conversation at the moment,' Coralie put in hastily. 'Perhaps, Madam, you would care to call. My friend has some wondrous beautifying products.'

'How very interesting.' And their hostess allowed herself to be diverted at the thought of spending money on such things.

Dr Ridgeway, a society physician of some renown, strode into the room where they were sitting. 'That hellcat creature,' he pronounced furiously. 'What a beastly girl she is. It was all I could do to calm her. Why, I've never known a female scream so much without rupturing her lungs. In the end I sent my coachman home for my bag. It took two of your lusty boys, Duchess, to hold her down while I poured white poppy syrup down her throat. A fair dose I gave her, too.'

'Did it put her out, Sir?' John asked.

'Yes. She completely lost consciousness, thank God.'

The Duchess looked wildly alarmed. 'Where is she now? Not in one of my bedrooms, I trust.'

'No, I sent her home to her papa. Fortunately young

Westminster was going into the City. Said he'd take care of her.'

'But how did you know where she lived?' asked John, a slight sense of unease nagging at him.

'Her suitor, old Cruttenden, told me over cards. Said he'd taken a fancy to a poor man's daughter, beautiful as sunset but without a penny to her name.'

John and Coralie exchanged a glance but said nothing.

'I must agree with him there. She's a damned fine-looking piece of womanhood, but by God I couldn't put up with all that noise,' the doctor continued. 'Anyway, she's gone. Nobody'll hear a sound out of her for hours.'

The Apothecary downed his brandy and stood up, then turned to Coralie. 'Are you ready to leave?'

'Yes.'

'Then I'll go and find the footman who has my clothes. There's something I need to ask him.'

Outside it was bitterly cold, a truly raw November night, and the Apothecary shivered in the doorway.

'Here you are, Sir,' said a voice, and the servant who had raised the alarm held out his coat, cloak and hat almost as if he had been waiting for him.

Gratefully John put on the cloak, holding his best coat and waistcoat at a distance from his bloodstained self.

'You say that the man who attacked Master Cruttenden jumped into a coach bearing a coat of arms,' he said, producing another guinea.

'Yes, Sir.'

'Did you by any chance recognise the crest?'

'As a matter of fact I did, Sir.'

John rolled the coin between thumb and forefinger. 'Whose was it?'

'The Marquis of Kensington's, Sir. I'd swear to that.'

'Was he at the party tonight?'

'Oh yes, Sir. Spent all the evening in the gaming room like he always does.'

'So he must have seen Master Cruttenden leave.'

'I suppose he must, Sir.'

'How very interesting,' said John, 'thank you very much indeed.'

Chapter Sixteen

———⟡———

It was too late for conversation and both Coralie and John were far too exhausted after the evening's alarms. Instead, a hackney coach drove them to Cecil Street where they disembarked and went straight to bed, sleeping side by side without touching. And in the morning when in the normal course of events he would have made love to her, the Apothecary, being the first to wake, got up, stripped, washed all Francis Cruttenden's blood off himself, then dressed in some old clothes he kept at Coralie's house.

She woke and saw him and patted the bed beside her. 'Come and sit here. Tell me what is worrying you. Oh John, I hate to see you this unhappy.'

At that moment she was so gentle, so sweet, that he literally did not know how to conduct himself or what course to take. He felt as if he were being split in two, unable to escape Coralie's spell, yet fatally drawn to Emilia Alleyn with whom he had exchanged such passionate kisses. Somebody started to speak and John realised that it was himself.

'Elope with me now, this morning, before it is too late. We can take a coach to St Mary's in Marybone. The parson there does not ask too many questions, so I'm told.' He uttered the words as if he had no control over them.

Coralie opened her mouth to answer but John rushed on.

'Don't argue with me. Darling, if you love me, please do what I say.'

The green eyes looked at him, a most perceptive expression in their depths. 'Another attachment has brought this on, I imagine.'

John wrung his hands and turned his head away. 'Yes, it's true enough. I have met someone.'

'Then why—?'

The Apothecary was sufficiently foolish to tell the truth. 'Because I just don't know what to do. I feel our relationship has run its course but yet I am still in your thrall.'

Coralie spoke, and her voice chilled him to the bone. 'Don't let me stand in your way, my dear. If you believe our association is at an end, then I beg you to go. Now. Thank you for everything you have done in the past. Good morning to you.' And with those words she turned her back on him.

What an ingnominious end to such a great love, John thought, as he slowly plodded down the stairs, saying farewell to the very fabric of the house, to every nook, cranny, picture and ornament. So many years of friendship, of feeling, had been wiped out at a single stroke, and irrevocably at that. The turn of Coralie's defiant chin, the look in her lustrous eyes, said more than words ever could. She was cut to the quick by his behaviour and wanted no more of him. Miserable as sin, the Apothecary felt tears start to run down his cheeks as he made his way up the street, evening clothes over his arm, in order to hail a hackney coach and within its dark interior hide his abject misery from the world.

As soon as he got through the front door of number two, Nassau Street, John knew what he must do. He was too upset to see Emilia, would have felt that he was betraying both her and Coralie if he had run from one to the other like a snivelling schoolboy. Instead, he longed to see Samuel Swann and hear his jolly laugh, tell him all that had transpired, not just about the ending of his relationship with Coralie but also the assault on Francis Cruttenden. Suddenly full of purpose, the Apothecary sent for hot water, washed again and had a close shave, then dressed himself in Sunday clothes and set off by yet another hackney for Puddle Dock Hill.

He discovered Samuel attired for churchgoing, looking very much the part of a respectable citizen of London. Clad in dun brown, the Goldsmith appeared slightly portly, a fact which though it made John smile also made him realise that none of them was getting any younger.

'I'm off to St Andrew's. Are you coming? It would do you good to pray, you heathen.'

'I go to church most Sundays.'

'Not if you're in bed with Coralie, you don't.'

John winced, the subject too painful even to contemplate. 'All right, I'll join you.'

The curiously named St Andrew by the Wardrobe stood a mere stone's throw from Samuel's shop, and the two friends walked briskly down the hill towards the river, fighting off the cold by the speed of their descent. Hurrying inside, John spared a thought to the fact that the large and imposing church had acquired its unusual name from the circumstance of the royal wardrobe being situated in the neighbourhood, its location there dating from as early as 1361.

Despite the bitter weather all the pews were packed, particularly with pretty young girls, all under the watchful eye of their parents.

'Regular churchgoing is truly good for the soul,' John murmured innocently, but Samuel stoically ignored him.

The service started and the Apothecary sang lustily with the rest, wishing that Coralie's devastated expression would not keep returning to haunt him. And then, quite suddenly, everything else was sent from his mind by the sight of Garnett Smith, clad all in black, stone cold sober, sitting in a crowded pew but somehow remaining alone.

'One of the suspects,' he muttered to Samuel under cover of the hymn book.

'Where?'

'Three pews in front. It's Garnett Smith. Of course! He lives just round the corner from you. He probably comes here every Sunday.'

'Yes, I've seen him before. He usually wanders off into the graveyard at the end of the service.'

'That's where the son must be buried.'

'Should we go and talk to him?'

'It's a heavensent opportunity,' John answered, and hoped he wasn't being blasphemous.

The service continued with a sermon, during which the Apothecary indulged his favourite hobby of observing people, his eye continually drawn to a slight figure sitting at the back of the church, its face concealed from the world by a heavily veiled hat. The fact that it reminded him of Emilia had to be a coincidence, yet even the young woman's movements and mannerisms were almost identical to hers. Intrigued, John kept staring, but while he was looking away to find a different hymn she must have slipped out, for when he looked again she was no longer there.

'Do we talk to Mr Smith in the porch?' Samuel asked out of the side of his mouth.

'Yes, let's get there first, then there's no way he can escape us.'

They duly got to their feet as soon as the service was at an end and hurried out to be greeted by the parson. Then they loitered, John looking all around for the mysterious girl but seeing no sign of her. After a few minutes, Garnett appeared, alone but chatting politely enough to those around him. He shook the vicar warmly by the hand then made to go off in the direction of the churchyard.

John stepped forward. 'Good morning, Sir. Do you remember me?'

Garnett stared at him blankly, then recognition gleamed in his eye. 'You're the young fool who came round enquiring after my welfare, aren't you?'

'Yes Sir.'

'And was it not you who tried to convince me that Alleyn did not kill my son through negligence?'

'I pointed out that to identify the wen in his neck as a cancer would not have been easy.'

'Yes, I believe you did.'

He stared at John, minutely examining him, almost as if he were looking at him properly for the first time. Which, the Apothecary thought, he probably was, Garnett's eyes being so befuddled by drink on the first occasion.

'Well, you're not a bad young fellow, after all. Would you care to step round to my house for a glass of sherry?'

'I am here with a friend, Sir.' John indicated Samuel, who was being extremely chatty to one particular group of saucy young females, bowing and making much of raising his hat.

Garnett actually smiled. 'Then bring him as well. But first I must go and pay my respects to my son. I do that every Sunday.'

'May I join you?'

'Certainly.'

They went down the path side by side, walking towards the back wall of the church where there was the greatest preponderance of gravestones. Then Garnett Smith suddenly stopped and put an arm out to check John's progress. 'There's somebody already there. Look. A woman's kneeling beside the grave.'

And indeed there was. The slight figure that John had noticed at the rear had obviously gone out before the service ended to place flowers at the headstone of poor Andrew Smith. Everything became crystal clear as the Apothecary saw that it was indeed Emilia, that she had come to pay tribute to her youthful lover.

'Damme,' said Garnett angrily. 'Who the devil is it?'

'It's Emilia Alleyn,' John answered quietly. 'Please remember, Sir, that she has recently been bereaved.'

'I know, I know,' the older man replied testily, but for all his gruff manner he hurried forward as if he were pleased to see the girl.

She glanced up, hearing someone approach, and the Apothecary saw her look of pure astonishment at finding them there. 'Mr Smith, John,' she said, very flustered.

Garnett made the sort of bow that indicates politeness and nothing more. 'Miss Alleyn,' he said stiffly. Yet still John could have sworn that there was a certain excitement about him, that the sight of the girl brought back memories of his son and made him feel happier.

Emilia got to her feet and curtsied respectfully. 'Mr Smith, I do hope you don't mind my coming here. My mother is staying in London at present and I took the opportunity to visit Andrew's grave.' She turned to John in bewilderment. 'I did not realise that you and Mr Smith were aquainted.'

'Well, we are,' he answered enigmatically.

She looked blank for a moment or two, then her expression changed and she said, 'Oh, I see.'

'Mr Rawlings called on me the other night,' Garnett offered by way of explanation. 'Strangely enough I found his conversation very helpful.'

Still looking at John, Emilia asked, 'In what regard, Sir?'

'He illustrated quite clearly some of the difficulties that apothecaries experience.'

Miss Alleyn tilted her chin upwards and stared Garnett Smith directly in the eye. 'Do you still blame my father for Andrew's death?'

'In some ways I do. If a correct diagnosis had been made earlier . . .'

'As I assured you before, Sir, even that couldn't have saved him,' John put in. 'Once a cancer has a hold, particularly in a younger person, no one can loosen its grip.'

'Please don't continue your enmity,' Emilia added sadly. 'My father is dead, murdered by some madman. If he made mistakes, then he has answered for them grievously.'

'Poor Josiah,' said Garnett, and turned away from them, going to stand beside the grave, his back averted.

'Why are you here?' whispered Emilia, putting her hand lightly on the Apothecary's arm.

'I am continuing my investigations. You see before you a man determined.'

'To do what?'

'To find out who poisoned the apothecaries.'

She lowered her voice even more. 'Was it Mr Smith?'

'I can't be absolutely sure but I don't think so.'

'Then who?'

John decided to be honest. 'I truly don't know.'

'Will my father's murderer ever be discovered?'

'I must confess that at this moment it doesn't seem very likely.'

Very faintly, while he had been speaking, John had been aware of distant voices, one of which appeared to be an hysterical female. Now came the sound of running feet, accompanied by puffing and blowing, and a few seconds later Samuel came into view, sprinting down the church path.

'John, come quickly,' he gasped.

'What's the matter?'

'A woman's collapsed at the church gate. I think it might be Clariana Gill, but she looks in such a terrible state I can't be certain.'

'What on earth would she be doing here?'

'You tell me. But you'd better hurry. Whoever she is, she's lost consciousness.'

It was indeed Clariana, John saw, as he ran up to the group huddled round a figure lying supine upon the ground. Closely reminded of the previous evening when her elderly lover lay in a very similar posture, the Apothecary leant over the prostrate figure.

'Who are you, Sir?' asked the vicar.

'An apothecary, Father. Would you like me to tend her?'

'By all means if you are trained. The poor woman ambled

in here on foot, then collapsed. She muttered something about her father before she fainted.'

Remembering only too vividly the opium that Clariana had been given the night before, John pulled up one eyelid. Sure enough the pupil of the eye had contracted to a mere pinprick and there was saliva flecking the corners of the girl's lips.

'It's an overdose,' the Apothecary said tersely. 'That old fool Ridgeway must have lashed it down her by the gallon. I must treat her with emetics and stimulants.' He looked up at Samuel. 'Can we carry her to your place?'

'I live near by,' said Garnett Smith, striding up the church path, Emilia one pace behind.

'Even though it's probably far too late, I shall have to make her sick,' John said by way of warning.

'I helped nurse a dying son,' Garnett answered simply.

'Then we'd better go quickly.'

'Can I assist?' Emilia asked.

Not only did he want her there desperately, just for the comfort of her presence, but the fact that an Alleyn would be setting foot over Garnett's threshold might go a long way towards healing old wounds, John thought.

He looked at Mr Smith. 'If it is in order with you, Sir, I would like Miss Alleyn to be present.'

Garnett hesitated momentarily, past hatreds crowding to plague him, then he said, 'Come along, my girl. I'm sure a woman's touch is always beneficial at a sickbed.'

Samuel may have been gaining a little weight but he was still enormously strong. Picking Clariana up as if she weighed no more than a feather, he carried the unconscious girl away from the curious gaze of the congregation and down the hill to the river and the home of Garnett Smith. There she was put to lie in a bedroom that by its very smell revealed it was never used and John, having no bag with him, was put to the task of finding ordinary household substances that would suit his purpose.

A strong mixture of salt and water he prepared for an emetic and gave this to Emilia to start spooning down Clariana's throat. For the stimulant however, the Apothecary was in a total dilemma.

'Do you have any thistles in your garden?' he called in desperation to Garnett, who was hovering in the kitchen doorway, watching John work with a considerable amount of interest for one who professed to hate apothecaries. 'I should hope not, Sir. I employ a gardener.'

'None the less, I'm going to look. This girl has been given too much white poppy syrup. It is possible she could die. From a thistle, I can make a concoction that is good for spasm or convulsions.'

They stepped into the garden, scouring the beds and borders.

'We're in luck,' said Garnett, and pointed to where a Scotch thistle had had the temerity to avoid discovery and was growing beside a hedge. John wound his handkerchief round his hand and produced his herb knife, something he always carried unless he was going out for the evening. Grabbing the thistle hard, he pulled so strongly that he almost fell over when the weed came up out of the ground. Cutting off the all-important roots and leaves, John hastened into the house.

Using the cook's pestle and mortar, he ground them into a pulp from which a greenish juice appeared. This the Apothecary added to watered down wine, poured the mixture into a beaker, then carried it to the room in which Clariana lay, dead to the world.

'Has she been sick at all?' he asked Emilia.

'Not yet. John, I'm finding it so difficult to get this down her.'

'Give it to me.'

He took the salt water from her somewhat shaky hands and opening the unconscious girl's mouth, poured it in as best he could, even though she coughed and choked as he did so.

John smiled at the expression on Emilia's face. 'Can you bear to stay? She'll start vomiting shortly. It won't be pleasant.'

'If you can put up with it, so can I.'

'Mine is not always a charming life,' the Apothecary said wryly, holding the bowl.

'Whose is?' answered Emilia sensibly, and mopped Clariana's brow with a cool cloth.

Much as John had expected, his patient went into a spasm as soon as the contents of her stomach had gone. And it was then that he administered the stimulant made from the thistle.

'Will she revive?' Emilia asked.

'I don't know. The opium will have entered her system long ago. The emetic was probably no use at all. All we can do now is wait and see.'

An hour later they had their answer. An examination of Clariana's eyes showed that her pupils were returning to normal, and she fell into a peaceful sleep.

'We'll leave her now. I'll come back in a while and see how she is, John whispered.

With a discreet cloth draped over the bowl which he carried gingerly, the Apothecary followed Emilia downstairs, loving the back of her shapely neck where the golden hair was swept up in curls.

'You're beautiful,' he said.

Emilia looked back over her shoulder and wrinkled her nose at him. 'Careful with that,' she answered, and laughed.

They found Garnett and Samuel in the salon, making short work of a decanter of sherry. But this time there were no slurred words or maudlin sentiments coming from the host, instead Mr Smith radiated enjoyment, and looked round his younger guests with a genial expression.

'I've been too long alone,' he announced to everyone in general. 'I should have invited people here before this.'

Samuel looked wise. 'Mourning ain't easy, Sir, but I do believe that the prolonged grief of it is only caused by guilt.'

'What do you mean, my boy?'

'Well, if you did your best for the dead person while they lived, I don't think sorrow drags on so long as it does for those who have a conscience regarding them.'

'I have no guilt about Andrew. I attempted my utmost. It was others—'

The conversation was taking a dangerous turn and John stepped in. 'I am sure that everyone tried their hardest, according to their abilities. No one in their right mind could let a loved one, friend or family, die.'

Why did those words ring so hollowly in his head? What was it that he should have realised by now? What lay just beyond his grasp that he should have seen?

'What are you staring at?' asked Samuel.

John snapped back to attention. 'Nothing. I was just trying to think of something.'

'What?'

'That's just it, I don't know.'

The Goldsmith laughed. 'You'll have to bear with him. He's always like this when he's trying to solve a mystery.'

'Well I think,' said Garnett, as if he were making a public pronouncement, 'that Mr Rawlings is a very remarkable young man. He called here pretending to be something else entirely and had me completely fooled. It's not until you informed me of the fact just now, Mr Swann, that I realised he worked for the Public Office.'

'I'm sorry about that,' John answered, 'but one does not always get the best results by offering that particular piece of information.'

'Quite understandably.'

'I'm worried about the patient,' said Emilia. 'I think perhaps I should sit with her. I cannot imagine anything worse than waking up in a strange bed in a strange room and not knowing how one got there.'

'You're quite right,' said John. 'I'll go with you.'

They kept a silent vigil hand in hand, until finally Clariana's lids fluttered and her eyes opened.

The Apothecary spoke at once, sitting on the bed beside her so that the sick girl could see him clearly. 'Don't be frightened, Miss Gill. You have been rather ill. I'm afraid that the physick the doctor gave you to calm your nerves at the Assembly last evening, did not agree with you. But that has all gone now and you are well on the way to recovery.'

She tried to raise her head but fell back against the pillows. 'Where am I?'

'You're in a house near to the church of St-Andrew-by-the-Wardrobe. Do you remember getting that far?'

Clariana looked terrified. 'Yes, no. It was like being in a dream.' She sat up and clutched John's coat. 'Oh Mr Rawlings, tell me it was all a nightmare. A horrible, horrible nightmare.'

'What was?'

'Going home and seeing my father like that.'

'Like what?'

'Hanging from that hook.'

Emilia gave a muffled shriek.

'Tell us what you saw,' John said soothingly.

Clariana went white as a ship's sail. 'I can't remember everything. That young man, the one with the coach, ordered his postillions to carry me into my house. I think the medicine was working on me by that time for I could hardly walk. Then he left me alone. Said he had to get home and I would be better by myself. I got no further than the shop before I fainted. I woke some time later and managed to light a candle and when, when . . .'

'Yes?'

'When I looked up I glimpsed a pair of shoes above my head, swinging very slightly in the draft from the shop door.'

'You're sure about this?'

'No, because I could have been dreaming.'

'Then tell me what you think you saw,' John demanded, barely able to control himself.

Clariana gave him a truly ghastly look. 'I thought I saw my father hanging from one of the hooks where the herbs are put to dry. He had a rope around his neck and, Mr Rawlings, he was quite, quite dead.'

Chapter Seventeen

The deep shadows of Pudding Lane were even darker in the twilight of that late November day when John Rawlings and Samuel Swann nervously came to a halt before the closed door of the apothecary's shop. Black shapes lurked at every corner and John, spinning round rapidly, swore that something had breathed upon the nape of his neck.

'What was it?' asked Samuel, perspiring lightly despite the clammy chill of the fog that had started to seep up from the river.

'I don't know,' John answered. And where normally he would have made a joke of his friend's patent fright, today he remained grimly silent.

They had journied into the City together in a coach provided for them by Garnett Smith, who had remained behind with the terrified Clariana and an equally panicky Emilia, only keeping control of her anxiety for fear of upsetting Miss Gill even further. 'Go armed,' she had whispered to John as he left the house in Thames Street.

'I've no weapon on me. I've been in church, remember.'

'Then borrow one from Mr Smith.'

This plan had proved farcical, however, as Garnett, who clearly had very strange ideas about self protection, could produce little more than an antique fowling piece and a cudgel. In the end, the Apothecary had settled for the bat while Samuel, unnerved by Clariana's terrible story, had dashed home at speed to fetch a pistol. Then they had set forth to investigate what they hoped was merely a drug-induced hallucination.

There was no wind at all, the fog ensuring that the evening was calm and still, yet it seemed to the Apothecary that the door of Tobias's shop rattled as they stood looking at it, wondering quite what move they ought to make next.

'There's somebody in there,' whispered Samuel hoarsely.

John shook his head. 'More likely a draft blowing through.'

'Do you think by any chance it's unlocked?'

'It has to be if Clariana rushed out this way. She was hardly in a fit state to secure it.'

'Yet she managed to pick up a hackney. You don't think there's anything odd about her story, do you?'

'No. She was definitely given white poppy juice last night and she definitely showed all the signs of an overdose. What is far more odd is the attack on Francis Cruttenden.'

'You mean that his assailant disappeared into a coach bearing Kensington's coat of arms?'

'Exactly. Does our esteemed Liveryman have enemies in high places? And if so, why?'

Samuel shook his head, bewildered, and John, drawing breath, continued, 'I suppose we'd better go in. Let it be hoped that everything is as it should be and we find Mr Gill alive and well in his apartment.'

'But it's pitch dark up there,' the Goldsmith answered gloomily, and having pealed the bell to no avail, put his shoulder to the door and stumbled inside when it swung open without difficulty.

Prepared as best he could be, John struck a tinder and taking a candle from his pocket, lit it. The flickering flame illuminated little, casting even darker shadows than those in the street outside.

'I don't care for this,' Samuel confided.

'Neither do I.'

'Where did she say she saw the body?'

'Hanging on a hook normally used for herbs, which means the compounding room.'

'Oh God!' said the Goldsmith, and swallowed noisily.

With the pit of his stomach contracting, John moved silently through the shop, wondering, even while he did so, why he was walking so quietly. For if Tobias was at home, better to call out cheerily and not startle the man.

'Hallooh,' he tried, the sound dying on his lips as he made it.

'Shush,' said Samuel from somewhere in the gloom.

'But if she dreamed it all, then Mr Gill is upstairs somewhere and needs to know of our arrival.'

'Then why is the place in darkness?'

The horrible truth of this could not be denied and John braced himself as he passed through the open door leading into the compounding room and went into the dimness beyond. He stood for a moment, his candle fluttering violently, trying to get his bearings. Behind him Samuel's breathing became magnified a hundred-fold, the only sound in the total stillness. And then some unseen object brushed against John's face.

To his shame he yelped like a dog and jumped backwards, clutching Samuel's arm as he did so.

'What is it? What happened?'

'Something touched my cheek.'

'Shine the light, shine the light,' Samuel ordered, and his voice was a rasp.

With a shaking hand, the Apothecary raised the candle to arm's length, and they both stared upwards. Sad old feet in worn out shoes were up there, a long apothecary's gown flapping very slightly around two thin ankles. Tobias Gill had compounded his last physick. Somebody had done for him on the end of a rope and now he hung where once there had been a bunch of fragrant herbs.

'Christ's mercy,' said John.

'Amen to that.'

'We must cut him down.'

'But surely there's no chance?'

The Apothecary shook his head. 'None whatsoever. He's been up there for hours. None the less, we must do the right thing.'

They hurried round the place, the confirmation of Clariana's story a relief in a sense, releasing the friends from their fear and tension and giving them a purpose, albeit a most grisly and horrid one. More candles were found and placed strategically round the room until at last there was enough light to see clearly what they were doing. Then both John and Samuel pulled chairs beneath Tobias's slight and sorrowful corpse and while the Apothecary hacked through the rope with a stout knife, discovered amongst the compounding equipment, Samuel caught the dead man. He swayed for a moment on the chair, then successfully clambered down with his burden and laid poor Mr Gill on the table.

'We've done all we can here,' said John. 'Now we must lock up and head straight for Bow Street.'

'Where are the keys?'

'There,' and the Apothecary indicated a large bunch hanging on a nail on the compounding room wall.

'But who could have done this, John?'

'He may have killed himself, of course.'

'That, I don't think,' said Samuel, simultaneously earnest and excited.

'Why?'

'Because to do so he would have had to climb on a chair and there was none beneath his feet, either standing or kicked over. We had to drag the two chairs we used into position.'

The Apothecary stared at his friend in true amazement. 'That was brilliantly observed. Please make the same point to Mr Fielding.'

'Do you think it important?'

'I think it very important indeed.'

At this hour, well past the time to dine, it was customary to find people out and about, visiting friends upon the town, attending the play, the ridotto, the pleasure gardens, or simply sampling the million and one pleasures that the lawless capital offered. However, quieter-living folk could be discovered safely tucked into their abode, making music, playing cards or reading a book. And in the case of John Fielding, Principal Magistrate, it was frequently the latter, for much as he was a cultivated man, loving the theatre, music, and all the delights allied therewith, the very fact of his blindness precluded him from many of the events that he would so dearly have liked to attend. Fortunately in the choice of his wife, Elizabeth, he had found the right companion. She, too, quite preferred the simple life, sitting and reading to her brilliant husband, keeping him up with the day's events through the newspapers, or enjoying the sheer pleasure of sharing a book together.

The only discordant note in this domestically blissful world was struck by the couple's niece, Mary Ann Whittingham, who was currently passing through a particularly tiresome phase that all adolescent girls have in common.

The young woman, for thus the little beauty had become, stood up as John and Samuel entered the Fieldings' salon, shown upstairs by a servant.

'Why Mr Rawlings – and Mr Swann is it not? – how delightful to see you again.'

The Apothecary shot her an acerbic look. 'Mary Ann, I'm glad to find you well.'

'Oh, never better, Sir.'

She fluttered lashes which concealed eyes of a piercing gentian shade and John was horrified to see Samuel make the kind of bow he would to an adult female.

DERYN LAKE

The Blind Beak spoke from his chair by the fire. 'You've come on business, I take it, Mr Rawlings?'

'Business indeed, Sir. May we speak privately?'

'By all means. Let us go into my study.'

Mr Fielding got to his feet, tall, large framed and agile, and led the way from the room, using a switch which he carried before him to help him avoid any obstacles in his path.

John was fascinated to find himself in a part of the house he had never seen before. Downstairs, leading off the Public Office, the Magistrate had a study full of legal papers and law books, a domain that the Apothecary always associated with Joe Jago, who masterminded the reading and writing of all official documents and letters for his sightless master. But climbing up one flight from the salon, John and Samuel found themselves in a snug little room, warmed by a fire of coal and wood, containing only a desk and two chairs for furniture. Here, books written by the Magistrate's half brother, Henry Fielding, crammed the shelves, along with works by Defoe, Swift and Richardson. This was clearly the place to which the Fieldings escaped when they wanted to read privately.

The Magistrate rang a bell and ordered the responding servant to fetch another chair, then, when all three of them were seated, he turned his head in the direction of John. 'So what has been happening, my friend?'

In as concise a manner as he could, the Apothecary spoke of everything that had taken place since their last meeting in the court at Bow Street. When he had finished, the Blind Beak sat in silence for a moment, then turned the black bandage that hid his eyes in John's direction. 'There's something else, isn't there?'

It was uncanny, for the Apothecary had omitted all mention of the attack on Francis Cruttenden, feeling it hardly relevant to the case they were discussing.

'Yes, there is, Sir. There's a Liveryman called Francis Cruttenden . . .'

'So I believe. Joe has spoken to me about him. You asked

him to make some enquiries into the man's background, I believe.'

'Yes I did.'

'May I ask why that was?'

'No reason really.'

The Magistrate's eyebrows rose and a small smile appeared at the corner of his mouth.

Without knowing quite why, John felt obliged to explain. 'Well, that isn't quite true. I met the man when I called on Master Alleyn to check his progress. Alas, he had died that morning, and even the Liveryman was unable to save him. Be that as it may, I took an immediate dislike to Cruttenden. And now I dislike him more than ever.'

'Oh?'

Shooting Samuel a look that defied him to elaborate, John said, 'He's obsessed by young women. I believe him to be a seducer on a grand scale.'

'And you don't approve?'

'Call me prudish if you wish, Sir, but no, I don't.'

Mr Fielding cleared his throat. 'Neither do I, come to that. However, Joe's enquiries revealed that his current young creature is none other than Clariana Gill, daughter of the murdered man, but then you would know that fact.'

'I certainly do. Yet there is something even more interesting.' And John explained in detail exactly what had taken place at the Assembly on the previous evening.

The Magistrate sat silently for a moment or two, then said, 'You are telling me that he was attacked by someone in the pay of the Marquis of Kensington?'

'That I don't know. The witness simply said that he saw the assailant get into a coach bearing the Marquis's coat of arms.'

'Then deep enquiries must be made. I shall call on Kensington myself, and you must accompany me, Mr Rawlings.'

'It would be a pleasure, Sir.'

Samuel spoke for the first time. 'Is there any sign of the missing watchman, Griggs?'

The Blind Beak shook his head. 'None at all. He has vanished from the face of the earth, or so it would seem.'

'Into the river in my view.'

'But not yet out again.'

John changed the topic. 'How do we proceed now?'

'As soon as you have gone, Mr Rawlings, I shall despatch the two Brave Fellows to fetch the body and take it to the mortuary. Then tomorrow, when it is light, I would like you, if it is convenient . . .'

'I shall make it so.'

'. . . to search Tobias Gill's house and shop from top to bottom. Who knows what might be revealed in the way of a clue to this ghastly crime? Then, Mr Rawlings, I think you should talk to Harriet Clarke. From what you have said of her she sounds an intriguing woman, possibly with something to hide. That done, I suggest we call on the Marquis. I shall dissemble and pretend that I am looking for a property in Kensington. I shall then drop Cruttenden's name into the conversation and proceed from there.'

Samuel spoke again. 'Sir, do you think the murder of Master Alleyn and that of Tobias Gill are connected in any way?'

'Very probably, yes. I warned you, Mr Rawlings, that this killer is dangerous. Maybe both Gill and Cruttenden discovered more about Alleyn's death than we know. Perhaps that is why both were attacked, one fatally.'

'But what could the Marquis of Kensington have to do with a modest Liveryman living in Chelsea?'

'That is what we must find out, for there is a connection in all this. I feel it in my gut.'

'I wonder what the link could possibly be?'

'When we know that, we know the truth,' said Mr Fielding. He got to his feet. 'Gentlemen, we can achieve nothing further tonight. Go and break the sad news to

Clariana Gill, and while you are doing so, see if there is anything further you can discover about her relationship with her elderly beau.'

'She is clearly fascinated by him.'

'Power and money are potent aphrodisiacs.'

John shook his head. 'Just *why* is he so high and so mighty? Liveryman is a worthy position indeed, but not sufficiently exalted to sustain the style in which Francis Cruttenden lives.'

'I'll instruct Jago to enquire further.'

'I think perhaps Harriet Clarke might hold the key. She and her mother once worked for him as servants.'

'Was she seduced by him?' Mr Fielding asked out of the blue.

John stared. 'By God, Sir, I hadn't thought of that. But do you know, you might be right.'

'Then you'll have to find out, won't you?'

'Tread carefully,' warned Samuel. 'Remember what women are like.'

But his friend did not answer, already starting to put an earlier idea together with this latest thought and coming up with the most extraordinary answer.

Chapter Eighteen

In the house of death, something moved. John, on his hands and knees in the compounding room where Tobias Gill had been hanged by the neck and left to die, heard the sound distinctly and jumped with fright. Above his head, in the apartments where the dead man had lived with his daughter, someone had just walked across the floor. Quite alone, for the two Brave Fellows had departed with Tobias's body during the previous night, the Apothecary felt panic rise within him, and had to breathe deeply in order to bring himself under control.

The place had been empty when he had arrived, there was no doubt about that. Before he had begun his painstaking search of the premises, looking for anything that might throw light on Tobias's murder, John had walked through both the shop and the residence over it. All had been quiet, filled with that eerie silence associated with violent death. But now someone was moving about. Feeling for the pistol in his coat pocket, the Apothecary made his way to the bottom of the stairs.

As he put his foot on the first step it cracked like a bullet, sending waves of sound throughout the house. John froze, listening for a response. None came. Nothing stirred in the apartment above. With extreme caution he continued his journey upwards, till at last he stood in the room where only a few nights previously he had dined with a grateful Tobias and petulant Clariana. It seemed a long time ago now, so much had happened in the interim, yet something of that occasion still hung in the air, adding a touch of sadness to the uncanny atmosphere.

And then John shouted with terror as something wrapped itself around his ankles. For no reason ridiculous visions of a serpent came into his mind, but when the Apothecary looked down it was to see a large red cat stropping round him. A great believer in the theory that owners and their pets grow to look alike, John knew at once that it was Clariana's.

He stooped to stroke it and felt a lump in the fur by its ear. Bending lower, the Apothecary saw that it had been wounded in some way and had bled profusely before the flow had congealed.

'Now what happened to you?' he asked, but the cat made no reply.

Finding some water in a ewer, John cleaned the injury, while the cat stood in reasonable patience, hissing occasionally under its breath. The wound was consistent with a blow and the Apothecary wondered whether the cat had got in the murderer's way and had earned a well-aimed kick for its pains. Assured now that the recent intruder had been merely feline, John went back to the compounding room, the cat following behind.

The job of searching for clues was not a pleasant one. So far the Apothecary had painstakingly swept the entire down-stairs floor area, looking for anything, however minute, that Tobias's killer might have dropped as he crept up on Gill from behind. That the assailant had pinioned his victim tightly, then probably half strangled the frail fellow before hoisting him into the noose that would finish him off, John was reasonably certain, for the signs of struggle were negligible.

'It points to him knowing his killer,' the Apothecary said to the cat, which was gingerly washing its ear with a paw.

Much as John had thought, the shop itself had revealed

little more than an abandoned suppository, not as skilfully made as those produced by his brand new machine, several pills squashed into the floor by a careless foot, and a few dropped coins. Of the compounding room itself he had higher hopes. Taking up a small hand brush and pan which he had brought with him, John sank to his knees once more and started to sweep gently.

Behind him, the cat started to play with something, patting a mouse substitute along the floor then hooking it with its claws.

'What have you got?' John asked, and looked over his shoulder.

The cat scudded its toy towards him, and the Apothecary stretched out his hand to pick it up. A gleaming diamond button lay in his palm, twinkling in the pale sunshine coming through the window.

'How very interesting,' he said, turning it over. 'Not at all the sort of thing one would expect to find in a workplace. I think, Sir Puss, you have been of great help to me.' So saying, John stowed the button in an inner pocket before continuing his meticulous task.

Five hours later, with dusk beginning to fall, it was done. The entire house had been searched, inch by inch. Exhausted by his quest, John, having first fed the cat with some meat obtained from the butcher, headed straight for an alehouse and downed several draughts before leaving the City behind him and heading for Samuel's establishment, where he cajoled his friend into joining him for dinner at Truby's in St Paul's Churchyard.

'Well?' said Samuel, once they had ordered their fare.

'My prize exhibit,' answered John, and produced the button.

'Where was it?'

'On the compounding room floor, no less.'

The Goldsmith let out a whistle. 'Dropped by the murderer?'

'Quite possibly. It certainly isn't the sort of button Tobias would wear and no apprentice worth the name would own so fine a thing as this.'

'What about a customer?'

'Customers don't go into compounding rooms. They remain in the shop.'

Samuel looked thoughtful. 'This is almost certainly a vital clue. Does it belong to a man or a woman, do you think?'

John turned the button over in his hand. 'It could be either. Come on, you know about these things. Is the diamond real or paste?'

Rather surprisingly, his friend produced a jeweller's glass which he put to his eye. 'I'm a goldsmith not a gemster, but I'd say it was real.'

'Then it comes from a very expensive garment indeed.'

'Almost royally so. What will you do with it?'

'Keep it for the time being. I want to show it to a few people and gauge their reaction.'

Samuel rubbed his hands together. 'This is most exciting. I do believe we have reached a turning point.'

'If Mr Fielding is right and the two murders are connected, then we have.'

'Unless the button is Clariana's.'

'Even then,' said John darkly, 'there could be a path to follow.'

'What do you mean?'

'She is besotted with Cruttenden but Tobias disapproved of the match and threatened to stand in her way. Perhaps in a moment of blind fury . . .'

'She killed her own father? Oh, surely not. The very idea is unthinkable.' Samuel's hearty countenance looked aghast.

'It would not be the first time in our investigations that we would have come across such a thing.'

'Not involving a woman, though John. A female could never do anything so vile.'

To have argued would have been to have upset his friend, so the Apothecary remained silent.

'And anyway,' the Goldsmith continued, making a good point, 'if the two murders are linked, what reason could Clariana possibly have for killing Master Alleyn?'

The truth of this was inescapable and John nodded slowly. 'Yes, you're right about that.'

Samuel got into his stride. 'No, I'm afraid if Clariana owns that button then it is no longer of any importance.'

Very reluctantly, since the rest of the house had yielded little of any significance, the Apothecary was forced to agree.

Reading his mind, Samuel said, 'Did you find nothing else?'

'Only the fact that two glasses of wine had been poured and consumed and not cleared away.'

'Clariana again?'

'I don't quite see father and daughter sitting down to share a bottle before she goes out for the evening, do you?'

'No, not really. Do you think it was the murderer?'

'If it wasn't it must have been someone who called just before the killer.'

'After Clariana had left the house?'

'Almost certainly, yes.'

Samuel frowned. 'You don't think Tobias kept an appointment book, do you?'

'If he did I definitely didn't come across it, yet that in itself is odd now I come to consider it.'

'Why?'

'Because all apothecaries who visit patients have a list of engagements written down somewhere. He *must* have had a book and the fact that it is missing is very significant.'

'Perhaps the killer made an appointment to see him, then removed the evidence to hide the fact that his or her name was there?'

'Precisely,' said John, clapping his friend on the back, an action to which Samuel responded by beaming.

'We are closer after all.'

'Not if we can't find the book, we're not.'

The Goldsmith refused to be daunted. 'It will turn up, never fear.'

'Perhaps it has already been consigned to the flames.'

'Don't be such a pessimist,' answered Samuel, and prepared to attack the food which had just been set before him on the table.

It was late when they left Truby's and set off in the direction of the river. John drew his watch from his pocket. 'I think I might beg a bed off Mr Smith. He seems quite happy to have his house full at the moment.'

'He certainly likes the company of Miss Alleyn and Miss Gill. *You* might be a different matter.' Samuel was half serious. 'If he hasn't the room, come back to me.'

'Thank you, I will. I want to cross the river early tomorrow.'

'To talk to Mrs Clarke? Or to visit the wounded Cruttenden?'

'Perhaps both, who knows, but certainly to see the lady. Dr Hensey will have called on her son by now. I would like to know his verdict.'

'Will you show the button to Miss Gill?'

'As soon as she is herself again.'

However, in that the Apothecary was to be thwarted. No sooner had he rung the bell of the house in Thames Street, a house he had left in deepest silence earlier that morning after he had broken the news of her father's death to a pale and trembling Clariana, than he was caught up in yet another situation.

Late though it was, both Emilia and Garnett waited up for him in the small salon.

John's apologies for tardiness died on his lips. 'What's happened?' he said, gazing from one face to another, a part of his brain that always appreciated the female sex thinking how gorgeous Emilia looked.

'Clariana's gone,' she said, rising to greet him and kissing him swiftly on the cheek.

'Gone?' he repeated.

Garnett stood up and gave a small bow. 'She wept in her room for an hour or so after you'd left. Then the next thing we knew, she had dressed, come down the stairs, told us both that she had urgent affairs to attend to, then was out through the front door.'

'Still in her evening clothes?'

'Yes. Those were all she had with her.'

'Then she won't have gone far,' said John grimly. 'My guess is that she hired a wherry and crossed the river to her lover Cruttenden. She certainly didn't return to Pudding Lane. I stayed there several hours and there was no sign of her. Yet I shall have to find her in the morning. She is still my patient.'

'But in Cruttenden's thrall,' Emilia commented bitterly.

The Apothecary shot her a look. 'Unfortunately, yes.'

Garnett suddenly asked, 'This Cruttenden, is he the fellow who was a great friend of your father's, my dear?'

'Yes,' she answered tonelessly.

'An extraordinary man, if I recall correctly. Very magnetic but somehow malign.'

John laughed, breaking the tension in the room. 'What a perfect description. It sums him up exactly.'

Emilia, who did not lack courage, said, 'I was broken-hearted by Andrew's death, and Francis Cruttenden took advantage of that.'

'Do you mean . . ?'

'He seduced me? Yes. He did not scruple that I was his friend's daughter.'

'The ravisher needs stringing up,' Garnett exploded angrily, and even though John agreed, he could not help but smile at the phraseology.

'May I stay here tonight, Sir?' he asked, rapidly changing the subject. 'I should enjoy talking to you for a while after Emilia retires.'

'I should like that,' Garnett answered, and by the very look on his face the Apothecary knew that the drunk, despairing, lonely man he had first met was fast disappearing in the wake of all the new, young, lively company.

The two of them conversed long and late, not about the murders but about life and its odd twists and turns.

'I already regard Emilia as the daughter I never had,' said Garnett sentimentally, a little tipsy by now but not unpleasantly so.

'She has set my life on its heels,' John answered, and sighed with the memory of all the sadness that he had experienced of late.

It was nearly December and the sun had broken through the fog. Even though it was cold and windy, the sky over the river was blue as linen bags, and the winding waterway beneath reflected the light and glittered like a jewel in the early morning. Young though the day was there was plenty of traffic on London's highway. As John Rawlings crossed the Thames he glimpsed a gilded barge heading downstream towards Greenwich and a flotilla of long, shallow boats bearing meat and malt to feed the capital, coming in from the upper reaches. Dodging them, in common with all his kind, the grizzly waterman exchanged oaths and insults with his fellow oarsmen as he cut his way across the river. John, leaning back against the board behind him, let the whole rude cacophony pass clean over his head as he concentrated on one thing and one thing alone: the rapid conclusion to this most elusive of cases and the stroke of good fortune that would lead him to discover the murderer of Josiah Alleyn and Tobias Gill.

Yet at the same time other matters nagged him. On a minor scale the fact that he had not replied to a letter from Sir

Gabriel inviting him to Kensington for a day or so, on a major, the guilt he felt about Coralie. Remembering, the Apothecary believed he would never forget his last glimpse of her, the harrowed look on her lovely face, the tightly controlled tears that he knew would cascade as soon as he was out of sight.

What a brute I am, he thought, and felt angered with himself that he had given his former lover so much pain. Yet what else could he have done? She had cut him to the quick with her constant rejection of him. The survivor in John told his inner being that if Coralie had only acted differently, if she had agreed to elope with him as he had wanted, then he would have handled the situation differently. But still he found it hard to come to terms with her loss.

'Mason Stairs,' called the wherryman, and John, startled, looked up and realised that his journey was done. He had arrived at the river's south bank and must now face a difficult interview with Harriet Clarke and one even worse with Clariana Gill. With certain trepidation, the Apothecary scrambled up the slippery stairs and stood at the top, looking around.

Almost immediately before him stood the narrow track leading to Pye House and its gardens. To his right and left ran Willow Street, in one direction towards a fairly rural landscape, in the other to the noisesome skin market, not the most pleasant of places for those who had no business there. The most direct route to Bandy Leg Walk was to go down the track past Pye House, then cross Maid Lane and enter Bandy Leg. But at this stage of the proceedings John had no wish to be seen by anyone connected with Francis Cruttenden so, instead, he turned left down Willow Street, passing the skin market but not going inside, then turned down Thames Street and in this way entered Maid Lane.

Bandy Leg Walk, entirely true to its name, curved outwards then in again. Parallel with it ran Gravel Lane, which did exactly the same thing. John fancied that a bird's eye view of the two must look just like the legs of a bandy old soul whose gait would be marvellous to behold.

He was now in the area of the tenter grounds, used for stretching cloths, which were put over frames and secured by sharp, hooked nails known as tenterhooks. Though there were few houses in this part, the Apothecary spied three opposite the Bowling Green, outside one of which stood Harriet Clarke, pegging some clothes onto a line.

There was indeed a striking Junoesque beauty about her, for though not buxom in any way, Harriet was tall and strong-looking. Unaware that a visitor was approaching, John watched her as she called out, 'Matthew, come here a minute,' then saw a boy step out of the house. So this was the lad who had the falling sickness, the child who had nearly been voided before birth by an abortive substance. Were his suspicions correct? he wondered. Then the boy turned his head to look towards the Bowling Green and John knew the answer. Matthew was tall and dark like his mother, his features handsome as hers, but in the very way he stood and moved he resembled his father. There could be no doubt about it. Matthew Clarke was the son of Francis Cruttenden.

'God's sweet life,' said John, and whistled quietly to himself. Was there no woman whom the wretched man had left in peace?

A new train of thought presented itself. Had one of the Marquis's women – wife, sister, daughter – been violated by the grand seducer, leading to the attack that John had witnessed a few nights before? The letter to Sir Gabriel and the visit to Kensington suddenly became enormously important, and a stratagem presented itself. The Apothecary sighed. A visit to the Public Office was yet another thing that he must do today.

John strode forward a few paces and called out, 'Mrs Clarke, how are you this morning?'

She wheeled in surprise and touchingly protected her son by drawing him close to her side. How many years had she spent in anguish, the Apothecary wondered, and found himself praying that Dr Hensey could perform a miracle.

Harriet recovered herself. 'Mr Rawlings, good morning to you. What brings you here?'

'A visit to a patient actually, but as I was so close I could not resist the opportunity of calling.'

'I'm glad you did so. Pray come in and have some tea. I regret my tardiness in asking you to dine. I have been somewhat preoccupied since I saw you last.'

'Have we not all, indeed.'

'Still no further forward with the affair at Apothecaries' Hall?'

John looked grim faced. 'There has been another development.'

'What?'

'I will tell you of it later,' the Apothecary answered, and briefly looked at Matthew, peeping at him round his mother's skirts.

She understood at once. 'Then please come inside.'

'I'd be delighted,' John answered, and removing his hat stepped over her threshold.

It was a charming house, quite recently built, with large rooms and a sizeable garden. A fitting home for someone with a position as responsible as that of Michael Clarke.

'What a gracious dwelling,' said John, staring around in admiration.

'We are very happy here. We live quietly but contentedly.'

The Apothecary lowered his voice. 'I would like to speak to you alone, Madam.'

'Of course. When Betty has made the tea she shall take Matthew into the garden. Then we can be private.'

The boy spoke up. 'Dr Hensey said that I might have a tutor, Sir.'

'Quite rightly so,' the Apothecary answered. 'He is a wise and good man and if he thinks that, then nobody can argue.'

'I believe him to be a saint,' Harriet said fervently.

Mentally John uttered thanks that the physician's visit had proved successful.

With a great deal of clattering, a large friendly girl struggled in with a tray. 'Hope this suits, Mam,' she said to Harriet.

Mrs Clarke shot John an apologetic smile. 'We're not used to a lot of company here.'

'Aye, but we does our best,' the girl responded and banged her way out again, all big breasts and large grins.

'Run along, my sweetheart.' Harriet turned to Matthew. 'You can have some cake in the kitchen.'

'But I'd rather stay here.'

'I need to speak to Mr Rawlings on his own.'

He went, reluctantly but politely, making a bow to John as he did so. The Apothecary was left with the strong impression that the boy longed to grow up a little but was being restrained from doing so by a fiercely protective mama.

Harriet turned to John. 'Now, my dear Sir, what is it that you need to talk to me about?'

'First I must deliver some grave news. Another apothecary has been killed. Tobias Gill, who you may or may not have encountered, has been murdered.'

Harriet lost colour but, strong woman that she was, mastered herself in a moment. 'Is this death connected to that of Master Alleyn?'

'It is believed so, yes.'

'Then the killer must be found before he strikes again.'

John spoke slowly, choosing his words carefully. 'Mrs Clarke, in order to see the present clearly, we often have to rake over the past, an experience which is sometimes both unpleasant and painful.'

She looked at him questioningly but said nothing.

The Apothecary continued. 'Further, details that may seem utterly irrelevant and bearing no relation whatsoever to the matter in hand, are often the ones that throw a sudden beam of light on a matter buried in murk.'

Harriet stiffened. 'Pray go on.'

John steeled himself. 'The other night – and please

remember that this may have no bearing on the two deaths, yet it is still of interest – Master Cruttenden was attacked. I believe you once knew him well. Do you have the slightest idea why somebody would wish to harm him?'

Her jewel eyes flashed in his direction. 'No,' she said stonily.

The Apothecary's heart sank but he continued on his course. 'You told me that you were once in his employ. Did you not see anything at that time that might have led you to believe the man had enemies?'

'No I didn't.'

The Apothecary gulped silently. 'Mrs Clarke, what were your feelings towards Master Cruttenden?'

'I had none.'

The ruthless side of John Rawlings's character took over completely. 'That isn't true, is it? You told me yourself that an apothecary prescribed for you for morning sickness and that you have never been sure from that day to this whether what you swallowed was responsible for your son's condition. But that was only part of it, I believe. I think Francis Cruttenden did not prescribe for sickness at all but attempted to procure an abortion for you because the child you were carrying was his and not that of your husband.'

She flew to her feet and bore down on him like a goddess of legend. 'How dare you? How dare you say such terrible things?'

'Perhaps because they are true,' John answered, and caught her wrists in his hands as she made to strike him.

She wept at that, savagely and wildly as only a woman of her temperament could.

'Calm yourself,' he said, his voice kind. 'I mean no harm to you. What passes between these walls is privy only to us. What a burden you must have carried all these years. Did you tell Dr Hensey of it?'

'How could I? How could I without betraying what I tried to do to my beautiful son?'

'I doubt very much you harmed the foetus. The falling sickness is a birth defect indeed but not one associated with attempted abortion.'

Harriet wept, violently, yet with a certain controlled strength. 'I did not want Michael, dear good kind Michael, to be foisted with a child he had not fathered. I married him when I was pregnant, you know.'

'Did he not guess at the time?'

'No. He thought the child was his. He prevented me from aborting.'

'But he knows now surely. The resemblance to Cruttenden is marked.'

'I don't know whether he does or not. The grim truth has never been spoken of between us.'

'Whatever the case, he loves the boy. That is obvious from the way he talks about him. Torture yourself no further.'

Harriet flung herself into his arms. 'My whole life has been a torture since I met that evil bastard. If somebody attacked him then good is all I can say. Oh, my dear Mr Rawlings, he took away my innocence, my girlhood, and he almost took away my son.'

The Apothecary removed her to arm's length so that he could look her in the eye.

'But he didn't take him away, did he? And, indirectly, Francis Cruttenden gave you your greatest treasure. For the boy is a fine one, for all his condition. Now what did Dr Hensey say?'

'That somehow he would contact his old tutor. He believes that Matthew's condition could be brought totally under control.'

John frowned. 'But surely his professor was in Paris, and we are at war with France. How will he get the message through?'

Harriet dashed away her tears. 'That he did not tell me. He simply said that he would try.'

'Then God bless him. He helped me once when I thought I was beyond hope.'

'He is a man of great integrity,' Mrs Clarke said solemnly. She withdrew her arms from John's grasp and he watched her compose herself. 'Now, Sir, how further can I help you?'

'By telling me how Francis Cruttenden became so wealthy.'

She looked at him wide eyed. 'Are you serious?'

'Very.'

'What are you implying?'

'I don't know. All I do know is that the man has enemies in high places. Now why should that be?'

She shook her head. 'I cannot help you there. I know of his reputation with young women. I know all the terrible things he did to me. But as to how he acquired his wealth, I have no idea. I always imagined that it was inherited.'

'Then I suppose it must be. And yet . . .'

'Mr Rawlings,' said Harriet.

'Yes?'

'Promise me one thing.'

'Which is?'

'That you will unlock the cupboard of that unpleasant individual and watch as the skeletons come tumbling forth.'

'I will not only watch,' answered John, thinking of the youth and joy of Emilia and how low she had been brought by the seal-grey Liveryman, 'I will personally crush his skeletons to powder beneath my heel.'

Chapter Nineteen

———◇◆◇———

He was in a white hot rage, angry on behalf of every female that Cruttenden had enticed into his bed, livid that one of them should have been the delightful Emilia Alleyn. In fact John's blood was running so high that he felt more than capable of punching the Liveryman in the face and taking the consequences. Then he recalled that somebody else had already done this for him and knew that however furious he might feel it would be beyond the pale to strike a wounded man.

He was marching towards Pye House, built on the site of the old Pye Pleasure Garden, so Harriet Clarke had informed him. In the sixteenth and seventeenth centuries Southwark had been London's haunt of pleasure, conveniently placed outside the City Boundary and with few people living there to raise complaint. As well as Pye Garden there had been the Old Bear Gardens, and the cruel torturing of animals, something which John abominated, had flourished. The playhouses had also been situated on the south bank, together with the stews or brothels. Lusty men and true had been rowed across the river to take their delights as they saw fit. But since the rule of Oliver Cromwell and his Puritans many of Southwark's attractions had been closed down and most had not reopened after the Restoration.

'Trust him to have a house on a prime site,' John muttered

spitefully, and wondered for a wild and capricious moment whether he dared heave a brick through one of the windows. Tempting though the prospect was, however, he remembered that he was an apothecary, that he had a respectable place in society, and reckoned beside all those factors that it was bright broad daylight and he would be bound to be seen.

However, his temper was sufficiently fired to send him through the gate and up the path to the front door at a stamping pace. Once there he rang the bell as if he were pealing for the hordes of hell to come forth from their flaming pit, and he barked at the footman who answered the door, 'John Rawlings for Miss Clariana Gill, if you please.'

'But . . .' said the man, opening and closing his mouth like a fish.

'She's my patient and I demand to see her,' thundered John, and pushed past the servant most rudely.

The house, which he had only glimpsed from outside, was even more voluptuous within than he had imagined it to be. Fine Turkey carpets, glistening chandeliers and expensive oil paintings abounded in all the major rooms leading off the hall. While the staircase rising from it was a triumph of delicacy, curving more beautifully than any John had ever seen before.

The footman recovered himself. 'I will see if Miss Gill is able to receive you, Sir.'

'Then she is here?'

'Madam is the Master's affianced bride, Sir. There has been a tragedy in her family and she is staying with the Master whilst she recovers from the shock.'

'Then would you be kind enough to take her my card and tell her that there is something of importance I need to discuss with her.'

'Certainly,' said the footman aloofly, and placing the card on a silver tray, disappeared from view.

Not having been extended the courtesy of a chair, the Apothecary remained upright, slowly wandering the length of the vestibule examining the many and beautiful *objets* casually placed in niches or on small tables, valuable though they obviously were. The fact of Liveryman Cruttenden's enormous wealth was endorsed everywhere John looked, and yet again he wondered at it.

The footman reappeared. 'Miss Gill will spare you five minutes, and that is all. Kindly follow me.'

John was led into a spacious room where Clariana, clad in flowing black, lay on a day bed, looking as ashen as if she herself had recently died. In contrast, her red hair flamed round her face, giving the girl an almost grotesque appearance.

She opened her eyes and looked up as John came in. 'Mr Rawlings, I am far from well. The news of my poor father's death coming on top of my recent ordeal . . .'

'You should not have left Mr Smith's house without my permission,' John stated abruptly.

'You are not my gaoler, Sir.'

'No, but you were in my care. I was treating you for a severe case of opiate poisoning. You had no right to discharge yourself without my authority.'

Clariana raised her livid face and glared at him and John found himself thinking what a particularly nasty young woman she was, quite capable of murdering anyone. He then considered the fact that she and Cruttenden thoroughly deserved one another and would make a perfectly beastly couple that should in no circumstances have children.

Her voice was like ice. 'Is that all you have to say to me? If so, you may as well leave now. As you know, my future husband is a Liveryman of the Worshipful Society of Apothecaries and is more than capable of prescribing for me.'

What a bitch, thought John, and produced the diamond button from his inner pocket with a great deal of flourish. 'I found this, Madam, at the scene of your father's murder. Do you know to whom it belongs?'

Clariana held out an imperious hand. 'What do you have there? Be so good as to show it to me.'

Advancing towards the day bed, John gave a curt bow. 'It is a button, Miss Gill. A diamond button of fine quality. Not the sort of thing that your father would have worn, I am sure you will agree.' He held it out but did not pass it to her.

Clariana stared, her bleached face turning even whiter.

Sensing her discomfort, John pressed on. 'Well?'

Miss Gill swallowed. 'It's mine,' she said.

'Really?' His disbelief sounded in his voice.

'I lost it from one of my gowns.'

'It must have been a very fine gown, if I might comment. Did you lose it the night of the Duchess's Assembly?'

'Yes. It was part of my evening ensemble. May I have it back please.'

'No,' said John, returning the button to his pocket. 'You may not.'

'Why? It belongs to me. It is my property.'

'On the contrary. It is now the property of the Public Office at Bow Street. It was found at the scene of a murder and is therefore material evidence.'

Clariana sat upright. 'How dare you say such a thing? The button is mine.'

'Then I suggest you put that to Mr John Fielding. I shall pass it into his safe keeping tonight.'

Behind him John was aware of a rustle in the doorway. A swish of garments together with the faint smell of medicinal balm, told him that Francis Cruttenden was standing behind him. Indeed, he could feel the man's eyes boring into his back in the most unnerving manner. Not even bothering to force a smile, John turned and experienced a spiteful thrill of pleasure at seeing just how bruised and battered the ladies' man looked.

The Apothecary gave a minimalistic bow. 'Sir.'

Cruttenden grimaced. 'I must thank you for your help the other evening. I was in a parlous state.'

'A very strange affair,' John answered, 'made even stranger by the fact that your assailant jumped into a coach belonging to the Marquis of Kensington. Now how do you account for that?'

Just for a fleeting second, before he masked his face utterly, the Liveryman reacted, John would have sworn to it. However, the older man's recovery was instant. Cruttenden laughed.

'Who told you that? What utter nonsense. The man was a common cutpurse, a vagabond whose only motive was robbery. Marquis of Kensington? God's life, where *do* these rumours start?'

It was so convincing a performance that momentarily the Apothecary wondered. But there was no denying the shutter that had closed at the very back of Cruttenden's eyes. The mention of the Marquis had both startled and disconcerted him.

John inclined his head. 'Indeed there are many strange stories circulating around town. Probably my informant was wrong.'

Walking painfully, the Liveryman came further into the room. 'There's no probably about it, Sir. You have been misinformed. Now, to what do we owe the pleasure of your calling upon us?'

'Two reasons. One I wanted to see how you progressed, Sir, after so painful a beating. Secondly, I was somewhat concerned that Miss Gill discharged herself from my care without my consent. She was very poorly, Master Cruttenden. I assure you I brought her back from the brink.'

Clariana had the good grace to look a little shamefaced. 'I wanted to be with you, Francis. I longed for your comforting presence.'

About as comforting as a cobra, John thought maliciously.

Cruttenden looked as urbane as his bruises would allow. 'I am sure you will understand, Mr Rawlings. Poor child. What an ordeal to return home and discover her father's body.'

'Fortunately Miss Gill was under the influence of opium at the time and therefore the full horror of the discovery would have been dulled.'

The Liveryman took a seat, not inviting John to do

likeways. 'I intend to demand a full apology from Dr Ridge-way. How dare the old fool treat my betrothed in such a manner.'

'Miss Gill was extremely hysterical,' John answered, straight faced. 'I believe the physician was hard put to it to quieten her.'

'I wish you would not speak about me as if I were not here,' Clariana said grumpily.

She really was a sullen baggage, the Apothecary considered, staring at her truculent face. The only time she had been even reasonably pleasant was when she had been full of opium and ill because of it.

He bowed in her direction. 'I have taken up enough of your time. Now that I am assured you will be properly cared for, I shall take my leave. Good morning Miss Gill, Mr Cruttenden.'

The Liveryman heaved himself to his feet. 'Allow me to recompense you for your services.'

The Apothecary raised a dignified hand. 'No, Sir. I would not hear of it. It is my calling to heal the sick and I only make a charge to those who send for me. To administer to those who have met with an accident is part of my duty. Good day to you.'

And with that he swept from the room, feeling rather proud of the way he had conducted himself.

'Do you mean to say that bloody button belonged to Clariana?' said Samuel, flushing angrily. 'Just as I feared. There's our one and only clue gone out of the window.'

John stroked his chin. 'She certainly *said* it belonged to her. Told me it had come off her evening gown.'

'It's possible. She probably went into the compounding room to tell her father she was leaving for the Assembly, and it fell off then.'

'The trouble is I don't remember her evening clothes

having diamond buttons on them. But then I didn't look at her all that closely. Quite honestly, I don't care for the girl.'

'There's one person who would know,' said Samuel cautiously.

'Who?'

'Coralie. Women always observe one another's fashions with a hawk's eye.'

'Well, I can hardly ask her. Our relationship has reached its inevitable conclusion.'

'John,' said Samuel earnestly. 'You may marry another, have children, do what you will, but your association with Coralie will never conclude, not as long as there's breath in your body.'

The Apothecary turned away impatiently. 'I don't wish to hear that. I have begun a new connection with a woman to whom I am violently attracted. I speak of Emilia of course. In fact I like her so well that I intend to go to Chelsea then take her to Kensington to meet my father.'

'I wonder what he will think.'

'He will like her. He told me that my affair with Coralie had run its course. Now stop trying to annoy me.'

'Very well. No more talk of ladies. What do you intend to do next?'

'To take the button to Mr Fielding this very night. Do you want to come with me?'

'I certainly do,' Samuel answered eagerly. 'I wouldn't mind another eyeful of that damned pretty niece of his.'

John looked shocked. 'She's a child, Sam. A horrible, snivelling child.'

'She's fifteen if she's a day. My mother married when she was fifteen.'

'That was then. Things are different now.'

'In two years that girl will be a bride, mark my words.'

'God's mercy! What with Nicholas hankering after her and now you. I'd like to throttle the little witch.'

'You probably fancy her yourself.'

'I think,' said John vehemently, 'that I am about to be violently sick.' And with that he slapped his hat on his head and made to leave.

Fearing that they might interrupt the Fieldings at dinner if they were too early, the two friends walked to Bow Street, breathing in the frosty December air, grateful that the cold was killing some of the smells that usually rose from the streets. They did not speak much, both preoccupied with the thought of the two deaths and who could be guilty of the crimes.

Eventually John said, 'I still can't see how the person responsible for poisoning the flour managed to contrive that Master Alleyn had more than anybody else.'

'He must have been present at the dinner.'

'And made himself ill? Yes, he must.'

'Do you think it was Master Cruttenden?'

'He's unpleasant enough most certainly, but there's absolutely no motive. He was Josiah's friend and had been for years.'

'Perhaps they had a quarrel that nobody else knew about.'

'Even Mrs Alleyn? I don't really think so. She was very close to her husband.'

'Yet he must have kept some secrets from her.'

'I suppose so,' John answered. Once again something intangible was nagging at him, some fact that he really should have thought of by now but had still failed to do.

The pensive silence was not broken until they arrived at the Public Office and were duly shown up the stairs to the salon where the Fieldings received guests. Seated on either side of the fire were John and Elizabeth, while Mary Ann perched at a table demurely doing her embroidery. She raised her long lashed eyes as the two young men came into the room, and shot them a look that was quite unmistakeable.

'Behave,' mouthed John, but Samuel bowed and made much of greeting her.

The Blind Beak moved his head in the direction of the newcomers. 'Mr Rawlings?' he asked.

'Here with Samuel Swann, Sir.'

'How fortuitous. I have news to impart. Let us repair to my study. Elizabeth, my sweetheart, would you arrange for refreshments to be served us?'

'Certainly, my dearest.'

As they walked up the stairs to the Magistrate's snug, John found himself strangely moved by the tenderness the couple obviously felt for one another and he wondered what it must be like for a blind man to fall in love with a voice and make love to someone he had never seen. The thought of never having been able to set eyes on Coralie's shimmering beauty or Emilia's heavenly looks made him cringe, and yet again his admiration for one of the most brilliant but challenged men in London soared.

They sat as they had done before, Mr Fielding behind his desk, his two visitors facing him.

'You said you had news, Sir.'

'Yes, the body of George Griggs has been found. It came up in Limehouse Reach near Cuckold's Point. It is lying at present in Poplar Mortuary.'

'How do you know it is Griggs? Has someone been to identify it?'

Mr Fielding gave a humourless laugh. 'Sotherton Backler was given the unpleasant task. Apparently he fainted clean away at poor Griggs's greenish condition.'

'God!' said Samuel under his breath.

John leant forward. 'Were there any signs of attack, Sir?'

'There was a bad blow to the head but whether this had been delivered after death is anyone's guess. I'm afraid that the poor fellow has been too long in the water for us to tell.'

'A strange coincidence, though, that he was nightwatch-man at the very place where the poison was put in the flour.'

'I quite agree with you about that,' answered the Blind Beak.

There was a short pause while a servant appeared with a claret jug and three glasses and served the assembled company. When they were alone once more the Magistrate turned in the direction of John. 'You have something to tell me?'

'Yes, Sir. I found a diamond button, real at that, in Tobias Gill's compounding room. His daughter claims that it was hers but I am not so sure.'

'But why should she lie?'

'To protect another. Francis Cruttenden perhaps.'

Mr Fielding chuckled gently. 'Mr Rawlings, my old friend, may I comment that you seem somewhat obsessed with that man. We are, after all, attempting to find the murderer of Master Alleyn and Tobias Gill, a task with which all of us are being singularly unsuccessful. There is nothing whatsoever to link Master Cruttenden, however much you might dislike him, with those crimes.'

'No, you're right, of course. And yet . . .'

'Yet what?'

'He seems to sit in the centre of the web, a silky grey spider that hastens away whenever you try to approach it.'

The Blind Beak was silent for a while, then he said, 'I agree with you that the attack by what appears to have been a lackey of the Marquis of Kensington demands further explanation, though I do not see the connection with the two deaths. To me they are a separate issue altogether. However, I intend to beard the Marquis in his den and travel to Kensington to do so.'

'Sir, I have a better idea,' John said boldly. 'My father has written to me to say that the building work on the place we have acquired is moving along splendidly and he desires me to stay for a day or so to inspect it. Why do you and Mrs Fielding not come down at the same time and take rooms in a local hostelry? I would then wager a goodly sum that Sir Gabriel can arrange an invitation for us to call on the Marquis. Why, he only has to be in a place a few days and he is on the visiting list of every hostess for miles around.'

'Capital,' the Blind Beak answered with enthusiasm. 'Far better than visiting officially. A very good plan, Sir. However, we shall have to bring Mary Ann. The girl's too young to be left in the care of servants.'

'It all sounds most amusing,' put in Samuel heartily. 'Has anyone any objection if I join the party?'

Chapter Twenty

They travelled to Kensington in Mr Fielding's coach, Mary Ann squeezed between her aunt and uncle, John and Samuel on the seat opposite, the luggage stowed on the roof. They journeyed by daylight and so considered it safe to traverse the park, notorious for highwaymen and duellists. Indeed it was so dangerous to use at night that bells were rung at the various gates to allow coaches to gather together and proceed in convoy. Yet even though it was day time, an armed Runner sat beside the coachman as a safeguard.

Passing Hyde Park Wall, the driver took the coach road crossing the park which led through to Knight's Bridge and eventually brought them into the village of Kensington, where they stopped at The New Tavern to deposit the Fieldings, the Magistrate considering the inn more in the centre of things than The Dun Cow, pleasant though that hostelry was. The coach then continued along the High Street before turning right into Church Lane, where it drew to a halt before the house at the end of the terrace near the King's kitchen garden.

'Mighty fine, if I might say so,' said Samuel, alighting and taking his bag from the carriage roof.

'My father insisted on something a little rural but not too far removed from the great houses. This seemed to fit the bill.'

'It's splendid.'

But there was even greater pleasure to be discovered within. John, fully aware that Sir Gabriel would be spending more time in the house than he would, had left the entire design of the interior in his father's hands. But any slight fear that the whole place would be done throughout in black and white was immediately allayed as the two friends stepped into the long, thin entrance hall. A sensous shade of saffron covered the walls and this was repeated within the principal salon, its long windows overlooking the royal domestic garden. To complement the colour, the cornice had been picked out in warm amber, a shade repeated with topaz and cream in the moulded ceiling. The curtains, made of velvet, rich gold in hue, hung to the floor.

'A triumph,' said John. 'Father, you have performed a miracle.'

'When one considers what a dingy little place it was, perhaps.'

'You are too modest, Sir,' said Samuel enthusiastically. 'You have a gem here. A palace in miniature.'

'Wait till you have seen it all,' Sir Gabriel answered, and with ill-concealed pride took them on a tour of the rest of the house.

There were more delights in store. A dining room of deep damson, the colour lifted by the use of silver; while white and green provided a splendid foil for the vivid red walls of the master bedroom.

'Your room, John,' said Sir Gabriel, throwing open a door on the first floor landing. It was all the Apothecary could have wished for, painted a deep yellow throughout, with blue and white curtains and bed hangings, and china of the same colour combination, decorating the walls and shelves. By contrast, the guest room was the palest shade of green, highlighted with salmon pink. On the top floor dwelt the three servants in far simpler but perfectly comfortable accommodation.

'I am more than impressed,' said Samuel as they returned to the salon. 'I intend to visit frequently.' He burst into hearty laughter and slapped John on the back, then bowed and wrung Sir Gabriel's hand. His exuberance was so infectious that the popping of a champagne cork seemed the only suitable accompaniment and the three men sat with full glasses by the fire, while the conversation turned away from the house to other matters.

'How are you proceeding with the investigation?' asked John's father.

'There has been another murder, Sir.'

And the Apothecary described to Sir Gabriel all that had happened since the older man had departed for Kensington, including the extraordinary attack on Francis Cruttenden and the even more extraordinary departure of his assailant.

Sir Gabriel refilled everyone's glass. 'The Marquis of Kensington, you say? Surely the fellow who claimed he saw this must have been mistaken.

'It's possible of course, but the fact remains for all that.'

'Extraordinary! I have met the Marquis. A regular sort of chap in my opinion.'

John smiled to himself. His personal wager that his father would know everyone within days of his arrival, just won. 'I thought you might be acquainted. Tell me what he's like.'

'He's young, in his mid thirties. He came into the title following the death of an uncle. He's quite good looking in a dark, fleshy sort of way. Loves playing cards, in fact he's invited me over for whist. Would you care to meet him?'

'I'd love to – and so would Mr Fielding.'

'You wrote me that they intended to stay near by. Are they at The Dun Cow?'

'No, The New Tavern. The whole family is with him. They have made an excursion of it.'

'And the purpose of their visit?'

John looked vague. 'I believe Mr Fielding is interested in buying a property somewhere round here.'

'And wants to meet the Marquis into the bargain?'

'Yes, Sir.'

'Then I shall see what can be arranged,' said Sir Gabriel, and looked wise.

They dined on simple country fare, extremely well prepared by a woman who came in to do the cooking, and after dinner the three men set forth, armed with lanterns and sticks, to make the short walk to the Blind Beak's hostelry, where they found him comfortably installed in a suite of rooms over-looking the King's stables on the other side of the High Street. After the usual cordial greetings, during which Mary Ann made much of flirting with all three of the new arrivals, the gentlemen repaired with a bottle of port to the Magistrate's private dining room.

Sir Gabriel opened the conversation, addressing himself to Mr Fielding. 'I believe you seek acquaintance with the Marquis of Kensington, Sir.'

The Blind Beak nodded. 'Yes, I do. Did John tell you of the strange attack on an individual named Cruttenden?'

With a shock, the Apothecary realised that this was the first time the Magistrate had ever referred to him by his Christian name and wondered whether, after all these years, their relationship was about to become less formal.

'He did. I am hard put to it to find an explanation.'

'Jago did a little research on the Marquis before I left town,' Mr Fielding continued. 'It seems that he was not in line for the title at all, being the child of a youngest son. However, his father was killed in battle leaving him and another boy, child of the deceased middle brother, as possible heirs. Then the hand of fate struck. The eldest brother, holder of the title, died of a fever shortly before he was due to be married and the immediate heir, child of the middle brother, followed him to the grave a few weeks later. Thus, the present incumbent took the title.'

'For him a fortunate series of misadventures.'

'Indeed.'

'What has all that to do with the attack on Cruttenden?' asked Samuel.

'Absolutely nothing,' the Blind Beak answered, 'except that I like to have the background details of those under investigation.'

Sir Gabriel spoke. 'He's a decent fellow, though damned addicted to gambling. He's always desperate for whist players, so I might suggest that I take the three of you along.'

'It's a pity Serafina is not here,' John commented. 'She would give him a run for his money.'

His father sighed. 'Our sweet friend. It seems an eternity since I have seen her. How is she these days?'

'Extremely pregnant. Her child is due in February I believe.'

Samuel chuckled. 'Not that that's ever stopped her. Do you remember the twins connected with The Devil's Tavern affair, John? She soon sorted them out and she was big bellied then.'

'That's true enough.'

'Anyway, to the present,' said Mr Fielding. 'You have heard, Sir Gabriel, that we are absolutely no further forward with the Apothecaries' Hall poisoning and that another apothecary has been murdered?'

'Yes, I have. Are there simply no leads whatsoever? It seems extraordinary to me.'

John took advantage of the fact that he knew everyone present extremely well, and thought aloud. 'The stumbling block for me is that Master Alleyn died.'

'What do you mean?' asked the Magistrate.

'How was it done? It means the poisoner must have been close to him in order to ensure that he was given more arsenic than everybody else. Did the Runners' investigation of all those Liverymen present reveal nothing?'

'Nothing that we could act upon.'

'But he *must* have a hidden enemy,' John said emphatically. 'He simply *must*.'

'I suppose,' said Sir Gabriel mildly, 'that you have looked through his private papers?'

Everybody stared at him, even Mr Fielding turning his bandaged eyes in the direction of the speaker.

'To be honest, no,' the Magistrate answered eventually. 'Truth to tell, having been assured that the only person with a grudge against him was Garnett Smith, a man whom it now appears seems highly unlikely as a suspect, we did not look any further.'

'I think you should,' John's father continued imperturbably. 'Also those of the other dead man. Perhaps you will find a foe common to both.'

'What papers I could discover at Tobias Gill's have been delivered to the Public Office,' John said. 'However, his appointment book was missing.'

'Very significant,' boomed Samuel, determined to get a word in. 'I'm sure the murderer's name was written in there and it was removed to conceal their identity.'

'Sir Gabriel is right,' said the Blind Beak. 'As soon as we return to town, those papers must be gone through.'

The Apothecary cleared his throat. 'It was my intention to call on Miss Alleyn in Chelsea tomorrow. I shall ask her mother's permission to search Master Alleyn's documents whilst I am there.'

'Excellent,' Mr Fielding replied. 'I trust you will be back in time to meet the Marquis.'

'I shall certainly be back,' John answered. He looked straight at Sir Gabriel, his expression endearingly earnest. 'And I would like to invite the Alleyn ladies to dine with us, perhaps tomorrow, if that is in order.'

He spent an amazingly comfortable night in his new bedroom, sleeping better than he had done for some days. Waking refreshed, John devoured a large breakfast, then, having left Samuel happily conversing with Sir Gabriel over the tea cups, made his way to a small but efficient livery stable situated not far from the King's own stable yard. There he hired a large competent-looking horse and went at speed back to Knight's Bridge, then down a serpentine path known as Sloane Lane by the locals, named in memory of Sir Hans Sloane, whose patients had included Queen Anne and a diarist named Pepys, and who had founded the Chelsea Physick Garden, much loved by all apothecaries. He had died in 1753 when John had still been an apprentice, living to the great age of ninety-two.

Now, proceeding down the path named after Hans Sloane, on his way to see Emilia Alleyn, a song of happiness rose to John's lips. Despite the circumstances of his visit, probing even further into her father's death, he felt carefree and young and in that divine state known as falling in love. The weather echoed his mood, the December sky a deep rich blue, the sun out and the ground hard with overnight frost.

Sloane Lane continued on its twisting way until it joined Jews Row, which John crossed, heading for Wilderness Row, which ran round the back of Ranelagh Gardens. From there it was but a short trot to the river and the house to which he had first escorted a dying Josiah Alleyn. Though I could have sworn I'd saved him, John thought. And at that an idea came that almost made him fall from his horse so sharply did it strike him. Clutching the reins to regain his balance, the Apothecary made a slower pace to his sweetheart's house as he considered every aspect of the sudden suspicion which had come to him.

It was customary to wear mourning for some time after the death of a member of the family, but today Emilia had adopted a very deep purple which suited her and enhanced her golden looks. Well aware and by now a little wary of the budding relationship between her daughter and the young apothecary who had tried so hard to save her husband, Mrs Alleyn, fond of John as she was, firmly acted as chaperone.

The two women received their visitor in a delightful parlour overlooking the garden and river.

'My dear,' said Maud Alleyn, rising to her feet. 'To what do we owe the pleasure of this visit?'

John, extremely conscious that he looked rather fine in his riding clothes, made much of kissing her hand. 'I am staying at my father's country house in Kensington and thought I would like to call. I trust you have no objection.' Knowing full well that she had only recently caught him embracing Emilia, he was very slightly on edge and determined to ingratiate himself.

'Of course not. It is always a pleasure to see you Mr Rawlings. Will you take tea?'

'I would very much enjoy that.'

Emilia came towards him, and he could not resist, mother or no mother, taking both her hands in his.

'Do you have any further news of Clariana Gill?' she asked, looking up at him with those heavenly eyes of hers.

'Yes, she's with the elderly lover, of course. And short shrift they gave me when I called. Cruttenden even offered to pay me for my services.'

'You should have taken the money,' said Maud roundly, 'he's got enough of it.'

The Apothecary seized the moment. 'Interestingly, the matter of his wealth is under investigation at this very minute,' he said, telling half the truth.

'Quite rightly so.'

'In fact, Madam, in that regard I have a favour to ask of you.'

'And what is that?'

'That I might be allowed to look at your husband's personal papers. Please do not be offended. I have no intention of prying into Master Alleyn's affairs. The fact of the matter is that Mr Fielding believes there might, just might, be some reference to Master Cruttenden within them.'

Maud looked round the room, her expression none too

happy. 'I do not really relish the thought of Josiah's documents being examined by strangers.'

Emilia spoke up, quite sharply, showing that there could be a bite in the angel's tongue. 'Really Mother! John is hardly a stranger. He tried to save Father's life, remember. To deny him and the Public Office access to anything that might throw light on any aspect of the mysterious circumstances surrounding Papa's death would be utterly wrong of you.'

Mrs Alleyn looked contrite to the point that John almost felt sorry for her. 'Of course, you're right. I shall unlock his desk and let you look through the contents. Forgive me. I still grieve for him you know.'

'Quite understandably.' John paused, then said, 'If it would not intrude on your mourning, I wondered if you and Miss Alleyn might care to dine with my father and myself tomorrow or the next day. After that I shall have to return to town alas.'

Emilia's pleasure was so obvious that it would have been a churlish mama indeed who could have put a stop to it. None the less, Mrs Alleyn hesitated.

'My father could send his carriage,' John continued, hoping even as he said the words that Sir Gabriel would agree.

Maud gave in, laughing at his eagerness. 'You are two very persuasive young people. Yes, Mr Rawlings. I should be happy to dine with Mr Rawlings senior.'

The Apothecary was so delighted that he bowed. 'What excellent news. By the way, my father adopted me as a child and we have different surnames.'

'Oh I see. So how shall I address him when we meet?'

'As Sir Gabriel Kent,' John answered airily, and could not help but feel a slight sense of self-importance at the look of interest that suddenly crossed Mrs Alleyn's features.

It was not a pleasant task, going through a dead man's papers, the act smacking too much of robbing a grave. With as vague a brief as he had, namely to find a reference to anyone who might have been Josiah's enemy for however slight a reason, John felt obliged to look at everything, particularly personal letters. Further, Master Alleyn's bills and receipts had to be inspected as they might reveal a dissatisfied patient or a shopkeeper who thought he was owed money. Hating what he was doing, the Apothecary slowly and painstakingly sifted through it all. Tea was served to him twice, once by Emilia alone so there was a chance for a swift embrace. Yet though he toiled on, the task proved fruitless. There was one thing that puzzled him, however: a list of names with no heading and no indication of what it meant. Probably past patients, John thought. Yet one of those names was highly significant in view of the current investigation.

Taking the list to the window to take advantage of the daylight, the Apothecary read it again. 'Mr Montague Bending, the Hon. Sophie Ebury, the Bishop of Bodmin, the Marquis of Kensington, the Prince of Castile.' It meant nothing to him but that one significant name was enough to make John fold the paper very carefully and slip it into an inside coat pocket.

'Did you find anything?' asked Emilia from the doorway.

'No,' said John, and went towards her, his hands outstretched. 'I am so glad that you are coming to meet my father.'

'I feel rather nervous. I didn't realise he had a title.'

'He's a baronet. The whole thing will die out with him, as his only child was a daughter who died at birth.'

'Why did he adopt you?'

'He married my mother, who at one time was one of his servants. My real father was one of the Rawlings of Twickenham. I don't know any more about it than that.'

'John, are you a bastard?'

'Yes, does it matter?'

'Not to someone who loves you,' answered Emilia, and went from the room as swiftly as she had come in, leaving

John to touch the place on his cheek where she had planted a swift cool kiss.

He returned to Kensington in the dusk, just before the hour to dine, and, having delivered the competent horse back to its stables, went hastily on foot to The New Inn where Mr Fielding, still tying his cravat, most admirably John thought, emerged from his bedroom to meet the visitor.

'You have news, my friend?'

'Yes and no, Sir. There was nothing in the papers anywhere – and I went through everything – to reveal the identity of a secret enemy. All I could find was this most extraordinary list.' And John read it aloud to the Blind Beak, who sat in a chair opposite him, finishing the adjustment of his neckwear.

There was silence when he had finished, then Mr Fielding said, 'The Marquis of Kensington again. Can this be a coincidence?'

'I don't know, Sir. I simply don't know. I have no idea what the list means. Are they possibly Master Alleyn's patients?'

'That is one possible construction certainly. But if not, then there must be some other reason for them to be linked together.'

'But what?'

'I have no idea, although I intend to find out. I had thought of spending another day in the country, but instead I shall leave Elizabeth and Mary Ann here to enjoy themselves, and go back alone. I want to get Jago working on this. I feel in my gut that you have discovered something important, Mr Rawlings, though for the life of me I can't imagine what it is. However, we can test the theory of Master Alleyn's patients tonight.'

'Are we booked to play whist with the Marquis?'

'Yes, we most certainly are, so I suggest that you hurry

home to dine and then set forth for his extremely gracious home.'

'I shall do as you say,' said John, standing up.

The Blind Beak rose also. 'You have done well, my friend. Thank you for all your help.'

With a very strong feeling that an extraordinary hidden truth was slowly beginning to emerge, John set off for Church Lane.

Four hours later, each one of them dressed within an inch of ostentation, Sir Gabriel, his son and Samuel Swann swept from the end of terrace house and into Sir Gabriel's black coach, complete with its team of snowflake horses. The coachman went down the lane, along the High Street, and drove a course towards Knight's Bridge that ran parallel with the huge, ornate and extremely beautiful gardens that lay adjacent to Kensington Palace. Fine and stately mansions stood to the right, opposite the palace grounds and it was before one of these that the équipage finally pulled in. A pair of vast wrought iron gates were swung back by the lodge-keeper and the coach proceeded around the carriage sweep to the front door of a magnificent dwelling house.

'Imposing,' said John.

'It was built by the Marquis's grandfather. He must have played here when he was a child, though he never thought to inherit.'

'I shall be fascinated to meet him,' the Apothecary answered with feeling.

He had not mentioned the existence of a mysterious list to either his father or Samuel, feeling it better to say nothing, until the whole matter had been looked into by Joe Jago. His discretion was confirmed by Elizabeth Fielding, this night acting as her husband's eyes, who breathed in his ear as she arrived immediately following them. 'John asks that you remain silent about your discovery.'

'Tell him that I have.'

'He further requests that you bring the name of Master Alleyn into the conversation.'

'I will gladly.'

They filed between two solemn footmen into a huge circular entrance hall. Lined with twenty veined alabaster columns, classical nudes dotted about in niches, some flaunting all they possessed, others with modest hands covering breasts and thighs, it was a truly awe inspiring sight.

Mary Ann immediately began a tour of inspection of the more well endowed male statues and started to giggle.

John sidled over. 'If you don't behave yourself, you will be sent to sit in the carriage.'

She grinned up at him, quite the prettiest little thing out. 'I didn't know that you had been put in charge of me, Mr Rawlings.'

'I'm not, Madam, luckily for you, but out of respect for your aunt and uncle behave with some decorum.'

For once the little flirt looked suitably contrite, and walked away to join the line of people proceeding into the circular saloon where beneath the Waterford crystal chandeliers and before Venetian mirrors of enormous splendour, card tables had been set up.

The Marquis stood in the doorway, dark and stocky, handsome in his way.

Sir Gabriel took the lead and introduced the company. 'My lord, may I present Mr John Fielding, the Principal Magistrate, together with his wife and niece.'

John noticed to his horror that Mary Ann even made eyes at the Marquis as she dropped him a curtsey that was very slightly impudent.

'And this is my son, John Rawlings, and a family friend, Samuel Swann.'

There was much bowing and salutation, and refreshment was offered to the guests before everyone sat down. As luck would have it, John found himself on the same table as the

Marquis, who was partnered by Sir Gabriel. He himself was paired with John Fielding, whose wife sat right behind him, whispering in his ear exactly what cards he had.

'Let us play a long hand,' said the Marquis, and relapsed into a frowning silence as he stared moodily at his cards.

Faced with a dilemma as to whether to speak or not, John decided that now would be as good a time as any. 'I saw some old friends of yours today, My Lord.'

The Marquis did not look up. 'Oh yes?'

'Mrs Alleyn and her daughter. As you probably know, Josiah Alleyn died recently in rather odd circumstances.'

The nobleman shot him a quick dark stare then returned his attention to his hand. 'Josiah who?'

'Alleyn, Sir. I was under the impression that you knew him.'

'Never heard of the fellow. Who was he?'

'An apothecary, Sir.'

'No, don't know him. There must be some mistake.'

Smooth as silk, Mr Fielding came in. 'But surely you know Liveryman Cruttenden, my Lord. Why he's a famous socialite.'

There was a reaction, John saw it. The dusky eyes looked up and a small flame flickered briefly in their depths before it was rapidly extinguished. The Marquis laughed. 'Who are all these extraordinary people you keep mentioning to me? Damme, Sir Gabriel, I swear that I'm in the clutches of the Grand Inquisitor.'

John's father responded smoothly. 'Attempts at conversation, my Lord, that is all. Some people talk over cards. Others, like ourselves, prefer to play in silence.'

'I stand corrected, Sir,' said John Fielding, but he had felt the Apothecary tense beside him and knew that their objective had been achieved. Elizabeth, too, had noticed something, and the pressure of her hand on her husband's arm tightened very slightly.

There was a guffaw from the other table where Samuel

and Mary Ann, together with the Marchioness and another jolly fellow, were indulging in horseplay.

The Marquis rolled his lustrous eyes. 'I fear our usual concentration is doomed to be broken, Sir Gabriel.'

'Alas, my Lord, youthful high spirits will out.'

'Indeed,' answered the nobleman, and shot John Rawlings a black expressionless look that revealed absolutely nothing.

Chapter Twenty-One

The winter weather was kind, and Emilia entered the house in Church Lane in a burst of sunshine, then proceeded to glow with so much pleasure that everything looked brighter in her presence. Mrs Alleyn discreetly allowed herself to fade into the background, letting her beautiful daughter gleam like the heavenly being she resembled. Sir Gabriel was utterly charmed; Samuel, who had seen her before but never like this, was clearly quite smitten; John fell more deeply in love.

They dined, then Emilia entertained at the harpsichord which she played extremely well. She also sang in a high, clear, untutored voice which all present found very appealing. After that they indulged in a hand or two at cards and then the ladies went home, having first pressed upon Sir Gabriel an invitation to dine with them.

'And you must come too,' said Mrs Alleyn, smiling fondly at John.

'Alas, Madam, I must return to town tomorrow. Firstly my shop demands my attention and, secondly, so does Mr Fielding. I simply cannot stay one day more. Much as I would like to.'

He looked straight at Emilia, who returned his gaze with an unmistakeable message in her eyes. Samuel, watching all this, made a strange little coughing sound and John, much to his own annoyance, immediately thought of Coralie.

'Then, Sir,' said Maud, just a fraction coquettishly, 'it will be just ourselves.'

'I can think of nothing nicer,' answered Sir Gabriel, gallant to his fingertips, and kissed her hand.

They all went into the street as the Alleyn coach was brought round from the yard at the back, and waved the party goodbye with a great deal of enthusiasm. John, under cover of darkness, blew a kiss to Emilia, but she either did not see it or was too shy to return it under the gaze of her mama.

'A fine young woman,' said Sir Gabriel as they went back into the house. 'What are your intentions, John?'

'Honourable, Sir.'

'And your relationship with Miss Clive? Is that finally at an end?'

An urgent desire to tell the whole truth came over the Apothecary. 'Samuel believes that it will never be.'

'Well, I . . .' his friend protested in the background.

'Samuel may well be right,' Sir Gabriel said wisely. 'There are some people whom it is impossible to give up entirely, some affinities too deep ever to be broken. But the time for you and Coralie was not right and may possibly never be so.'

'Then what am I to do?'

'What I advised you originally. Miss Clive misjudged your patience and expected you to continue your connection with her on her terms and her terms only. She may be the great passion of your life, who knows? But I believe that you are doing the right thing in drawing that chapter to a close.'

'Then you approve of Miss Alleyn?'

'I think she is absolutely charming.'

'Hear, hear,' said Samuel. 'Propose, lad, before somebody else snaps her up.'

'Meaning yourself?'

'Now would I poach on another man's terrain?'

'Definitely. Without a second thought.'

'I'll drink to that,' responded the Goldsmith cheerily.

'Another decanter of port could be in order,' said Sir Gabriel, and the two younger people happily agreed.

The next morning, quite early, John and Samuel caught the public stage back into London, arriving at the Gloucester Coffee House, Piccadilly, in good time to start work. There they bowed and shook hands, arranged to meet shortly and went their separate ways, both to their individual shops to see how their apprentices had enjoyed, or otherwise, the responsibility of running the establishment singlehandedly.

As usual when Nicholas was in sole charge, John found his emporium in Shug Lane full of eager young females. Wondering yet again what it was about the Muscovite's pale, rather angular features that attracted them, John courteously raised his hat and retreated to the compounding room, leaving his apprentice to deal with their clamours for his attention. Eventually, though, the place cleared and the usual patients, gout, wind and clap ridden, surfaced. The Apothecary briskly dispensed a decoction of Dog's Grass for the gout, also beneficial for expelling urine and staying laxes and vomiting; Saxifrage for colic and expelling gas, to say nothing of its uses against the stone, gravel and scurvy; and Hound's Tongue for the clap.

'Does it work?' asked the beau buying it, his expression a little weary.

'On everything,' John answered cheerfully. 'The root baked in embers, wrapped in paste and made into a suppository, will ease painful piles. The distilled water will take away any foul ulcers, while the physick will cure your clap, fluxes and haemorrhages. By the way, if a mad dog bites you, rub the leaves on to the wound. And don't forget that the bruised leaves boiled in hog's lard and applied to the scalp stop your hair falling out.'

The beau gave a sickly smile and left, looking fractionally faint.

'Is all that true?' asked Nicholas, amazed.

'It is,' said John seriously. 'A wonderful plant is Hound's Tongue.' He looked at his watch. 'The dinner hour approaches. I shall take you to have something to eat, my boy. You have a lean and hungry look, to quote the Bard. But perhaps it's that that brings the young ladies rushing to your side. I suspect they all want to mother you.'

'Then I must stay thin, mustn't I?' Nicholas answered cheerfully, and set about closing the shop.

They dined at the Smyrna in Pall Mall, the haunt of Whig politicians, before John left his apprentice to return to Shug Lane for the late afternoon trade. The Apothecary hurried back to Nassau Street, fairly confident that a message from Mr Fielding would be awaiting him. He was not disappointed. A letter asking him to go to Bow Street as soon as he arrived back in town lay amongst a pile of others. Only pausing long enough to freshen his appearance, John sent one of his father's footmen to hail him a chair.

He found the Blind Beak and his redoubtable clerk in conference in the study on the ground floor, close to the Public Office and the court. Both heads moved as he went in and Mr Fielding, in that unnerving way of his, said, 'Mr Rawlings?'

'Yes, Sir. I only returned from Kensington today and went straight to my shop before going home. I came here as soon as I received your message.'

Joe Jago stood up, his light blue eyes smiling in his craggy face. 'You've arrived just in time, Sir. The Magistrate and I were on the point of discussing the list you found.'

'Take a seat, my friend,' Mr Fielding said. 'I think we are about to learn something of interest.'

'Indeed you are,' Jago answered with a chuckle. 'Indeed you are.'

John sat, removing some law books from the chair to make room. 'Did you make any sense of the list, Joe?'

'Not at first I didn't. Just seemed like a series of names put together at random. And then I began to make a few enquiries. And what do you think I found?'

'I've no idea. What?'

'Well, I'll begin at the beginning. The first name on the list, Mr Montague Bending, I discovered belonged to a gentleman recently deceased. He had died leaving a considerable fortune to his heirs. But do you know what?' Joe had his audience in the palm of his hand and was enjoying every minute of it.

'Tell us,' ordered Mr Fielding with a rumbling laugh.

'He was never due to inherit that fortune in the first place. His grandfather had fallen out with him and was just about to make a new will, cutting Mr Bending out, when lo and behold the old man suddenly died.'

An extraordinary sensation rang the length of John's spine but he said nothing.

'Then I came to the Honourable Sophie Ebury, a flighty young lady of some thirty years or so. Hers was rather a different tale. Daughter of a younger son with very little fortune, she scraped her way into society on the strength of her title and family name. There she acquired an elderly admirer, old Lord Briggs, who was keen as mustard to make her his wife and who made her his chief beneficiary to prove the warmth of his affections. But alas, she had formed an attachment for a handsome young army man, Captain Robert, who wanted her to elope. The elderly lover threatened cutting her off without a penny unless she married him. And then . . .'

'He died before the will could be changed?'

'Precisely so. Next I came to the interesting story of the Bishop of Bodmin. Here clerical skulduggery enters the tale. Throughout his rise through the ranks of the clergy he was always stalked by a rival, the Reverend Timothy Simpkins. Both had risen to the rank of archdeacon when suddenly the Bishopric of Bodmin fell vacant. There was intense speculation as to who would receive preferment, but the consensus was that Archdeacon Simpkins was more favourably regarded by the Archbishop. And then the Archdeacon, though still only in his forties, took sick of a sudden and died.'

Still not quite sure what the thread was, John shook his head. 'Go on.'

'The story of the Marquis of Kensington's sudden acquisition of the title you already know.'

'And the Prince of Castile?'

'More difficult to unearth because it all took place in Spain. But from what I can gather the Prince's grandfather, the old King, had about ten sons, none of whom lived as long as he did. Because of this the eldest grandson was in line to become Crown Prince. There were four ahead of the Prince in the line of succession but they were all mysteriously struck down with dysentery and died, leaving him as Heir Apparent.'

John gazed at him, thunderstruck. 'Is this true, Joe?'

'As far as I can ascertain, Sir.'

'Then what's the common denominator, other than the fact that these people profited by the death of another?'

'My enquiries so far – and please remember that I have not had the time to probe too deeply – reveal that the persons who died were, every one of them, treated by an apothecary.'

'But what's odd about that?'

'It was the same apothecary, Sir.'

'The same one? Oh, surely not?'

'It looks very much that way Sir.'

John went white. 'Not Master Alleyn?'

'No, not him.'

'Dear God, then who?'

He still hadn't made the connection but Mr Fielding was a leap ahead. 'It's Cruttenden, isn't it, Joe? Mr Rawlings's instinct was correct all along.'

'Then why was the list in Master Alleyn's desk?'

'Because he had become suspicious. He was probably

making his own enquiries and coming up with the right answers. That is why he had to die.'

John let out a groan. 'Just as I thought. The poisoning wasn't done at Apothecaries' Hall at all, that was merely a blind. Josiah was killed on the morning I called to see him, having been made ill again the night before. Cruttenden told me he had administered a clyster as a last resort. I'll warrant it contained pure poison.'

'I think you're probably right,' said the Blind Beak slowly. 'We are quite obviously dealing with a man who is a paid assassin. Now it becomes clear how his great wealth was amassed.'

'What about Tobias Gill? Did he murder him also?'

'More than likely. From what you have told me, Mr Rawlings, the poor old man stood between Cruttenden and the object of his desire, the unlovely Clariana. I would imagine that that was enough to sign Gill's death warrant.'

'He has to be stopped,' said Joe Jago solemnly. 'He is a menace to society.'

'The thing is, how do we prove what we think? None of the people concerned will admit to hiring a paid killer. We are between a rock and a hard place when it comes to establishing our case.'

'What about the Marquis?' asked John. 'He seems to have wanted Cruttenden dead.'

'Probably because he was being blackmailed. That is a well known risk if one engages an assassin to do one's filthy deeds for one. I doubt that he would talk.'

'Then what do we do?'

'We must use a decoy. Somebody must go in, somebody from the *beau monde* claiming to have a tiresome relative – it has to be believable for he is a clever devil and may well check – and ask for his services. Then when he agrees to the deed and we hear him say so, we can strike.'

There was no need to ask who: Coralie's name hung in the air almost as if it were visible. Indeed there was much hesitation over who would be the first to say it.

'Of course there is one obvious candidate,' said the Blind Beak eventually.

'I don't want her anywhere near him,' answered John vehemently.

'There would be no danger. He would never harm a potential client.'

'Unless he suspected that she was not all she appeared to be.'

Mr Fielding turned the black bandage in the Apothecary's direction. 'But she must go as herself, my friend. She must say that someone, perhaps another actress, perhaps even her sister, is standing in the way of her career. That to reach the top of her profession means more to her than anything else in the world.'

The words were too close to home and John winced visibly.

Perhaps he made a small sound, for the Magistrate added, 'Please don't be afraid for her, Mr Rawlings. I would have armed men at every door.'

Joe Jago, who always knew exactly what was going on and who had undoubtedly heard through his own private network that the Apothecary's affections were now engaged elsewhere, caught John's eye and winked.

'Of course it will be up to Miss Clive in the end, Sir. Is that not so, Mr Fielding?'

'It is, Jago, it is.'

John sighed deeply. 'I suppose you want me to ask her?'

'You would appear to be the obvious choice.'

'My close relationship with Miss Clive has actually come to an end, Sir. We are no longer as intimate as once we were.'

'None the less, you are the nearest to her in terms of age and friendship. Will you put the matter to the young lady?'

'If I do,' John answered honestly, 'I will probably try to dissuade her.'

'That's as may be. Let fate decide.'

'Then on those conditions, I will do as you ask. I shall call on Coralie tomorrow morning.'

'The sooner the better,' answered the Magistrate. 'It is high time that Liveryman Cruttenden was brought to book for the evil he has perpetrated.'

'Let's get the bastard,' said Joe in layman's terms.

'Amen to that,' echoed John, and wished that his heart were not so full of dread.

Chapter Twenty-Two

As usual when it came to Coralie, John felt torn in two. Part of him wanted to see her again, for the sake of gazing at her lovely face and smile as much as anything. The other part dreaded the meeting, for, after all, she had asked him to leave when they had last been together, had rejected him and shown him the door. There could be no denying that their relationship had reached – and indeed passed – the point of no return. Further, there was the fact that he had now surren-dered himself totally to the delicious madness of being in love with Emilia. Yet there still lingered the thought that Sir Gabriel and Samuel might be right, that Coralie was like a recurring dream, something that would never quite go away.

With a resigned shrug of his shoulders, the Apothecary set off next morning to walk to Cecil Street. The path he took brought back memories: of returning from Coralie's early in the morning after he had first made love to her; of standing outside the house in Cecil Street and hearing Kitty sing to a man with a German accent. The King himself, perhaps? Or the great Mr Handel? Whoever, John was riven with bitter-sweet recollections and felt thoroughly sad by the time he arrived at Miss Clive's front door.

Not for nothing was Coralie acclaimed as one of the brightest stars of the London stage. After keeping him waiting half-an-hour she appeared looking radiant in white muslin trimmed with forget-me-not ribbons, her dark hair *au naturel*, tied up with an ice blue scarf.

'John, my dear,' she said, 'how sweet of you to visit me. My goodness, doesn't time hasten? Is it a month, or more?'

'A week or two actually.'

'As little as that? When one is busy it is so hard to tell.'

He looked at her suspiciously, wondering if the eyes were just a little too bright, the smile just a fraction too merry, but the actress revealed nothing. It seemed that she had already forgotten him, dismissed him into the ranks of former admirers, of which, of course, there were many.

She poured coffee into a small and exquisite bone china cup and her hand shook not at all. 'Now, my dear John,' Coralie said, her green eyes fastening on him, wide and clear, 'to what do I owe the honour of this visit?'

Was there a trace of sarcasm in the voice? None that he could hear. Within, John felt more than a flicker of irritation that he had been forgotten quite so easily. 'I come on behalf of Mr Fielding.'

She could have spoken words to the effect that she had guessed he had not called on his own accord, but Coralie merely smiled serenely. 'A wonderful man. Truth to tell I would like to see more of him and his family, but when one is in the theatre life goes pacily by. Anyway, what can I do for him?'

'He wants you to undertake an errand on his behalf, an errand which I believe might be dangerous and which I would prefer you did not engage to do.'

The smile softened and the eyes grew wide. 'How thoughtful you are. Tell me of it.'

Why, oh why, thought John wretchedly, did he have the terrible feeling that somewhere, deep down in her heart, she was laughing uproariously at him? He cleared his throat. 'It concerns the poisoning at Apothecaries' Hall.'

And he told her everything, just as he had discussed it with the Magistrate and Joe Jago on the previous evening.

Coralie looked thoughtful. 'If what you suppose is correct, then this Cruttenden must be one of the most evil monsters ever spawned.'

'You remember him?'

'Of course I do. The lecherous grey lizard dressed to kill.' She clapped a hand over her mouth, her eyes dancing above her fingers. 'Dressed to kill! Oh la, what have I said?'

It was funny, very, but John could hardly raise a smile, so upset was he by her attitude towards him. 'Very droll,' he said drily.

Coralie contrived to look contrite and mischievous simultaneously. 'I'm sorry. This is a serious matter. I must try not to be frivolous.'

Now she was making him feel middle aged. John composed his features into a scowl. 'I believe that ladies always study one another's clothing,' he said severely. 'Did the redhead, Clariana, have diamond buttons on her gown that night?'

'No, indeed not. Remember, I was the one who found her screaming in the street. I had to physically wrestle with the horrid girl. Buttons would have gone flying at that, but none did.'

John nodded grimly. 'Much as I thought. Did Cruttenden wear any?'

'Oh yes. As he raised his quizzing glass to stare at me I saw the flash of them at his wrist.'

'Then Clariana is an accessory to her own father's murder!'

'What do you mean?'

'I found a diamond button in the very room in which Tobias Gill met his death. When I showed it to Clariana she claimed it was hers and was therefore not an important piece of evidence.'

'Then she deserves to roast in hell,' said Coralie emphatically. 'Tell Mr Fielding that I will undertake his commission. Such villainy must not go unpunished. I am free tomorrow evening if that is convenient. I shall await his instructions.'

'But . . .'

She put a finger to her lips. 'Too gallant of you to protest, but I assure you it is in vain.' Behind her, a long case clock struck the hour. The actress stood up. 'Good gracious, is that the time? I must go and dress. We are to rehearse a new play this morning. John, my dear, it has been such a joy to see you again. Do call at any time.' And in one movement she planted a kiss on his cheek, waved her fingers and was gone from the room.

Feeling thoroughly wrong footed, the Apothecary crammed his hat on his head and left the house.

Before he had left Bow Street, Joe had drawn John to one side in the entrance hall.

'It is poor Gill's funeral tomorrow. The Beak has asked me to go, but first I am to call on the Master at Apothecaries' Hall. In the greatest confidence I am to tell him what has transpired.'

'Are you sure he'll say nothing?'

'A man in his lordly position? No, Mr Rawlings, he'll keep mum.'

'What time are you to be at the Hall?'

'Twelve noon. The funeral's shortly afterwards. I believe the Master wishes to attend. He is much disturbed by all that has happened.'

'Hardly surprising! I'll meet you there, Joe, and go to the burial with you.'

'I'll be glad of your company, Sir.'

Thus they had parted and now, thoroughly discomfited, John looked at his watch and saw that he had plenty of time to walk. At a brisk pace he set off for his destination.

His first call, on arrival, was to Michael Clarke who beamed a good morning at him. His attitude was so cheerful and friendly that John decided Harriet had said nothing to her husband about their recent conversation.

'My dear friend,' Michael greeted him, 'I can never thank you enough for your introduction to Dr Hensey. Did Harriet tell you that he is sending to his old Professor to discover how we might bring Matthew's sickness under control?'

'She did indeed. What wonderful news.'

'The good man is calling on us tomorrow afternoon at three. It is my fervent wish that you will be there for, alas, I cannot. I am duty bound to pay my last respects to poor Gill and two days with the shop closed are not possible. Further, whatever prescription Dr Hensey gives us, it is you, Mr Rawlings, whom I want to compound for us.'

'But what about yourself? You are more than capable.'

'I trust nobody more than you, Sir.'

'Then I would be honoured.'

They bowed to one another.

'I am closing the shop at noon,' Michael continued.

'Are the Liverymen intending to be present at the funeral?'

'In force, Sir.'

'Despite Gill's quarrel with the Society?'

'They are too big for such pettiness,' Michael answered simply, and John felt a huge surge of pride that he was a member of such a great and powerful body that put minor disagreements behind them and rose to an occasion without rancour.

'In that case I'll be on my way. I intend to greet the Backlers before I wait on the deceased.'

'Then I'll see you in church.'

Crossing the courtyard, John proceeded to the Butler's pantry and there found Jane Backler, dressed all in black and looking most becoming. She smiled her wide-toothed smile. 'My dear Mr Rawlings, Sotherton and I were discussing you only the other night. Where have you been? And what has happened about the poisoning? Are you any nearer the truth? Everything has gone so quiet.'

Very taken with how charming she looked, the Apothecary kissed her hand. 'Madam, we are near the answer indeed. In fact we have it.'

The eyes widened and the great grin also. 'You know who did it?'

'Yes.'

'Well?'

He smiled disarmingly. 'I cannot tell you, not yet. Mr Fielding has still to make an arrest. So I would ask you to keep the knowledge that we are close to a solution to yourself for the moment.'

'But what about Sotherton?'

'Yes, what about him?' said a voice from the doorway, and they both turned to see that the Beadle stood there.

His wife immediately adopted a conspiratorial look which John found faintly amusing. 'Nothing, my dear,' she said – the least likely phrase to put someone off the scent.

He came into the room, his rounded belly leading. 'Mr Rawlings.' Sotherton inclined his head, the gesture of a superior to one of lesser status.

John responded with a full blooded bow. 'Sir, I trust I find you well.'

'You do indeed. Now what was it you were saying?'

Jane turned to him. 'Mr Fielding is close to the truth, but neither you nor I are to breathe a word.'

Sotherton looked pompous. 'I trust no one we know is involved.'

John shook his head. 'I cannot expand, Sir. I simply cannot.'

'Just tell me it wasn't poor mad Mr Smith,' said Jane anxiously. 'I always felt so sorry for that man. Oh Mr Rawlings, tell me it wasn't him.'

'I have said too much already,' the Apothecary answered, wishing he had never gone to see them.

The Beadle became even more grandiose. 'Jane, you ask too many questions. Mr Rawlings, here, is clearly ill at ease. Now I must go and put on dark weeds. We are about to lay a fellow apothecary in the earth.'

Pretentious old beast, John thought, as with effusive

politeness Sotherton Backler bowed his way out of the room.

At two o'clock that afternoon, in the church of St Dunstan's in the East, at which Tobias Gill had been a regular worshipper, a strange notion for such a bitter man, the murdered apothecary was finally put to rest.

The Liverymen were true to their word, waiting outside in the bitter December cold until the funeral procession, consisting only of Clariana, like a dark vixen in her stark black, and one elderly man who could have been Gill's brother, walked in behind the coffin.

Amongst their number trooped Francis Cruttenden, his long black robe swirling about him, his face drawn and serious. It was hard, John thought, seeing him in that context, to imagine him killing at will. Yet was it? His expression was so closed, his demeanour so suave, that any wickedness could have been hidden.

As they took their seats in one of the hard wooden pews at the back, Joe nudged him. 'The Master's all for clapping him in irons now,' he whispered.

'If only we could.'

'We daren't. Our case is too flimsy. What did Miss Clive say to you?'

'She'll do it, tomorrow night if possible.'

Joe rubbed his hands together. 'The sooner the better.'

'I insist on being there to protect her.'

The clerk's light blue eyes shot him a look that spoke volumes yet said nothing. 'I'll pass that on to Mr Fielding, Sir.'

'I shall be at Bow Street first thing tomorrow morning to receive my instructions.'

Joe chuckled softly, even though he was in church. 'I see there'll be no dissuading you, Sir.'

'There most certainly won't,' John answered, then was forced to silence as the funeral service began.

Knowing, because of the diamond button, that Clariana must be fully aware who had murdered her poor wretched father, John found himself studying the girl with a horrible fascination. That anyone in their right mind could so give themselves over to another human creature that they would allow a parent to be killed, then cover up for the murderer, was totally beyond him. So it was that as they processed to the graveside, something the Apothecary usually avoided, he allowed his expression to change briefly to a look of intense dislike. As chance would have it, that was the moment Clariana chose to glance up at him through the dark veils beneath her huge brimmed hat.

The Apothecary looked away upon the instant, but not before he had registered the fact that she had seen him stare at her, had interpreted his gaze correctly, and had returned a look of malice, so strong that it had caused him to shiver.

Chapter Twenty-Three

———— >◦◦◦< ————

Strongly resisting the urge to call on Samuel Swann, whose shop and dwelling place lay directly on his route home, John made straight for Nassau Street after the funeral of Tobias Gill. There, having eaten a very light dinner, somewhat to the chagrin of Sir Gabriel's cook, who was heard to mutter openly about 'country ways from Kensington', he ordered a hot tub and soaked in it for an hour, the water being topped up with steaming kettles at regular intervals. That done, John put on his nightshirt and retired to bed, only to have a confusing dream in which both Coralie Clive and Emilia Alleyn featured. Despite this, he woke at first light, dressed himself, and skipping breakfast altogether, a fact that sent the cook into a state of high alarm, headed for Bow Street to await Mr Fielding's instructions.

The Magistrate was still at table but welcomed the visitor with a wave of his hand.

'Mr Rawlings, this is a familiar scene for us. How often have we breakfasted together, I wonder? Now take a seat, do. Will you join me in some ham?'

Mary Ann slanted her pretty eyes. 'I'll carve it for you, Mr Rawlings.'

He glowered at her, Elizabeth having left the room. 'I'll cut it myself, thank you, my dear.'

She flicked her tongue over her lips. 'Oh, do let me.'

Narrowing his eyes to slits, the Apothecary said, 'I alone know how much I want.'

Mary Ann looked at him most impudently. 'I am sure I can guess what you would like.' Then, with a waggle of her hips, she left the room.

Thinking that one day he would be forced to slap her, John turned to his host. 'Sir, Miss Clive is ready to go into action tonight.'

'So Jago told me. I have already sent a letter to her requesting that she meet him in The Spaniards, close to The Tabard, at seven o'clock. I shall remain here as a blind man would only get in the way on such an occasion. In the meanwhile, my good friend, I would like you to go and see Mrs Clarke.'

'I had already intended to. What do you want with her?'

'You mentioned to me the night before last that she and Cruttenden had connections, that she once worked for him.'

'True.'

'I desire that you might ask her the best vantage points in that house where a man might hide unnoticed. Similarly regarding the exterior. If she can draw you a plan, so much the better. By the time Miss Coralie goes in to face Cruttenden, I intend to have the place infiltrated by stout men and true.'

'I'm mighty glad to hear it.'

The Blind Beak moved his face close to that of John. 'There is no question that this woman Clarke is still in love with the Liveryman? That she might betray our plan to him?'

'I'd stake my life on the fact that she hates him.'

'Then let us hope you are right, my friend. A great deal depends on her and the information she can give us.'

'She will not let us down,' said John, and hoped most earnestly that he was right, knowing the contrary way in which women's hearts sometimes led them.

★   ★   ★

Because it was still early, the Apothecary decided to spend some time at his shop before he made the journey across river to Southwark. But as no apprentice worthy of the name would dare be at work later than his Master, he arrived after Nicholas, who was already dusting and cleaning and setting the place to rights before opening for the day.

'Sir,' said the Muscovite in surprise. 'I hadn't expected you in today.'

'Oh, why was that?'

'Because you had risen early and left the house as I was stirring, which usually means you are about Mr Fielding's business.'

'Well, I have been but I am back for a brief while before I go off again.'

Nicholas's eyes gleamed. 'Is there much afoot?'

'A great deal.'

His apprentice took on a most solemn look. 'Mr Rawlings, if there are to be doings after dark, Sir, please let me join in. Much as I enjoy studying with you, life has been just a shade dull since our adventures connected to the Peerless Pool. No reflection on yourself, Sir. My apprenticeship is one of great interest, but . . .'

'You're bored to sobs,' put in John.

'I wouldn't state it quite that strongly.'

'Nevertheless, you would like some adventure.'

'I would indeed, Sir.'

'Then be at The Spaniards in Southwark, close to The Tabard, tonight at seven. But Nicholas . . .'

'Yes, Sir?'

'I warn you that if Joe Jago does not want you involved in this enterprise he will tell you so and you are to abide by his decision without argument. Is that understood?'

'It is indeed.'

'Then be there, but say nothing of this to anyone.'

'My lips are sealed, Mr Rawlings.'

'In that case let us both do a good morning's work and say no more of it.'

They set to, opening the doors of the shop early to receive the sick and the suffering who had wreaked havoc upon themselves the night before.

A belle of fashion who had clearly not gone to bed, as it was far too early for a lady of the *beau monde* to be upon the town, came in looking somewhat green about the gills.

'Madam, how may I help you?' asked John.

She leaned close over the counter, her expression ghastly. 'Are you to be trusted?'

'Certainly. All my patients are treated in confidence.'

'Then give me something strong. I was indiscreet last night.'

John's brows rose but he said nothing.

'With a footman at that. I was in my cups, of course.'

'Of course.'

'So what do you suggest?'

'Common mugwort, Madam. I'll compound you an infusion straight away.'

'Common? I don't think I care for that very much.'

'Well, you don't have to have it.'

'There's nothing else?'

'None so effective. Drink the infusion twice a day and sit over it for six hours daily.'

The belle turned even greener. '*Sit* on it, you say?'

'Indeed I did, Ma'am.'

Grabbing the parcel, the belle limped from the shop, and John went into the compounding room where he and Nicholas indulged in silent hysterics.

'I thought ladies were only meant to sit over mugwort for a half hour or so,' whispered the apprentice.

'They are, but I considered that might keep her out of mischief.'

'Oh, dear Lordy!' said Nicholas, and wiped his streaming eyes.

The rest of the morning proceeded without incident and shortly after one o'clock John left the shop and walked briskly to the river, where he hired a boat to take him across to the south bank.

He landed at Cuper's Bridge, adjoining Cuper's Gardens, a pleasant site and one much favoured in the summer months, then set off past the timber yards and tenter grounds until he came to Upper Ground, from which he turned down into The Green Walk, then Bare Lane. From there it was a quick cut across to Bandy Leg, indeed the Apothecary was a fraction early for the appointed hour of three.

Dr Hensey had already arrived and was in discussion with Harriet, while Matthew played in the garden outside, well wrapped against the chill. They both turned as the cheerful servant showed John into the room.

The physician bowed, then held out his hand. 'Mr Rawlings, well timed, Sir. I was just relaying the findings of my old tutor to Mrs Clarke.'

John produced paper and pencil from an inner pocket. 'I am most interested in this. I intend to record all you say.'

'Pray do, Sir. Professor Vallier is a leading authority on the falling sickness. Anyway, he maintains that prevention is better than cure and sufferers should adopt a daily routine which will minimise the chances of a fit.' As the Apothecary took notes, Dr Hensey continued. 'He believes that the dried root of Pellitory of Spain should be chewed in the mouth three times a day, every day without fail. Further, he suggests that for thirty days Matthew should consume four ounces of the juice of Cinquefoil, then have thirty days without it, then thirty days with, and so on.'

'For the rest of his life?'

'Yes. There is no cure for the falling sickness as such but a regime like this will bring it under tight control.' The physician looked from one to the other of the two avid listeners. 'And those, my friends, are his findings.'

'Remarkable,' said John. 'I would never have thought of

such a combination. And the professor has had great success with this treatment?'

'He has indeed, Sir. He has indeed.'

'Tell me,' asked John curiously, 'how did you manage to communicate with him in these difficult times? I would have thought it well nigh impossible to get a message into Paris, let alone receive an answer.'

Florence Hensey smiled and tapped the side of his nose. 'We have our methods, Sir.'

'You clearly do, and I congratulate you on them. You have done a great service, Dr Hensey.'

'Indeed you have,' said Harriet, her eyes brighter than John had ever seen them. 'I thank you most sincerely. Our life will be revolutionised. I might even consider having another child.' She checked herself. 'Oh dear, have I been indelicate?'

'You are amongst medical men,' said the physician, and laughed.

In a moment of true friendship, the Apothecary flung his arm round the other man's shoulders. 'I shall be eternally grateful to you for this,' he said quietly. 'You have brought happiness back to a rather sad family.'

'We must be practical,' Harriet put in. 'Will you send your bill, Dr Hensey? Or I could pay you something on account now?'

The physician shook his head. 'You owe me nothing, Madam. I am only grateful that I could introduce something of my tutor's treatment to this country. For I am sure that Mr Rawlings will prescribe it from now on.'

'I most certainly will. In fact when I have studied Matthew's progress, I intend to write a brief paper and send it to the Master of the Worshipful Society of Apothecaries.'

'Then the word will be spread,' said Dr Hensey simply. He picked up his hat and bowed to Harriet Clarke. 'Madam, I take my leave. I have to see another patient within the hour.'

She took his hand and held it to her heart, a touching gesture. 'From there I thank you.'

'No need, Madam. No need.' And he kissed her fingers and was gone.

There was a long silence as both stared at the space where he had stood. Then Harriet began to cry, very quietly.

'Relief?' asked John gently.

'Great relief, together with the belief that the man must be a saint. It would have drained us of money had he charged what his treatment was worth. Michael and I have been worried about it for days.'

'He's certainly a good soul.' John changed his tone. 'Now, Madam, dry your tears. I need your help in another matter entirely.'

Harriet turned away for a few moments and by the time she swung back to look at him was entirely in control of herself. The Apothecary thought yet again what a fine looking woman she was.

'What is it, Sir? How can I assist?'

'Do you remember the last conversation we had? The one in which you asked me to open Cruttenden's skeleton cupboard?'

'Yes.'

'That deed will be done tonight. But in order to achieve this end, Mr Fielding of Bow Street needs your co-operation.'

'In what way?'

'He would like you to draw him a diagram.' And in a voice that would not carry beyond the room in which they stood, the Apothecary explained the Blind Beak's plan. Harriet gazed at him in astonishment. 'Cruttenden is to be arrested tonight? But what can he have done that is so bad?'

'That, I am not allowed to tell you.'

She had already guessed, however. 'He's a killer, isn't he? He was responsible for the poisoning at Apothecaries' Hall and the death of Master Alleyn? To say nothing of Tobias Gill. Did he murder him as well?'

'Don't ask what I must not say.'

'Very well, I won't, but I'll draw your plan and gladly.

How long have I waited for this moment? Years and years. The mills of God grind slowly, but they grind exceeding small.'

'You must tell no one what is planned, Harriet. The entire evening depends on the element of surprise.'

'On my word, my lips are sealed.'

An hour later the Apothecary had what he had come for, and two plans of Pye House, one of the exterior, the other showing inside the building, had been tucked into a secure pocket in John's cloak.

He bowed to Harriet. 'Thank you for these. They will be of enormous help.'

'I am only glad I was able to assist in bringing that creature down.' She looked fierce. 'At what time tonight will all this happen? I want to be able to think about it.'

'I believe that everything will begin about eight. But not a word, mind.'

'There will be no word from me,' Harriet answered solemnly.

They met in The Spaniards in Southwark. Joe Jago and four tough-looking Runners, dressed in nondescript clothes, were already there when John walked into the taproom. A moment or two later, Nicholas came in, smiling hopefully. Last of all, as was her right, Coralie made her entrance.

She was particularly beautiful this night, dressed in emerald green, the colour of her eyes, which glinted behind a jewelled mask she had adopted.

'You have your story ready, Miss Clive?' asked Joe, coming straight to the point.

'Yes. I gave some consideration to asking Cruttenden to kill my sister, Kitty. But then I decided against that.'

'Why?'

'Because Kitty is somewhat older than I am and the story makes no sense. When she retires from the stage, I will reign unchallenged. No, I have decided upon Miss Sheringham, who is currently rivalling me for many leading roles. She is the one I would be glad to see out of the way.'

Joe chuckled. 'You sound as if you mean it.'

'I do,' said Coralie.

John asked a question. 'My apprentice Nick is most anxious to join the party. What role might he play – if any?'

'I would suggest that he accompanies Miss Clive to the front door, posing as her man servant. Then he can wait in the kitchen. If Miss Clive should so much as cry out, he is to come out and protect her.'

'I don't have a weapon,' said Nicholas.

'Do you know how to fire a pistol?'

'I was once at sea, Sir,' answered the Muscovite, with patience.

'Very good.'

'How do the rest of us get in?' said John.

'A kitchen lad has been bribed. There is a wooden spiral staircase leading from the kitchen area which is only used by the servants. It goes as high as the attic. At a certain signal we are to go in, climb the stairs, and take up our positions. I trust Mrs Clarke has given you a plan.'

'She has indeed.' The Apothecary laid the drawings flat on the table.

'These are excellent.' Joe turned to the Runners. 'Greenwood, Hart, you are to remain outside, there and there.' He pointed to the plan of the exterior. 'Marriott and Burrows, you are to come inside with Mr Rawlings and myself. You will be stationed here and here.'

'Where am I to go?'

'I have a nice store cupboard in mind for you, Mr Rawlings. From there you should be able to see Miss Clive through the crack in the door.'

Coralie smiled. 'Then I shall feel really safe.'

John shot her a glance but her expression was as pleasant as ever.

'Have you any questions?' asked Joe, leaning back in his chair.

'If he makes trouble do we shoot to kill?' said one of the Runners.

'Why not?' answered Joe urbanely. 'Why not indeed?'

By eight o'clock everyone was in place, despite the difficulties of four grown men creeping up a wooden staircase that creaked with every step. Not easy in view of the fact that none of the other servants was aware of what was going on and could have come along at any moment. However, all managed to scuttle into cupboards or recesses without being stopped, and John settled uneasily into a store cupboard leading off the salon, the place in which Cruttenden received visitors, so he was informed.

Much to Joe's relief both the Liveryman and his affianced bride were at home, ostensibly in deep mourning for her father, and so were within doors when the bell rang punctually at eight. A footman went to answer it and John from his vantage point heard the distant murmur of Coralie's voice. After a long pause, Cruttenden's silken tones were added to hers and finally, following what seemed an interminable wait, the door of the salon opened and the Liveryman ushered her in.

'Pray take a seat, Madam,' John heard him say. 'May I get you some refreshment?'

'A little wine perhaps.'

'Of course.' He pulled a bellrope.

Coralie sat down, as did Cruttenden, and both of them disappeared from the Apothecary's line of vision, although he could overhear them perfectly.

'Sir, I was given your name by an old school friend of mine, the Honourable Sophie Ebury. As you know, she inherited a considerable fortune and eloped with Captain Robert. However, that association did not last and now she is quite the belle of society in Cheltenham, where I happened to run into her.'

The wine arrived at this juncture and there was no further conversation until both had been served. When the footman had left the room, Cruttenden said, 'Dear Miss Ebury, such an attractive young woman.'

'She spoke very highly of you,' John heard Coralie answer.

'Did she now? Umm. Tell me, Miss . . .'

'Clive, Coralie Clive. I act, you know.'

'I thought your features were familiar. I wondered where I had seen you, and only recently at that.'

'I am currently appearing at the Theatre Royal, Drury Lane. You probably noticed me there.'

Cruttenden's face suddenly came into view and his smile was that of a wolf. 'No, not at the play.' He paused, looking thoughtful, then said, 'Oh yes, I remember now. It was at an Assembly. You were in the company of an irritating young man called Rawlings. He is supposedly an apothecary, but I have heard a rumour that he is somehow connected with the law. I do trust he is not a friend of yours.'

Coralie stood up and was clearly visible. She had removed her mask, and John, knowing her so well, could see at once that she was worried. Her plan was not working. She was being forced to think where she stood.

She turned to Cruttenden, her rustling garments exuding a perfume which John could smell even in his hiding place. 'It is about him that I came to see you,' Coralie said, and she gave a light laugh that would not have disgraced any stage.

'Really?' The Liveryman sounded interested.

'Yes. To cut straight to the heart of the matter, Sir, the bastard has betrayed me. He went off with another woman, leaving me high and dry. God's life but I hate him for what he did. How dare he abandon me so?'

In his hiding place, the Apothecary squirmed.

'I could kill him,' the actress shouted, then burst into a veritable flood of weeping.

'There, there.' Cruttenden stood up and folded Coralie into his arms. John felt physically sick.

From his considerable height, the Liveryman looked down into the actress's face. 'You are a very beautiful girl, my dear. One of the loveliest I have ever seen.'

She gazed up at him with trembling lips. 'Then will you help me? I can repay you.'

'How, my dear?'

'That would depend.' Rainbows were appearing from behind the tears and she was laughing and playful now.

'Let us sit down and discuss the matter.' Cruttenden indicated a couch and took a seat next to that of Coralie. He laid a long hand over one of hers. 'This is a very sad story you have just told me. It shames me that one of my gender could behave so badly.'

'It was particularly hurtful since we were lovers of long-standing.'

In his hiding place, John felt sicker than ever.

'Wretched little beast. I never liked the look of him. But tell me, pretty lady, how do you think *I* can help?'

Coralie raised winsome eyes. 'Miss Ebury – in her cups admittedly – did say that you had eased the passage of Lord Briggs from this wearisome life of ours.'

'Did she now?'

'Yes, but it may well have been a falsehood.'

'That is possible.'

'But if it were true, if you had done her that most remarkable favour, I just wondered – only wondered, mark you – if you might do a similar service for me.'

Cruttenden chuckled, a cold and sinister sound. 'Are you saying, dear Miss Clive, that you want the upstart Rawlings removed?'

'Yes, permanently.'

'And *if* I were to do such a thing, what would be my reward?'

'You would only have to name it, Sir.'

The Liveryman's lecherous eyes swept Coralie's body.
'Anything?'

'Anything,' she whispered softly.

He caught her to him and swept a long deep kiss on to her
lips. Without protest, the actress melted against him, as if she
were loving every minute, in fact she was returning the man's
kisses. Hardly able to contain himself, John watched in horror.

'You'll kill him for me?' murmured Coralie, as they drew
briefly apart.

'Yes,' answered Cruttenden, equally quietly, and bent his
head to kiss her breasts.

And it was then, at that most intimate of moments, that
the door opened, and what the Apothecary could only see as a
white-faced fury flung itself into the room.

'You faithless bastard!' screamed Clariana. She turned on
Coralie whom she began to beat about the head and neck.
'You filthy whore!'

Taken by surprise, Cruttenden stood defenceless for a
moment or two, then he swung a swingeing blow at Clariana
which, fortunately for her, missed its target.

The girl appeared to go crazy, rending at the Liveryman
with nails, kicking him viciously. 'You bloody murderer. I'll
tell the world what I know. I'll say to them how you killed my
father. You're not fit to live. Bastard, bastard, bastard!'

She wheeled from him to Coralie, on whom she landed
such a clout that the girl fell back on to the floor, semi-
conscious. Given this chance, Clariana kicked the actress
repeatedly, and was only stopped by Cruttenden, who picked
her bodily off her feet and flung her across the room.

John had had enough. He burst from his hiding place
shouting, 'Stop or I'll shoot.'

It seemed the same idea had simultaneously occurred to
Joe, who erupted from a large chest, waving a formidable
pistol. 'Mr Francis Cruttenden,' he shouted, 'I arrest you in
the name of the Public Office, Bow Street, on a charge of
conspiring to kill. Come with me, Sir.'

The Runners burst in through a long window which they had managed to force open.

'Take him,' ordered Joe.

'Piss you!' shouted Cruttenden, and was past them and out of the window as quickly as they had come through it.

'After him,' Joe commanded, then swung round on Clariana, who had totally lost control and was attempting to goudge out his eyes with her evil nails. Without pausing for breath, the clerk heaved a blow to her jaw which knocked the hellcat senseless. 'Silly woman,' he said, and turned back to John who, to his shame, laughed.

'Nicholas,' the Apothecary called, as he attempted to control himself. 'You're wanted, quickly.' He leant over Coralie and applied every bit of skill he had into tending her.

She opened her eyes and spoke through a lip that had started to swell. 'Mr Rawlings, how nice to see you.'

'Be quiet. I'm about to take you to bed upstairs. I feel we'll all be staying at this house tonight.'

She looked at him very seriously. 'If I go to bed, I will put myself there. You and I shall not be alone in a bedroom again, John.'

'Why not?'

'Just in case we did something we might regret. Your path is clear now, my friend. Our goodbyes are said.'

Then she closed her eyes and refused to speak further.

An hour later, Joe, John and Nicholas, together with two of the Runners, sat at Francis Cruttenden's dining table being served a hearty supper by his servants. The other two of the party had already left, taking Clariana, bound hand and foot, to Bow Street, after Jago had formally arrested her on a charge of accessory to murder. She had gone in the Flying Coach and was to be transported over Westminster Bridge rather than risk her escaping by water.

As John came downstairs after checking Coralie, who was now sleeping peacefully, Runner Marriott was speaking.

'. . . we couldn't stop it, Sir. It all happened so quickly.'

'What's this?' asked John.

Joe looked grim. 'Cruttenden's gone into the river and we've lost him in the darkness.'

'Surely he can't swim far in this icy cold?'

The Runner gave a humourless laugh. 'He won't be swimming anywhere, Mr Rawlings. Somebody dealt him a death blow.'

'What are you saying?'

'As we sprinted after him, a figure detached itself from some bushes and swung him such a clout with a club that he staggered and fell into the Thames. He wouldn't have lasted five minutes in that state. He must have drowned immediately.'

'Who did it? Did you catch them?'

'No. We gave chase but he or she was too quick for us. Sped off like lightning and knew their way round, too. Soon disappeared into the night without trace.'

'Didn't you even catch a glimpse?'

'Not a glimpse, Sir. Could have been anyone. But then Master Cruttenden had a lot of enemies, I believe. Wasn't he attacked recently?'

John looked thoughtful. 'Yes he was.'

'Then, Sir, I don't suppose we'll ever know,' said the Runner with an air of resignation.

Chapter Twenty-Four

It was so cold that ice had formed in the water of the fountain which played in the gardens round which the graceful houses of Hanover Square were built. Indeed the roofs of those same houses gleamed with frost despite the fact that it was already getting on for noon.

With the reputation of being something of a Whig stronghold, Hanover Square, deserted on this wintry day, not only housed many important people but even boasted its own church, St George's, at which the great Mr Handel, very ancient and very blind, had been a churchwarden. John, out of curiosity, had once attended a service there and watched the grand old man sitting in his own pew. Rumours had abounded even then that at an advanced age the celebrated musician had fallen in love with Kitty Clive, who had created the role of Dalilah in the first production of his oratorio, *Samson*. Whether this was true or not even John, with his knowledge of the family, couldn't say. But he could vividly remember the night he had lingered outside the home of the Clive sisters and heard Kitty sing to an unknown German admirer.

But now he stood outside another house, number twelve Hanover Square, ringing the bell for admittance and wondering whether his great friend, Serafina de Vignolles, would allow him to visit her in her extremely pregnant state. He had much to discuss with her. Firstly how Francis Cruttenden, whom he had disliked on sight, had been responsible for the poisoning at Apothecaries' Hall. And, much more importantly, how his relationship with Coralie was finally at an end and how he had a new sweetheart, a young and beautiful woman with whom he was falling somewhat seriously in love.

The footman who had answered the door reappeared in the entrance hall where John waited.

'Madame la Comtesse will see you for a short while, Sir. She is in the salon. If you would be good enough to follow me.'

The servant led the way and they climbed the sweep of the exquisite staircase to a first floor landing. Here the footman threw open a pair of double doors.

'Mr Rawlings, Ma'am.'

'Ah John,' Serafina called from within, 'come in, do.'

She was lying on her *duchesse en bateau*, the curtains partially drawn to protect her eyes, and the Apothecary was vividly reminded of the first occasion on which he had met her. He had been investigating a mysterious death in the Dark Walk at Vaux Hall Pleasure Gardens at that time, but he had still found time to fall in love with her, or rather with her alter ego, the Masked Lady. Now Serafina was his friend, his confidante, someone with whom the Apothecary needed to discuss the twists and turns of his personal life. With a smile, John drew close to her couch.

He had never seen her so drawn, in fact Serafina looked utterly exhausted. She waved a hand at him feebly.

'My dear, if it had been anyone else but you I would most certainly have refused to see them. I have had quite the most wearisome night and morning. My back has ached and twinged constantly. I simply cannot find a comfortable position in which to lie. In fact Louis has taken Italia out in order to give me some peace and quiet, in the hope I might sleep.'

Because he knew her so well, the Apothecary was able to

say, 'Sit up a bit and I will rub your back for you. The pressure of hands can often relieve pain.'

Serafina struggled to rise, her distended body in the way whichever move she made.

'Oh I shall be glad to get shot of this little devil. I feel if I get any bigger I shall burst.'

'When is it due?'

'Supposedly another five weeks or so, but I think it will be before then.'

John slipped his hands behind her and started to massage the length of her spine.

'I have a new lady love.'

'I thought you might.'

'Why?'

'Because last time I saw you you were so over-friendly to Coralie.'

'You notice too much.'

'A sign of a good gambler.' Serafina closed her eyes. 'My pain is easing. You are doing me good.'

'Sign of a good apothecary,' John answered, and they laughed.

Serafina looked up. 'I forget my manners, Sir. Let me offer you some refreshment.'

'Only if you are having something.'

'I thought a glass of canary might raise my spirits.'

'Then I shall join you. Do you want me to summon a servant?'

'No, the exercise will be good for me. I insist. Don't pull that face.'

With a mighty effort Serafina heaved herself off the *duchesse en bateau* and waddled, there was no other word to describe her gait, towards the bellrope. Then she stopped, let out a mighty cry as her hand flew to her back, and turned on John a look of consternation.

'My God, it's coming. I had no idea. Send someone for Dr Drake. Quick, John, quick.'

He shot to the door and down the stairs, collaring the first footman who came into view.

'Madam has gone into labour. Send your fastest boy to Dr Drake's house and ask the physician to come immediately. Meanwhile, get me some towels, a bowl and several ewers of warm water. Oh, and some brandy wouldn't come amiss.'

'Are you going to deliver the child, Sir?' the servant asked, looking horrified.

'If Dr Drake doesn't hurry it looks as if I might have to.'

Serafina was back on her couch, supine and straining, when he returned to the room. She rolled a desperate eye at him. 'I want to push the little beast. I must have been in travail for hours.'

'You'll never get the child out like that,' said John. 'You're too flat. Do it the gypsy girl's way. They think nothing of it.'

'How do you know what they do?'

'My Master delivered one once. We were out picking simples and there she was crouching beside the footpath. Did the whole thing with great despatch. Now come on, Serafina. Hitch up your gown.'

'Oh take the damned thing off me.'

'What do you want for your modesty?'

'Ask Louis's man to bring me one of my husband's shirts.'

She pushed again at that, loudly and distinctly. John heaved her upright, arranging as many pillows as he could find behind her back. There was a knocking at the door and the footman, looking absolutely petrified, appeared.

'The things you ordered, Sir.'

John did not turn round. 'Go and get one of the Master's shirts,' he said over his shoulder. 'Be quick about it.'

For Serafina was struggling to undress herself, rending at her elegant gown which was now impeding everything she was doing. John thought, most wryly, that several years ago he would have given much to see her naked, and now his wish was being granted in the most extraordinary circumstances.

A female kitchen servant came in with the shirt. 'Do you want me to stay, Sir?'

'Yes, as long as you don't faint.'

'I'm one of sixteen, Sir. I've seen my mam pop 'em out many a time.'

'Good, then make sure that water stays warm. Now take my coat, there's a good girl, and fetch my herb knife out of the pocket. Wash it thoroughly in the bowl.'

'Yes, Sir.'

Serafina swore violently. 'John, hold me.'

'The girl can do that. I need your fundament in the air, Ma'am. That's where I shall be stationed. Now, come along. Into a ball, chin down.'

'Damn you!'

'Would you prefer to stand?'

'No, but prop me up more.'

John turned to the servant. 'Pillows from the beds, my dear. When you've brought them put them behind the mistress's back.'

'My mam's got a special birthing chair.'

'Well, it isn't here, is it! So we must do the best we can.'

He took Serafina's feet and put them against his chest, just beneath the shoulders. 'Push against me.'

The Comtesse gave an almighty heave and the first sign of the head appeared.

'He's dark,' said John.

'Can you see him?'

'Yes. We'll have him before long.'

'Oh God,' said Serafina.

'Stop talking, you're wasting energy. Put your chin down, don't push in your throat.'

'You're a bastard. I hate you.'

'I love *you*.'

'You love everybody.'

Now she worked in earnest, with no word to anyone. She approached the task, as Serafina did with most things, utterly determined to do it quickly and to do it well. With the kitchen maid holding her mistress tightly, John Rawlings, apothecary of Shug Lane, eased Serafina's child out into the world, gave the boy a good shake to start his heart up, as John's old Master used to say quite ridiculously, cut the cord with his herb knife and handed the Comtesse her son. Then he drank the brandy.

He turned to the girl. 'To the kitchen, quick. We must keep this little fellow warm. I don't think he was meant for the world just yet.'

'My mam always kept her early ones by the hearth, in a box with a hot brick by. She never lost one.'

'Then we'll do exactly what she did. Get the fire stoked up in Madam's bedroom. The little chap can lie there.'

The girl rushed from the room but not before she had given Serafina a quick kiss on the cheek. 'Begging pardon for the familiarity, Mam, but I never thought a lady could do it so good.'

'I think that was a compliment,' said the Comtesse as the door closed behind her.

'It was but you deserved it, gypsy girl.'

'This little person is going to be called John.'

'I am honoured.'

'John Gabriel Louis. Now, how about a glass of champagne?'

'I'll ring for service,' said the Apothecary, realising as he crossed to the bell rope that not only was he sweating like a racehorse but shaking like a beast that had just won a truly hard race.

Chapter Twenty-Five

They left London in a blinding snowstorm and drove through the most horrid conditions to spend Christmas at Kensington. Sir Gabriel, always thoughtful, shut down the house in Nassau Street, leaving only a skeleton staff to keep the place warm, and gave those of his servants who were not travelling with them, the twelve days off. Then he and John, with luggage piled high, set off on their hazardous journey, having said farewell to Samuel who was heading for Islington to join his father for the festivities.

Before they left town, Sir Gabriel had been to call on his new godson and had shared presents with the de Vignolles.

'John is remarkable,' Serafina had said, resting in her great bed, her child sleeping in a cradle by the fire.

'I hope he finds happiness with Emilia Alleyn.'

'Everyone wants that for him. He is such a gifted and generous person.'

Sir Gabriel had smiled. 'We are all at the mercy of fate, whether we believe it or whether we don't. John will triumph in the end, I feel it in my heart.'

And now he and the son he had adopted were battling through the snow to reach the village before Christmas Eve. In the coach, they talked.

'So what has happened, my child? You have been so preoccupied of late I have hardly had time to speak to you.'

'Well, Sir, Cruttenden has not come up yet, held down by the icy waters I expect.'

'No chance he escaped?'

John shook his head. 'The Runners who witnessed the attack on him said that he didn't have a hope. He may well have been dead when he entered the water.'

'Then a mad dog has been put down. That's my view. Have you any idea who assaulted him?'

'Now that, dear Father, would be telling.'

'There were no clues at all?' Sir Gabriel persisted.

'Only this.' And John drew from his pocket a small piece of olive green material, jaggedly torn.

'What is it?'

'I found it on a bush near Cruttenden's front door when I inspected the premises next morning.'

'Was it left by his killer?'

'Who is to say? It could belong to anyone. I do not regard it with any special significance.'

And the Apothecary refused to be drawn further.

Sir Gabriel changed his questions. 'What about the dangerous Miss Gill? What has happened to her?'

'She came up before the Beak and he sent her for trial at the Old Bailey. She is at present languishing in Newgate I believe.'

Sir Gabriel looked extremely pensive. 'Samuel told me that you found some sort of list amongst Master Alleyn's papers. Apparently all on it were people who had employed Cruttenden to do away with someone who stood between them and what they wanted.'

'It's true enough.'

'But what is happening to them all? They are as guilty as the man they hired.'

John sighed. 'Mr Fielding gave the matter much thought but decided that there was not enough evidence to proceed against them. If Cruttenden had been alive to give testimony, that would have been a different matter. But the fact that he was involved in every case does not, in itself, prove a felony.'

'So none of them will be punished for their crime?'

'Only by the mills of God.'

'What do you mean?'

'Something Harriet Clarke said to me about them grinding exceeding small.'

'Was the Marquis of Kensington involved in all this?'

'I think as you are continuing to play cards with him it might be better if I say nothing.'

'Oh dear,' said Sir Gabriel, and shook his head.

'Let me change the subject. Have you heard the latest gossip?'

'Plenty. But to which particular piece of tittle-tattle do you refer?'

'Well, the rumours are all about town that Coralie has a new beau. The heir to the Duke of Westminster, no less.'

Sir Gabriel took snuff. 'Then great joy to her, declare I. I've always regarded that young woman very highly.'

'As do I,' said John sadly. 'As do I. Now to my plans. I would like to propose to Emilia over this festive season. Do I have your approval, Sir?'

'You most certainly do, my dear. An admirable and fine girl who is ripe and ready for marriage, as are you.'

John looked reflective. 'Life's odd, ain't it?'

'Very, very odd,' Sir Gabriel answered, and pulled his hat forward over his three storey wig indicating that he wished to sleep.

On Christmas Eve at dinner time, the house guests arrived: Mrs Alleyn, Emilia, the twin sons, and Garnett Smith, who had emerged into the world a kinder and rather good-natured person. Bedroom space was at a premium but Sir Gabriel, with his usual charm, had managed to persuade bluff Mr Horniblow, who lived next door and was a widower with a dog, to give up his two spare bedrooms to the twins and Garnett. So everyone sat at peace round the dinner table and thought with pleasure of the days ahead, when entertaining would be shared between Sir Gabriel and Maud Alleyn.

It was then, with the snow still falling outside and night drawing in fast that there came a thunderous knocking at the front door. The company looked from one to the other.

'Whoever can that be?' said Sir Gabriel, an expression of anxiety on his face.

'What an hour and in what weather to call,' agreed Mrs Alleyn.

John stood up. 'I'll go and see.'

His father's best footman was already at the door and the Apothecary heard a woman's voice ask for him by name. He stepped forward, peering out into the blizzard. A glistening black figure stood there, snowflakes on its hat and cloak.

'Who is it?' he called.

'Harriet. Harriet Clarke.'

'Then come in, come in. You must be frozen. How did you get here?'

'By the public stage. It has taken me all day, in fact I never thought we would come through the ways are so bad.'

John drew her into the hallway and looked at her closely. She was molten with some inner emotion, her eyes gleaming and her face tense and taut. She looked to him, at that moment, as Boudicca, the ancient Queen, must have done before she went into battle, capable of anything.

The Apothecary seized her hands. 'Harriet, what is it? You look . . . wild.' He could not think of a better word.

'I've come about Dr Hensey.'

'Dr Hensey! But it's Christmas Eve!'

'I'm aware of that. Do you think I would have left my husband and child on such a day if the matter had not been urgent?'

'Well, what's happened to him?'

'He's been arrested. It was in the newspapers this morning.'

'What!'

'On a charge of high treason. It seems he has been spying for France for several years.'

'Dr Hensey has?'

'Yes, Mr Rawlings, yes. But it was his letter to his old tutor in France that finally did for him. The letter in which he asked for help for Matthew. Apparently the Secret Department in the Post Office has been opening his correspondence for some time. On seeing him write to Paris they acted, and they have come for him.' Harriet looked him straight in the eye. 'I have booked into The New Inn for tonight but tomorrow I shall make my way to London, somehow or other, and I am going to see the Secretary of State, the Earl of Holdernesse. I intend to plead for clemency for our friend, otherwise he will be shot. Mr Rawlings, will you come with me?'

'Oh yes,' said John, 'without hesitation.'

He shook his head in amazement, remembering how the signalling spy from the escapade on the Romney Marsh had never been caught. Small wonder if it had been Dr Hensey all along.

He led Harriet into the warmth of the small parlour, and returned to the dining room.

'It seems I will not be keeping my Christmas with you after all,' he said. 'Urgent business requires my return to London.'

There was a murmur of general consternation and Emilia jumped up from her seat. 'John, what has happened?'

'Something rather serious.' He looked across at his father. 'Sir, may I speak to Emilia alone?'

'Of course, my boy.'

He took her into the hall. 'Listen, I have to go and plead for a man's life. He is a good man, and a hero in his own country, and it is my duty to do all I can for him. I shall leave tomorrow morning. Would you go too?'

She did not hesitate for a second. 'Of course.'

He pulled her into his arms. 'Second question. Will you marry me?'

The angel's eyes widened and the heavenly being smiled. 'Of course,' she repeated, and took his hand in hers.

Chapter Twenty-Six

Harriet drew John outside the front door. 'We will not fail in this mission, will we?'

He looked at her, covered in falling snow, noticing inadvertently that the hem of her olive green cloak had a jagged tear in it and a small piece of the material was missing.

'I don't know,' he answered. 'But we can do our damnedest.'

'Will the Secretary of State listen to our pleas?'

'Yes, I think he probably might. He has a reputation for great fairness. If we tell him all we know about Dr Hensey's character, we might at least be able to save him from the firing squad.'

Harriet took the Apothecary's hands in hers. 'You are a strange creature.'

'In what way?'

'You represent the law, yet you are quite prepared to go to any lengths to see that even a so-called criminal is treated fairly.'

'What *is* a criminal,' answered John Rawlings. He fished in his pocket and drew out the small piece of material that lay within. 'Your cloak is torn, Harriet. Might this belong to you?'

She took it from him, holding it in the beam of light that streamed through the open front door on to the snow. 'Yes, it's mine. Where did you find it?'

'On a bush,' said John. He raised her hand to his lips. 'Farewell, my dear. A footman shall escort you to the inn. We will meet again tomorrow.'

She gave him a glittering smile, a powerful woman indeed. 'Goodnight, Sir,' she answered, and walked away into the darkness.

HISTORICAL NOTE

John Rawlings, Apothecary, really lived. He was born circa, 1731, though his actual parentage is somewhat shrouded in mystery. He was made Free of the Worshipful Society of Apothecaries on 13 March, 1755, giving his address as 2, Nassau Street, Soho. This links him with H. D. Rawlings Ltd who were based at the same address over a hundred years later. Rawlings were spruce and ginger beer manufacturers and in later years made soda and tonic waters. Their ancient soda syphons can still be found on the bar counters of unmodernised pubs.

Dr Florence Hensey, too, is a real historical character, a doctor of physick who was also a genuine French spy. He was caught by Anthony Todd, head of the Post Office, who was also in charge of the Secret Department of the Post Office, whose brief it was to open any suspect mail and read it. Interestingly, this department was not disbanded until the middle of the nineteenth century. A letter from Anthony Todd to the Lords of the Treasury, dated General Post Office, June 18, 1762, reads as follows:

> One Florence Hensey, Doctor of Physick, convicted of High Treason in 1758, was apprehended by my means, His Majesty's Secretaries of State having no information from any other quarter that he was carrying on a treasonable correspondence . . . and though it was thought proper not to execute Dr Hensey, his conviction seems to have had so good an effect that the many spies then in London have been

deterred, as far as it has appeared to me, during the course of this War, from giving intelligence to the Enemy.

As spies, in the main, were executed it seems that somebody, somewhere put in a plea for Dr Hensey. I have let my imagination link this actual event with the enigmatic John Rawlings.